For Scott

the further adventures of

SHERLOCK HOLMES

THE IMPROBABLE PRISONER

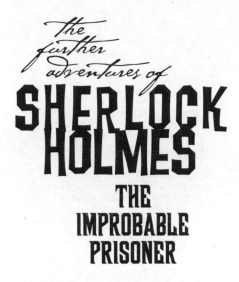

the
further
adventures of

SHERLOCK HOLMES

THE IMPROBABLE PRISONER

STUART DOUGLAS

TITAN BOOKS

THE FURTHER ADVENTURES OF SHERLOCK HOLMES:
THE IMPROBABLE PRISONER
Print edition ISBN: 9781785656293
E-book edition ISBN: 9781785656309

Published by Titan Books
A division of Titan Publishing Group Ltd
144 Southwark Street, London SE1 0UP

First Titan edition: July 2018
10 9 8 7 6 5 4 3 2 1

A CIP catalogue record for this title is available from the British Library.

Printed in the USA.

What did you think of this book? We love to hear from our readers.
Please email us at: readerfeedback@titanemail.com,
or write to Reader Feedback at the above address.

To receive advance information, news, competitions, and exclusive offers
online, please sign up for the Titan newsletter on our website:
www.titanbooks.com

Chapter One

In all my long acquaintance with Sherlock Holmes, there were few occasions when I was more grateful for his friendship and support than in the autumn of 1898. Even now, recollecting those months between the end of a pleasantly warm summer and the onset of a blustery, wet winter, I can picture in my mind's eye only darkness and squalor and cold. The faded newspaper clipping I hold in my hand is on its own enough to cause a dull, leaden dread to settle in the pit of my stomach and turn my mouth as dry as ash. Barely legible though it is after the passing of these many years, I can still make out the headline and bring to mind the events it presaged.

DOCTOR JOHN WATSON ARRESTED!
CHRONICLER OF THE FAMOUS DETECTIVE SHERLOCK HOLMES CHARGED WITH MURDER!

More Inside!

But perhaps it is time, as I near the end of my life, finally to record those events I have kept hidden for so long, and to allow the world one further chance to marvel at the wisdom of my dearest friend.

Yet the chain of events that almost led to my death began in an entirely commonplace manner.

I was building up a small practice that had initially proved somewhat less busy than I might have hoped, and thus I was often to be found visiting my more elderly and infirm patients in the evening. So it was on one occasion, as I left the rooms of a bedridden old soldier whom I had been treating every night for a week, and made my way from Warrington Crescent towards Baker Street.

With the distance under two miles, I had adopted the habit of walking, trying out lines for my latest story in my head as I did so. It was a sharp autumnal evening but I was well wrapped up and, the old soldier being my last port of call, I allowed my mind to wander as my feet did likewise, replaying in my head as I walked an earlier conversation with a charming nurse.

Had it not been for my distracted state of mind, I might have been more attentive and avoided the terrible months that followed. Holmes would no doubt lambast me for wasting time in idle speculation, but still the thought nags at me that had I taken a cab, or even a different route, then I would never have known the inside of Holloway Prison, never have heard the name McLachlan – or made the acquaintance of the notorious Matthew Galloway.

Holmes would be right, though. Any such speculation is a waste of time and effort, for the fact of the matter is that I was not fully attentive when I heard running feet in the darkness of a side street, nor when a dishevelled young woman called my name as she ran into the bright sphere of the gas-lit main thoroughfare.

"Dr. Watson! Are you Dr. Watson?" she cried in obvious

distress. "They said you'd be passing this way on your way home, and I have a terrible need of your assistance, sir!"

The girl was around eighteen or nineteen, with hair almost silver in the streetlight, a small, round face and large, dark eyes. She was well, if plainly, dressed, but wore no coat or jacket, which was not to be recommended on such a cold evening.

"I am Dr. Watson," I confirmed, with what I hoped was a reassuring expression, though whether I was successful was hard to judge, so distressed was she. She pulled at my arm and gestured back along the alleyway from which she had emerged.

"My grandmother!" she cried, with a choked sob. "I think she's dying! Please, please... come and help her, I beg of you!"

Were I not a doctor, and so bound by my oath to assist, still I would have gone with the girl and done what I could, so heartfelt were her entreaties. I nodded my assent and hurried after her as she ran into the alley.

The house to which she led me was in the centre of Linhope Street. It was three storeys high, a former family home now converted to individual rooms; not so grand as it once had been, but a respectable enough address for all that. Scaffolding shrouded the building immediately adjacent, which consequently was cast in shadow, but otherwise the street was unremarkable. The girl pushed open the main door and I followed her in. Inside, a door on each side of the hallway presumably led to what had once been private rooms, with a staircase directly ahead and to its left-hand side a further corridor, dimly lit and leading I assumed to the back garden.

"Upstairs," the girl said breathlessly, already mounting the first stairs.

Again, I followed, round the bend in the staircase and onto the first floor, which largely mirrored the one below. "In here," she said, pushing open the door on our left for me and inviting me to go inside.

The room was spacious and in the daylight would have been well lit by a large bay window, but at the moment was illuminated by a series of candles, which guttered and cast soft shadows on the walls and the over-sized print which hung opposite the bed. There was little by way of furnishings. A wardrobe with a cracked mirror stood against the wall by the open window, with a lady's robe of decent quality draped over its door. A small, tarnished table holding a washbasin, a jug and an old-fashioned lorgnette had been placed just beside it. These few items aside, however, there was only a large double bed, in the centre of the room, in which I could make out the shape of the girl's mother. She was unmoving and silent as I approached, and I feared that any speed we had made had been wasted and the woman was already beyond my help.

I fancied I heard the door fall shut behind me, but I gave it no thought other than to wonder if the girl had some premonition that we were too late and so found it excessively painful to enter. Having no such luxury myself, I placed my bag on the edge of the bed and pulled back the top of the heavy cover.

The scene that confronted me was one I am never likely to forget. Violent death is no stranger to me, nor does it hold many terrors, but I was younger then than now, and for all my time in the army, this was the first woman I had seen so brutally slain. The body of an elderly lady lay now exposed, her eyes wide open in terror, her mouth slackly agape. She had been stabbed many times, as was clear from the amount of blood which stained her night-clothes and the open wounds I could see around her neck and on her arms, but something – shock, perhaps, or the ingrained sense of duty I had as a doctor – forced me to check for a pulse and to lift her up enough to ascertain that rigor had begun to set in.

Only as I lowered her back to the sodden bedclothes did my common sense begin to function again. I strode to the door, intent on taking hold of the girl who had brought me here and who, evidently, was no more a concerned granddaughter than I was myself. The door, however, was locked and no key to be seen. I was trapped in the room with the murdered woman.

I gave the door a kick and pulled at the knob, but to no avail. The house may have seen better days, but its doors were as solid as the day they were built. I ran to the window and heaved it open, but the street below was empty and quiet and though I shouted for help, nobody answered. Left without choice, I returned to the door and began to kick it in fury, all the while shouting for help, crying out that murder had been committed.

I estimate that less than a minute passed in such frenzied actions before I heard heavy footfalls coming up the stairs and became aware of a hand turning the same doorknob I still held, only from the other side of the door.

"Open up in there," someone cried from the hall, then, "Police! Open this door!"

"Do you not think I would if I could!" I snapped. "There is no key and someone has locked me in! Quickly, man, murder has been committed!"

"Murder–" I heard the faceless policeman mutter in the sudden silence as I broke off my own assault on the door. "Stand back then, sir, for I will have to force my way in!"

I did as instructed, retreating to the end of the bed. The door shuddered under the policeman's assault but failed to open. Next thing, I heard footsteps rushing down the stairs and, crossing to the window, I saw a uniformed figure running down the street. A few minutes later, he reappeared, with several other men behind him. Moments later, the door flew back, crashing into the weak plaster of the wall and partially rebounding from it. The constable rushed in, followed by several working men and, roused by the commotion, a thin, elderly woman whom I later learned was the landlady of the house.

At that moment, everything seemed somehow *excessive* – the room too hot, the body too obscene in its mutilation, the landlady's scream from the doorway too piercing. I had seen corpses before, but I had been, at least in part, prepared for those deaths. Now, though, in this otherwise unexceptional room, I felt a profound disquiet, a deep-rooted sense that events were moving beyond my understanding. As though at one remove from my surroundings, I felt my senses become dull and muted. Perhaps it was this dislocation that initially prevented me from hearing the constable as he examined the body and began to ask me questions.

"Sir, excuse me, sir!" His voice interrupted my reverie suddenly, like the crack of a cab driver's whip.

I brought my chin up from where it rested on my chest and refocused my eyes on the room and the man now shaking my arm.

"Sorry. I don't know… that poor woman… my mind must have wandered… What were you saying?"

"Your name, sir, for one. And how you came to be in this place, for another."

He was young but slightly balding, I noticed, and seemed entirely competent. He had pulled the blanket back over the body (I should have thought to do that, I realised), and stood in front of me with a notebook in one hand and a pencil in the other.

"Your name, sir?" he repeated.

"John Watson. Dr. John Watson."

"Right then, Dr. Watson it is. Now, Doctor, can you tell me how you come to be in this room with this unfortunate lady?"

I was pleased to hear genuine enquiry rather than veiled accusation in his voice. At the mention of my professional status, he had relaxed, to the extent one could do so in the present circumstances. I explained as well as I could the events leading up to his appearance in the room, while he took extensive notes, asking me now and again to repeat some fact or expand on another. He was, predictably, particularly interested in my description of the girl who had claimed an infirm grandmother. Finally, he accurately summed up what I had said, and indicated that I would need to give a formal statement at the local police station that night.

Looking back on the next few minutes, I am astonished at my naiveté. I recall thinking that I would prefer to make a statement the following morning, and considering whether to suggest that Holmes be called at once, to provide assistance to the police in their endeavours. Madness to have thought of the events of that evening so dispassionately, as though I were not at all involved and it could be treated as simply one more mystery for my friend to investigate. In fact, I was on the verge of suggesting that Holmes and I return in the morning when daylight would aid our examinations, when a voice behind me rendered such considerations moot.

"Here, Constable," one of the working men called. "Did I hear your man say that the door was locked and there no key to be had?"

I turned round to look at the fellow. There, hanging at a slight angle from the lock on the inside of the door, was a key.

The policeman walked across to the door and turned the key in the lock, causing the bolt to recede back into the mechanism.

"Would you care to explain, sir," he said after this exhibition, "how the door could be locked on the inside, if you were trapped as you say in this room?"

Of course, I could not. I might have pointed out that it had been I who had brought the dead woman to his attention by calling out, but in truth my head was heavy, and I found myself struggling to concentrate. With no other choice, I suggested that we move the discussion to the station, where I might also telephone a friend to come to my assistance.

The constable agreed, and indicated that we would wait outside while he sent a man ahead to the station. With an ever-growing sense of the unreality of the situation, I slumped down on my haunches in the corridor, and waited.

Chapter Two

The next few hours in the police station were but the first of several new experiences for me. Never before had I been one of the accused, and consequently my time there was very different from previous visits. I was fortunate that the sergeant who took my details recognised my face and, after a whispered but energetic debate with the constable who had brought me in, escorted me to a disused office, with the promise to send word to Holmes immediately. He could not have been more friendly, bringing me a cup of tea and assuring me that we would "soon clear this misunderstanding up", but I noticed he locked the door when he left.

I did not have long to wait, thankfully. Within half an hour, I heard a commotion outside, and Holmes's voice demanding access. Softer, calmer voices could also be heard, and presently the office door opened and my friend hurried inside, a paper-wrapped packet tucked under his arm.

"You are entirely well, Watson?" he asked as he handed me the packet, which I was pleased to see contained a clean shirt. "You were not harmed?"

I was touched by his solicitude, of course, but feared he had misunderstood whatever message the sergeant had sent. "Harmed, Holmes? No, not at all. But I suspect that matters have not been explained to you properly. I was never in danger of harm, merely discovered alongside it."

Holmes waved a hand at me in dismissal. "Never in danger? Of course you were. Indeed, of course you *are*. Are you not suspected of a terrible murder? Is not your life in peril, should that suspicion become something more concrete? The danger is very real, Watson."

He paused for a moment, reached for a cigarette, then thought better of it and took a seat instead.

"You realise, of course, that this whole affair is a snare designed specifically to capture you? You are fortunate that whoever concocted the plan decided that it fitted his purpose better to humiliate you than to kill you. Had he not, you would even now lie dead and I would be undertaking an investigation into your murder, and not your innocence of that crime."

Only then did he light a cigarette, offering one to me and another to Inspector Lestrade, who I realised had now entered the room. The inspector shook his head in refusal, rubbing his eyes as he took a seat. He had not shaved and his collar was askew, I noticed; sure signs that he had been roused from sleep.

"I was sound in bed when Mr. Holmes's lad came rapping on my door, Doctor," he confirmed, though with no indication of annoyance or irritation in his voice. "I'd have sent him on his way with a flea in his ear, too, if he'd not said he'd been told to say that Dr. Watson had grave need of my assistance."

He opened a brown folder he had brought in with him, and consulted the first of two typewritten sheets it contained.

"And the boy spoke truly, did he not?" he asked rhetorically, glancing up from his reading. "This is Constable Howie's report, taken from his notebook, and it makes for uncomfortable reading, Doctor."

Holmes held out a hand. "If I may," he said. He scanned the pages quickly, then, with a nod of assent from Lestrade, read aloud from them:

At 11.04 p.m., I was making my way along Linhope Street, near Regent's Park. I would not usually have been in the area at the time, but I had been instructed to check on number 14, on which maintenance work was being carried out, and being unsure of the honesty of the nearby inhabitants I had made certain to keep a close eye on so insecure a dwelling.

I had barely begun checking number 14 when I became aware of a man's raised voice coming from the next door along, number 16. A lady, who I knew to be the landlady, Mrs. Elizabeth Soames, met me in the doorway of number 16, and informed me that "a maniac is screaming murder in one of the rooms".

Arriving at the door to the room in question, the sound of booted feet could be heard from within, banging heavily against the door. A male voice, crying "open, damn you!" accompanied this banging. Mrs. Soames informed me that the occupant, an elderly lady, had taken a room earlier that evening, having been brought to the house by a girl describing herself as her granddaughter. A gentleman had been the occupant's only visitor, though she had not herself spoken to him. Mrs. Soames had seen nobody leave before hearing banging from the room.

Upon investigation, I discovered that the door was locked. No key could be seen and Mrs. Soames admitted that she had no spare, that key having been lost some time previously. With no means of access, I made enquiries through the door as to the reason for the commotion. A man's voice – I believe the same as I had earlier heard cursing – replied, "There is no key and I have been locked inside! Murder has been committed!"

At this point, believing life to be at risk within, I asked Mrs. Soames to send a boy to the local station for assistance, and attempted to break down the door. I was unable to do so at first, until I enlisted the help of several men from the area who helped me to effect entrance.

The room contained little furniture. In addition to a small table and a wardrobe, the only other furnishing was a large bed, on which could clearly be seen the body of an elderly lady. The lady had suffered several severe, visible wounds.

The only living occupant of the room was a middle-aged gentleman. His clothes and hands were soiled by significant amounts of blood and he appeared confused, saying, "Sorry. I don't know that poor woman. My mind must have wandered."

Upon questioning, the gentleman identified himself as Dr. John Watson and claimed to have been led to the room by a young lady, who stated that her grandmother was seriously ill and in danger of death. Upon arrival, he further stated, he had discovered the room exactly as seen by myself and had been locked inside, he claimed, by the same young woman. He was unable to supply the woman's name, though he did provide a detailed description (overleaf).

A bag, of the type used by doctors and identified by Dr. Watson as his own, was found to contain several sharp knives, though each was clean of blood. No other potential weapon was discovered.

Further investigation revealed that, contrary to Dr. Watson's claims, the key was still in the door lock. This being put to him, he was unable to provide any explanation.

No sign could be found of the young woman.

"And then the usual formalities of such reports," Holmes concluded, dropping the folder onto the desk which took up a large portion of the room.

Inspector Lestrade pulled it towards himself and glanced down before he spoke. "A nasty tale, Doctor," he said, looking back up at me. "But I think I'm a good enough judge of character to know that you had no part in it. No malicious part, at least."

If I had been confused earlier, Lestrade's words, comforting though they were intended to be, brought my predicament into sharp focus. The inspector was not exactly a friend, but we had worked together sufficiently often – and shared enough of Holmes's thoughtless comments – for a bond of sorts to have formed between us. He might be willing to say that my involvement in the murder of the old woman was innocent of malice, but what of others, with less reason to believe my story?

As though reading my thoughts, Holmes nodded briskly. "You are quite correct, Watson, to wonder if the remainder of Scotland Yard will be so quick to put their trust in your honesty. Lestrade knows you well, but others do not, and will be less likely to give you the benefit of their doubt."

"How–" I began to ask, but Holmes was already answering my question.

"We really do not have time to waste on explanation of every deduction I make, Watson, but I shall indulge you on this occasion. You heard Lestrade's words with a small smile of pleasure, then your eyes dropped to the folder containing the constable's report, and your face fell. Next you glanced at the door, clearly considering those outside, and your brow became noticeably furrowed. What else could you be thinking, but that you might not be so readily believed elsewhere?"

As ever, Holmes's reasoning was faultless. Lestrade, though, seemed unimpressed.

"These parlour tricks are all very well, Mr. Holmes, but I should tell you that the very fact of my acquaintance with Dr. Watson makes it unlikely I will be appointed to this case. There is no saying how another officer might view the evidence, and Howie's statement is damning in several respects. The Doctor has good reason to worry."

Holmes had little time for Scotland Yard or its representatives, and the withering look he now aimed at Lestrade did nothing to mask this negative opinion.

"Of course he does!" he snapped. "He has been discovered with a dead woman, covered in blood, and with no explanation for his presence beyond a mysterious girl and an unsupported tale of a sick grandmother. Additionally, the only knives on the scene belong to him, and the room in which he was found was, it is claimed, locked from the inside, the key still present in the door after your doughty constable broke it down. He has a great deal to worry about!

"But still, there are already points of interest which we might consider to his advantage. For instance, the key found in the door. It was definitely the original, which should have been in the possession of the tenant, and not a copy?"

Lestrade shook his head. "It would seem so, Mr. Holmes, but Howie's just outside if you'd care to speak with him?"

Without waiting for a response, the inspector leaned into the hallway and asked Howie to come in. I nodded a greeting at the constable, who was taller than I remembered, but he failed to return the gesture and instead came to attention before Lestrade.

"Right then, lad. Mr. Holmes here is wondering whether it's certain that the key you found in the door was the usual one, the one given by the landlady to the tenant of the room. It could not be a copy, made by persons unknown?"

"No sir, it could not," Howie replied. "Mrs. Soames identified the key by various marks on the barrel as the same one she'd handed to the dead lady earlier."

"And the lock?" Holmes leant forward in his chair eagerly, his face lighting up as his great brain came alive. "The door was definitely locked? It could not have simply been jammed shut with a piece of wood?"

"No such jam was found in the room, sir, and the splintering of the wood around the keyhole indicated that it had been locked prior to the door being broken down."

"And how long would you say passed between you first hearing a raised voice from number sixteen and the breaking down of the door?"

"No more than five minutes, sir."

"You are certain, Constable? It could not have been closer to ten?"

"Not ten, sir, no. Maybe a minute or two beyond the five, but I'd swear it was no longer than that."

"As much as seven minutes, then." Holmes's long fingers tapped a rhythm on his legs. "In which time you saw nobody other than those persons mentioned in your report?"

"I took a note of everyone who entered or was present in the house, sir. There was nobody else there, or I'd have taken note of them too."

Holmes considered this, his head cocked to one side. "Thank you, Constable Howie," he said finally. "You have been of great assistance."

Lestrade gestured that the officer might depart, which he did with relieved alacrity, leaving the three of us alone in the room once more. In the sudden silence, I felt my spirits fall. I stared down at my shoes, my thoughts unhappy ones.

I heard Lestrade's voice as though from a distance. "For the moment, we should see what we can do to keep Dr. Watson out of a cell, and his name out of the newspapers."

"We will need to be quick to catch the early editions," Holmes replied thoughtfully. "Watson will be charged with murder, and while I cast no aspersions on your officers, there is always someone who will speak to a journalist, if the financial inducement is suitable. But I believe that there is someone I can speak to who will be able to ensure that the case is allowed to disappear, at least so far as the gutter press are concerned."

Holmes's reluctance to mention his brother Mycroft in front of Lestrade was understandable, for his role in government was a complicated and largely secret one, but he was spared the need to explain further as the door of the office chose that moment to creak noisily and open a little. A tall, dark-headed man stood framed in the doorway for a moment, then pushed his way inside.

"Good evening, Lestrade," he said with a nod. "I'm surprised to see you here. Isn't this your night off?"

The man could not have been more obviously a policeman, from the tips of his closely cropped hair to his polished regulation boots. He was thin to the point of emaciation, with the sharp bones in his face straining against his skin, and a wide, crooked nose, below which a sparse moustache struggled to be seen. His eyes darted quickly about the room as he made his way behind the desk and took a seat.

"Won't you make the introductions then?" he said, pulling the folder, which still sat on the desk, towards him as he spoke.

"Mr. Sherlock Holmes, Dr. John Watson, meet Inspector Potter," Lestrade growled quietly, making little effort to hide a clear dislike of his colleague. "Potter, before we proceed further, you should know that the Doctor has been a good friend to the Yard."

It was a name I had heard before, though I could not immediately say where. I nodded a greeting and mumbled, "Inspector," while Holmes merely closed his eyes and allowed a half-smile to play on his lips.

The effect of these introductions on Inspector Potter was, however, far more marked. At the mention of Holmes's name, he sat forward and stared directly at my friend, keeping his eyes upon him for what felt like at least a minute. Finally, he spoke, though he directed his comments not to Holmes but to Lestrade.

"Well, let's be clear from the off, Lestrade. There'll be no favours here. Your good *friend*" – and here he stressed the word mockingly – "will be treated the same as any other person suspected of murder, beginning with a night in the cells and a trip to court in the morning where, I'm certain, he'll be invited to spend a good deal longer in our custody."

Lestrade, to his credit, protested immediately and with force. "Dr. Watson and Mr. Holmes have given great assistance to the force in the past, Potter. Without them there's many a villain who'd even now be free and easy, and we none the wiser."

It must have pained him to make such an admission, especially in front of Holmes, but whatever discomfort he felt was surely doubled by Potter's reply.

"That may be so, Lestrade, but that is exactly the sort of appeal for special favour to which I referred. The fact that these gentlemen have been able to shore up your own shortcomings as a detective is hardly germane to whether one of them is a killer or not." He paused for a moment. "Be assured that *I* have no need of their assistance."

He rose from his seat and stretched his long frame. "Now, all we need is a handy constable and we can have your *friend*" – again he stressed the word – "tucked up in a cell, quick smart."

My heart fell as his hand closed on the door handle and I turned to Holmes, who had remained silent since Potter had entered the room. Now, with the smallest of nods, he spoke.

"Are we to assume that you have already been formally appointed to Dr. Watson's case, Inspector?" he asked.

"Not yet. Not formally, no," the inspector admitted grudgingly, turning back from the door.

"Then you have no more authority in this matter than, say, Inspector Lestrade. Is that correct?"

"I have been told by the Commissioner himself that I shall be given the investigation," Potter blustered.

"*Shall be*," repeated Holmes. "Not *have been*."

"In which case, Inspector Potter," interjected Lestrade, with the beginnings of a smile, "I'll continue to deal with Dr. Watson for the present. It's getting late, though, and there's no need for the two of us to be here. Why don't you take yourself off home, and I'll see to it that suitable accommodation is arranged for the Doctor?"

So long did Potter take to reply that I felt sure he would protest, but in the end he simply shrugged. "As you wish," he muttered. "I shall return later in the morning, with the appropriate paperwork to hand, and relieve you of the responsibility. I'm sure you have a good deal of your own work which requires attention."

With that, he left the room, closing the door firmly behind him. I heard him call the name of a colleague, and his feet retreating down the corridor outside, and then everything fell silent.

Holmes was the first to speak. "An interesting man, for a policeman. Do you know his story, Watson?" I shook my head. "Lestrade will no doubt correct me if my information is erroneous, but my understanding is that Inspector Potter had, until relatively recently, enjoyed a meteoric rise through the ranks of his chosen profession. Too fond of the rulebook, his critics have said, but that is perhaps no bad thing. He is currently the youngest inspector on the force, I believe. Lestrade?"

The inspector nodded, a sour expression on his face. "Very popular with the higher-ups is Potter, yes," he admitted.

"He had even been mentioned in senior police circles as a potential future Chief Constable, or so I am told." Holmes cocked his head at an angle. "That, of course, is not what makes him interesting. To be the most senior of a gaggle of incompetents and paper pushers is no great boast, after all. One may as well congratulate oneself on being chief madman in the asylum."

He smiled at his own jest and, suddenly, I was irritated by his insistence on drawing out his every minor thought as though it were spun gold.

"For goodness' sake, Holmes, why is he interesting then?" I snapped.

Holmes was immediately contrite. "I am sorry, my dear fellow," he said. "I'm sure you're tired and naturally you are concerned, yet here I am, wandering off on a tangent of my own devising." He straightened in his chair and continued. "Potter is interesting because his rapid ascent up the police ranks came to a juddering and, it once seemed, permanent end the year before last. He arrested, and insisted – in the face of opposition from his superiors – upon charging, the younger brother of one of our most senior judges, along with several other members of prominent society families. The crimes were... well, let us simply say that they were more of a moral nature than a strictly criminal one and leave it at that. In any case, it was felt that Potter had pressed on with the case for reasons of personal publicity, and not in the best interests of the force or the country at large.

"The upshot of the whole affair was that pressure was brought to bear, the charges were quashed, and Potter's ambitions left in tatters."

"Or so it seemed at the time, Mr. Holmes," Lestrade interposed. "But this last year he's arrested so many London criminals that the papers have started calling him the Capital's Saviour. That's the sort of thing to put anyone's career back on track."

Now I recalled where I had heard Potter's name mentioned before. Even *The Times* had carried a few small pieces on his spectacular successes in infiltrating and exposing the work of the criminal gangs who currently infested the capital.

"Why has he been allocated my case then?" I asked. "Am I viewed as so important?"

Lestrade shrugged. "Who can say? Your name is a well-known one, as is Mr. Holmes's, and Inspector Potter is back in favour among my superiors. What's more, he has a nose for the popular cases. I wouldn't put it past the man to have asked for the case, hoping thereby to have his name in the newspapers even more often. As though that's the measure of good police work…"

It was plain that Lestrade did not care for his colleague. I had no more desire to listen to the inspector bemoaning his lot compared to that of Potter than I did to hear Holmes's intellectual digressions, and so changed the subject as quickly as I could.

"Never mind Potter for now," I said. "He can wait until the morning. Of more pressing concern is the question of what is to be done tonight."

Lestrade indicated his agreement. "Of course, Doctor. Though there's not a great deal anyone can do at this time of night. You've been charged with murder, and can hardly be allowed to return to Baker Street, at least until further investigation has taken place. But," he smiled, "there's nothing to say that you cannot pass the night comfortably enough in this room, in discussion with myself, officially speaking." He considered his own words for a moment, then continued, "I can even get a couple of day beds brought in and you and Mr. Holmes can get your heads down for a few hours."

His smile was obviously intended to be encouraging, and though the expression looked out of place on his thin, rat-like face, I appreciated the effort, and the offer of sleep. It had been a long night, and in the distance I could hear bells chiming two o'clock.

Holmes, however, was predictably keen to press on. "There will be plenty of time for sleeping later," he announced, jumping to his feet. "Just now, we must make the most of the time we have to prepare Watson's defence."

"Thank you, Holmes, but I fear none of us are in any condition for such a task," I said with a yawn. My whole body ached with tiredness and it was all I could do, now the immediate danger had passed, to keep my eyes open.

Holmes stared at me for a long moment, then nodded his head

briskly and began to speak. "Quite right, Watson," he admitted. "It has been a trying night for you, and perhaps rest is the best preparation for tomorrow."

He shrugged on his coat and took his hat from the stand. "For myself, there are certain papers back at Baker Street which I might profitably consult in the meantime. Take advantage of Lestrade's kind offer and I shall return in a few hours having, I hope, made some progress in your most interesting case."

Had I not been so exhausted I might have made some small jest at the speed with which Holmes had relegated my arrest on suspicion of brutal murder to an interesting intellectual exercise, but instead I confined myself to bidding him farewell and slumped back in my chair as he left the room. I think I must have been in shock, for even as Lestrade murmured something about arranging for a bed, my eyes had closed, and within seconds I was fast asleep.

Chapter Three

The following morning, I was woken by Holmes's voice close to my ear.

"Wake up, Watson. Potter is on fast on my heels, and I have a question to ask you before he arrives."

I struggled to sit, feeling every muscle protest as I uncoiled myself from the chair in which I'd passed the night. Holmes stood before me, still wearing the clothes in which I had seen him the previous evening, and carrying a carpetbag which he placed on the floor by the desk.

"What is it, Holmes?" I asked. "Have you discovered something already?"

"Too early to say," he replied shortly. "But quickly, before Potter arrives. What do you know of Major Sir Campbell John McLachlan? He is a proud Scotsman, currently a Member of Parliament, having previously served with the army for many years in Afghanistan and India. Did your paths ever cross during your own army service?"

The name was unfamiliar, though I could not say with certainty that we had never met. I had treated many officers while in Afghanistan, but retained few names in my memory. I said as much to Holmes, who nodded as though expecting such a response.

"Very well," he said. "Potter will be here in a moment, possibly with news that the lady of whose murder you are accused was a relation of Major McLachlan. If you have no knowledge of him, it can only work to our benefit. But give the name some thought. It would reflect badly on you if you were to deny knowing the man, only to have Potter uncover some past acquaintance, however slight, which had unfortunately slipped your mind."

With that, he took a seat, just as the door swung open and Inspector Potter entered the room.

He was as immaculately dressed as before; my own trousers still bore specks of blood, as did the cuffs of my jacket. He strode across the room, took a seat behind the desk and, with an irritated glare at Holmes, flipped open a folder he had carried in with him. He wasted no time on polite greetings, but launched himself into what I felt sure was a prepared speech.

"Dr. John Watson, you have been charged with the murder of a person unknown, said event taking place at number 16 Linhope Street, London, on the evening of 4 November 1898. You will be taken from this place to appear before a magistrate, who will then decide whether the gravity of the alleged offence, and the evidence implicating you in its commission, provide sufficient cause to detain you in custody while further investigation is carried out." He slowly closed the folder, and looked up at me for the first time. "Do you understand what I have just told you, Doctor?" he asked.

I glanced across at Holmes, wondering at Potter's failure to mention the MP, McLachlan, then nodded towards Potter. "I do,"

I replied, hastily swallowing the bile which had risen in my throat as the charge against me was read out. I had every faith that our legal system would soon acquit me of guilt, but to hear the charges against me read out so coldly was an uncomfortable experience.

"Very well. That being the case, I must ask you to ready yourself for transport to court. In view of your professional status and standing in the community, it has been decided you will not be manacled, but I should stress that any uncooperative behaviour on your part will cause that decision to be reversed."

Potter did not look at all pleased as he spoke. Had it been his decision, I had no doubt I would be shuffling into court in a full set of irons. I wondered to whom I owed my thanks that I would not.

"I have brought Dr. Watson a fresh suit, and such toiletries as he will need to make himself presentable. I assume that is in order?" Holmes was already opening the bag with which he had arrived. He handed me a neatly folded jacket and trousers as Potter retrieved his folder and walked towards the door.

"Five minutes, and not a moment longer," he said with a scowl. "Once five minutes are up, he's leaving with me, whether he's had time to brush his hair or not! Constable!" he shouted through the open door, then waited until a uniformed policeman came running up.

"Keep an eye on the prisoner while he changes, and tell me as soon as he's ready to go. Or in five minutes' time, whichever comes first. Mr. Holmes," he continued, "is to be escorted from the station immediately. You may have friends in high places, Mr. Holmes," he concluded, "but that does not give you the right to do as you wish in my station. If you will follow me?"

The familiar half-smile on Holmes's face was enough for me to know that he was pleased with Potter's reaction to his presence, and he willingly followed the inspector from the room, pausing only for an instant to assure me that he would be present in court.

The door closed firmly behind the two men and, under the watchful eye of the constable, I made my toilet with as much haste as I could manage. I had no wish to appear at anything less than my best before the magistrate.

My court appearance was, in fact, remarkable only for its brevity.

Although Holmes and I had led many men and women into the embrace of our legal system, I had rarely concerned myself with what happened next; how the criminals we had exposed were treated and how they passed through the courts on their way to sentencing and conviction. So it was that, while I had a vague sense of what was to occur, I was still surprised to be whisked into an all but deserted courtroom and, within two minutes at most, informed that I would be held in custody while the police carried out further investigation.

"The gravity of the offence being such that no thought of bail might reasonably be expected," in the words of the magistrate.

With no opportunity to speak for myself, I was led from the court and back down the corridors and passageways through which I had entered. From there, I was placed in one of the so-called Black Marias – police carriages specifically designed for the transport of prisoners, with the rear carriage converted entirely into a series of secure cages, each entered separately from the outside. Holmes strode across as my door closed behind me and whispered a swift warning. "Speak to no other prisoner, if you can avoid it, Watson, but if you are forced to do so, take note of them in detail, for your life may depend on your knowledge of your fellow inmates. There is more than one man inside our prisons who has reason to curse the names of Sherlock Holmes and John Watson. You will be allowed no visitors on your first day, but rest assured that I shall come to see you tomorrow. With positive news, I feel sure." His voice fell away as the Maria moved off.

It is a mark of my disturbed state of mind that I welcomed the enclosure provided by the Maria. It concealed me from the potential embarrassment of public scrutiny and left me alone for the first time in almost twenty-four hours. I considered Holmes's words and recognised the sense in them. I knew that people believed the old saying that there is no smoke without fire, and though I had no doubt that Holmes would uncover a flaw in the case against me and I would be set free, the fewer people who knew of my predicament in the meantime the better. Exhausted as I was, the steady motion of the carriage soon lulled me into deep sleep.

For the second time that day, I was woken by a hand on my shoulder. A police constable stood before me in the doorway of my enclosure.

"Up you get now!" he ordered roughly. "Don't make me drag you out of there!"

Over his shoulder I could see an imposing brick building, the interior portion of Holloway Prison, to which I knew all prisoners awaiting trial were brought. I stepped from my temporary cell and, in the company of my fellow detainees, followed the constable through the imposing gateway and into the prison itself.

"Males? To the left," a voice rang in my ear before I had a chance to take in my surroundings.

On either side of me stretched a long passageway, lined with what I took to be cells. I shuffled in procession to the left and allowed myself to be placed at one corner of a square of prisoners, facing a bored-looking guard who immediately began to recite a set of rules and regulations in a dull monotone. That completed, another guard called each of us forward and handed us two grey sheets, in addition to our cell number.

Thereafter came a long period of standing in the cold corridor, while the guards led prisoners, a pair at a time, to have their measurements and weight recorded. When my turn was completed, all that remained was to sign a form listing the few possessions that I had in my pockets (these were taken away for safe keeping), and then I was led to the cell, which was to be my home for the night at least.

If truth be told, it was less spartan than I expected. Measuring about twelve feet by ten, my cell was clean, if cold, and lit by a gas light and a small, rectangular window on the far wall. The contents consisted of a single bed on one side of the room, adjacent to a writing desk and chair, with a battered sideboard, on which rested a water jug and bowl. The door itself was lined with metal on the inside, broken only by a small glass panel through which the guards could check on the prisoners at any time.

"You've got good friends, looks like," the guard remarked as I moved inside and took the seat. "A 'superior' already, and you not in the door five minutes."

"A superior?" I asked in confusion.

"One of the good cells. You, or your mates on the outside, pays a few shillings and you gets one of these. Room to yourself, nice bit of furniture, better grub too. Surprised you didn't know that. Most do."

He looked me up and down without embarrassment. "But you're not the type usually ends up here. Goes to show, though. There's wrong'uns everywhere."

With that, he closed the door, and left me alone with my worrisome thoughts.

Though not for long. Within minutes, another guard appeared.

"Up you get, Watson," he growled. "Governor Keegan wants to see you."

He stood to one side so that I preceded him along a bewildering array of corridors and stairs and so to the door of the governor's office. Lestrade had warned me that the governor, though officially only a temporary replacement for his consumptive predecessor, had been in the role for almost two years, and had gained a reputation for severity.

Even so, he greeted me warmly enough, offering me both a seat and a cigarette. I happily accepted, having been forbidden tobacco all day, watching him as he struck a match and held it out to me. A little under six feet in height, he was slim and clean-shaven, with thick black hair that shone in the office light. He was immaculately dressed, in a lounge coat and matching trousers, with one of the fashionable Homburg hats hanging on a rack behind him.

"I must say, Dr. Watson, that gentlemen of your calibre do not often pass through the gates of my establishment." He laughed. "Indeed, you will not be shocked to learn that most of the men within these walls are poorly educated, violent ne'er-do-wells. The very dregs and leavings of society, you might call them. Sadly beyond redemption," he concluded, and sat back in his chair, obviously inviting some comment from me.

"Surely not," I ventured, feeling a genuine sense of relief that I had been delivered into the hands of a sympathetic and learned man. Perhaps my period of incarceration need not be entirely without consolation, I thought.

I could not have been more wrong.

The two simple words I had spoken were, it seemed, enough to cause a change in personality worthy of the pen of Mr. Robert Louis Stevenson. Where he had been all affability and friendship before, now his face purpled and the veins on his forehead throbbed alarmingly.

"You doubt me? Or do you instead believe yourself to be a greater judge of criminal character than I? Has the mere proximity of Sherlock Holmes been enough to render you fit to refute the conclusions of an experienced penologist?"

The transformation was astonishing. Keegan rose from his chair so violently that it fell back with a clatter on the ground. He leaned forward so far that, even with a desk in between us, his face was within an inch of mine.

"Get on your feet, Watson!" he spat. "And stub that cigarette out. You're not at Baker Street now."

Thoroughly confused, I ground out the cigarette and rose to my feet. Keegan came round from behind his chair and prodded me in the chest with his finger several times. It took all my self-control not to push him away, but I knew that such a course of action would be disastrous. Instead, I focused my eyes on a point just above his head and waited for his temper to abate.

Whether it would have done so, I was not to discover.

"Shapley!" shouted the governor. The door opened and the same guard who had brought me to the governor rushed in. "Take the prisoner to his cell. And keep a close watch on him. His insolence and contempt for authority is plain to see, and I will not have it infecting the other inmates. Any infraction of the rules is to be reported directly to me." He swallowed hard and wiped sweat from his forehead. "Now get out!"

This last command was directed at me. In response the guard

seized my arm and swung me roughly through the office door. I caught a final glimpse of Governor Keegan, slamming his fist down on his desk in fury, and then I was shoved hard in the small of the back and forced along the corridor, back to my cell.

Chapter Four

❦

Having spent many nights under canvas in the army, a cold room and a hard bed were no great discomfort to me, and my cell was sufficiently remote to shield me from the worst of the prisoners' anguished cries I heard faintly echoing along the corridors. As a result, I woke next morning refreshed and feeling much more my usual self. I breakfasted on a small bowl of thin porridge and two slices of brown bread, washed down with water served in a rusty tin cup, then sat and waited for Holmes to arrive. A pair of cards on the writing desk laid out the rules of the prison and the few special privileges allowed to the unconvicted prisoner. These amounted, so far as I could see, to the right to wear one's own clothes, more licence to move around various approved sections of the prison, and a greater number of visitors than would otherwise be the case. The only other information of any great interest was that prisoners were required to take an hour's exercise at 10 a.m. and would be given lunch at midday. Beyond that, and compulsory attendance at church services, it appeared that the day was my own.

In fact, nobody came to take me to exercise and thus I spent the morning alone with my thoughts. I determined to remain positive, but it was difficult with no means of distraction, save counting the bricks in the cell wall. The arrival of lunch was a welcome break in the monotony, even if the food was of the same poor standard as I had received earlier.

Fortunately, I did not have too long to wait after I completed my sparse repast. Promptly at 12.30, a guard came to lead me to the visitors' room, a spacious if grubby hall with tables and chairs arranged in two lines facing one another, a clear space of a foot or so in between. A guard stood at either end, occasionally taking a turn along the corridor between the chairs. Holmes already sat at one table. To my dismay Inspector Potter sat beside him.

Potter wasted no time on pleasantries as I took the seat opposite the pair.

"Dr. Watson, we have this morning discovered the identity of the lady of whose murder you are accused. Her name is–"

Holmes cut across the inspector as though he had never spoken.

"–Miss Sarah McLachlan, the elderly maiden aunt of Major C. J. McLachlan, hero of Cawnpore, crusading Member of Parliament, English gentleman and, currently, chairman of a parliamentary inquiry into the organised criminal gangs who plague the streets of the capital."

"I'll have Lestrade's badge for this!" Potter hissed, glaring at Holmes who, for his part, raised an eyebrow quizzically.

"Why on earth would you do such a thing, Inspector?" he asked mildly.

"He had no right to divulge confidential police information to you! You may consider yourself an adjunct to the police force, Mr. Holmes, but to my mind you are no such thing. In truth, you are nothing but a self-aggrandising amateur!"

Holmes allowed the insult to pass without comment, though he was quick to correct Potter on the remainder of his statement. "I can assure you that I have not spoken to Lestrade since the very early hours of this morning, nor has he divulged information of any sort to me."

"Then perhaps you would be good enough to explain to me exactly how you came by facts concerning the late Miss McLachlan which have only come to light in the last hour, when Major McLachlan himself visited the Yard to report his aunt missing?"

"As you were so quick to point out, Inspector, I am neither your underling nor a member of the police force. And as a mere amateur, I hardly think it my place to educate you in how best to carry out your investigations."

"Amateur you may be, Holmes, but if you do not furnish me with a reasonable explanation for your surprising knowledge, I shall be forced to draw the obvious conclusion. That your friend Dr. Watson informed you of the name of the woman he brutally murdered. Now, sir, what have you to say to that?"

Holmes considered for a moment, his fingers steepled beneath his chin in a familiar manner. He glanced at me, but I had long experience of his methods, and was in no doubt that he had an answer for Potter, if he chose to give it. Finally, with a sigh of irritation, he turned his attention to the waiting policeman.

"Very well, Inspector Potter. If, as seems the case, you are incapable of the most basic police work, then I suppose it falls to me to educate you. The chain of deduction is really a very simple one." He gestured towards me. "In his statement, Dr.

Watson mentioned that the murder room contained little by way of furnishings, and what there was of inferior quality. However, he also noted that a lady's robe of expensive manufacture hung from a wardrobe door.

"The only logical explanation was that this garment belonged to the victim. Therefore, when I left the police station last night I contacted various street urchins who have in the past rendered me similar services, and detailed them to visit every police station they could, checking whether an elderly lady of quality had been reported missing. Fortunately, one of my young friends happened to chance upon a serving girl on an errand who informed him that her mistress had wandered off during the night. It seems that the lady in question is mentally somewhat past her prime and has been known to disappear on unplanned midnight rambles, but always she has returned by first light. This morning she failed to do so. The lady's name was Sarah McLachlan, aunt through marriage to Major McLachlan."

He sat back, his face expressionless, awaiting Potter's reaction.

To my surprise, Potter seemed mollified. "Very good, Mr. Holmes," he said, with a strained smile. "If only some of my lads were half as sharp as you, we'd already have this case tied up."

"I cannot comment on that, Inspector. You know your men better than I."

"I do. And any of my men would have come to me at once, had they any information likely to aid in an investigation. In fact," he concluded, the smile fading from his face, "I wonder that you did not. And I wonder what other facts you might know, but have kept to yourself? Facts which might, perhaps, further incriminate your friend here."

He stared steadily at Holmes as he spoke, ignoring me as

though I were not there. But if he expected Holmes to react, he was to be frustrated.

"As you said, Inspector, I am a mere amateur. What could I possibly know that the professionals do not? As for Miss McLachlan, this is the first time I have seen you since discovering her identity. When else might I have told you of what I had learned?" A cold smile played briefly on his lips. "And besides, you did come to the same conclusion without my assistance."

Potter held Holmes's eye for a moment longer than was comfortable then, with an exaggerated sigh, turned his attention to me.

"Very well, Dr. Watson," he said. "As I was saying before I was interrupted, the deceased lady has been identified as the aunt of a prominent Member of Parliament, Major Sir Campbell McLachlan. Do you have any personal knowledge of the major or his aunt? Have you ever met or treated Major McLachlan or any member of his family? There is a brother who lives with the major, I believe." He flipped open his notebook and held a pencil above a blank page. "I would remind you that we will be asking the same question of the major, so I would advise you to be sure of your recollections."

It was fortunate that Holmes had alerted me to the name earlier, otherwise I would have been less sure of my answer. As it was, I was able to reply with confidence that I had met neither McLachlan nor his late aunt.

"But you are aware of the major's work concerning the gangs who have recently been the cause of an upsurge in criminality in the capital?"

"I am aware of the gangs, yes, of course. I have even, in my own small way, been able to assist Holmes in disturbing their activities.

Major McLachlan's name is new to me, however – in this and every other regard!"

I had not cared for Potter's insinuation that I would be less than truthful, and I fear some of my irritation was apparent in my tone.

"There's no need to raise your voice, Dr. Watson," he said with a glint of pleasure in his eye. "I should tell you that I myself have worked with Major McLachlan in the past, with a great deal of success, and a fair amount of reporting in the press. I must admit to some surprise that a gentleman with your particular interests should claim that the name is unknown to him."

"Watson is as knowledgeable regarding current affairs as any man, Inspector, but if he has a flaw it is in his occasional failure to take note of details." Holmes's voice was smooth as he again took charge of the conversation. "I, however, know a great deal about the major. He is a soldier of some repute, and a hero of various Indian campaigns. Famously jealous of his privacy and of his family's reputation, all that is generally known of this private man is that he is a keen collector of military memorabilia, was in his time a gifted polo player and is expected to be raised to the Lords in the very near future. He is not, however, someone who has ever called upon the services of either myself or Dr. Watson, nor do I recollect ever making his acquaintance socially."

"Does that answer satisfy you, Inspector Potter?" I asked.

"It is certainly an answer, Doctor, but I would not go so far as to say that I find it satisfactory. But let us move on for the moment." He consulted his notebook. "You were discovered in the murder room with several knives. Now," he held up a hand to forestall my objection, "I am aware that as a doctor you can claim such blades to be necessary for your work, but you are not currently – and correct me if I'm wrong – a surgeon? So, three knives might be viewed as excessive, given your normal day-to-day practice?"

"In my day-to-day practice, yes. But recently I have treated an elderly patient by lancing a variety of painful boils, for which I needed a range of knives. Besides," I said, becoming more heated at the detective's insinuating tone, "even your own policeman admitted that each knife in my bag was free of blood."

To my surprise, Potter gave a small chuckle at this sally. He flipped his notebook to a new page and read the few words I could see written there.

"Thank you again, Dr. Watson, for reminding me of the second piece of new evidence uncovered since last night."

He reached into his bag, and pulled out a crumpled brown rag, which he laid before us on the table.

"This rag was found by one of my men, dropped under the bed. As you will see, it is heavily marked with dried blood. Almost as though someone had wiped a bloody knife clean on it."

He sat back, satisfied he had struck a blow to my defence. Holmes, however, was once again equal to the task.

"Might I examine it, Inspector?" he asked quietly. Without waiting for an answer, he lifted the rag from the table and turned it this way and that in his long fingers. He spent no more than five seconds in such scrutiny, before casually tossing it across to me. "Here is a key element in the inspector's case against you, Watson. Will you tell him the flaw in his reasoning, or shall I?"

It was on the tip of my tongue to tell Holmes that this was no time for games, but before I had even opened my mouth, I saw exactly what my friend meant. The rag had clearly once been grey, for here and there small patches of that colour were visible among the far more prevalent dark brown of dried blood. Nothing but the blood rendered it remarkable, making it all the easier to spot the flaw in Potter's theory.

"The bloodstains!" I cried with delight and no small relief. "They all but cover the rag!"

"Bravo, Watson!" exclaimed Holmes with a laugh of real pleasure; the first I had heard in this place. "You have it exactly! This rag has been soaked in blood, Inspector," he said, switching his attention back to the bewildered Potter. "There is barely a space the size of a shilling unblemished. You surely see the significance? No? Then let me demonstrate."

With that, he leant forward and picked up the detective's pencil. Holding it in one hand as though he would a knife, he took a piece of paper from his pocket and held it in the other. "See here, Inspector, I have the weapon, fresh from the kill, but I can hardly walk the streets afterwards with a bloody knife in my hand. I must clean it, but how? Aha! A fragment of cloth lies nearby, just the thing! I fold the cloth in two round the knife–" he matched his actions to his words as he spoke "–and slide it along the blade, wiping away all trace of my infamous act."

He pulled the paper open again and laid it back flat on the table. "You take my point, Inspector? As Watson so readily grasped, any bloodstains caused by cleaning a knife blade would stand out clearly in straight lines and congeal on either side of the fold. Not smudged across the whole, as is the case here."

He handed the rag back to Potter, who said nothing but glared at the blood-encrusted object as though it had personally offended him. He snapped shut his notebook, having written nothing in it, and rose to his feet. "Well, I cannot spend all day talking to you, so I'll bid you both good day. I'm sure I'll have further questions later."

With that, he departed, leaving Holmes and myself alone at last.

"Thank you, Holmes," I said. "Had you not forewarned me

about Miss McLachlan I fear I would have given the appearance of guilt, however honestly I searched my memory."

Holmes dismissed my thanks with a wave. "Even by the woeful standards of Scotland Yard, Inspector Potter is impressive only in his mediocrity. He contrives always to miss the obvious in his quest for the incriminatory. No matter what you said or how you reacted, he would have assumed your guilt and assured himself he had seen evidence of it. He is, however, dogged, if Lestrade is to be believed. He will not readily give up his pursuit.

"Still, he has been routed this morning. We should allow ourselves some pleasure in that. Perhaps it will prove some consolation to you, once you have read this."

I had noticed Holmes turning a square of newspaper in his hands since the door had closed on Potter, and this he now held out to me, an unexpected look of contrition on his face.

The clipping was from a newspaper I recognised as a notorious purveyor of social scandal and revolutionary rhetoric. The paper itself was cheap and thin, the ink tending to smudge even as I unfolded it, but enough remained legible for me to realise that it was an account of my arrest. The text was in the usual jumbled mix of typefaces, designed to heighten the impact of the author's lurid prose, but the content was less terrible than I might have feared. Beneath the banner headline proclaiming my arrest were only two paragraphs, the first of which merely recounted the bare facts of my "capture".

The second section, however, concentrated on my relationship with Holmes.

DR. WATSON IS BEST KNOWN to the public as the author of a series of fictions recounting his activities as assistant to Sherlock Holmes, the well-known London busybody. Those of our readership who are familiar with his writings will be aware that Dr. Watson and Mr. Holmes exclusively content themselves with investigations into "criminal" acts aimed at the ruling classes, thereby positioning themselves firmly on the side of the oppressors. It has long been suspected by certain parties, among whom this reporter counts himself, that Mr. Holmes considers the law to apply only to other people, and it seems that this lax attitude to personal morality has now spread to his amanuensis. Mr. Holmes is known to have close ties to Scotland Yard and prominent members of the government, so it will come as no surprise to our readers to hear that steps have already been taken to quash reporting of Dr. Watson's crime, and that he is likely to be released into his companion's custody in the near future.

I shrugged my shoulders slightly. "It was bound to get out, I suppose," I said in a steady voice. "If you blame yourself for its existence, then please do not, I beg of you, Holmes. No man could hope to silence the entirety of the British press. Not even you," I concluded with a wry smile.

Holmes frowned in return. "It is the only account I have found. We can at least console ourselves with that. Still, Mycroft is most vexed that even one reporter thought it worthwhile to oppose his will. There will be no repeat."

I hurried to reassure him further by stressing the one positive to be found in the newspaper clipping. "Never mind that, Holmes! Is there any truth in the last part – that I am likely to be released soon?"

"Forgive me, my dear fellow!" he exclaimed suddenly, slapping a palm on the table. "That is the news I intended to give you before Inspector Potter appeared and drove the matter temporarily from my mind. Mycroft is confident that you will be released by the end of the week."

The relief that flooded through me at those words was incalculable. I have, of course, spent time in far worse physical conditions than those I had seen in Holloway Prison, but the mental anguish, the horror of public humiliation should this affair become common knowledge; that had tied my stomach in knots since my fleeting appearance in court. Now it seemed that particular ordeal would soon be behind me.

"That is splendid news, Holmes," I cried. "But how have you managed it?"

"I must admit that little of the credit is mine, Watson. My role was simply to remind my brother that, save for your presence in the murder room itself, there was no real evidence against you. You had the opportunity to commit the crime, but that is all. What possible motive could you have for slaughtering a complete stranger, and how did you do the deed, and yet leave your knives as spotless as ever? These questions were put to… interested parties, and it was agreed that the answers provided by the police force were less than satisfactory." He smiled widely. "I expect the paperwork required for your release to arrive in the next few days."

On that happy note, Holmes took his leave, the time allotted for our interview having come to an end. The promise of freedom would sustain me until that promise became a reality, and so I allowed myself to be escorted to my cell with a far more hopeful heart than I had expected when leaving it only an hour before.

Chapter Five

It is a grave mistake to embrace hope when another person controls every part of your existence.

This was brought home to me almost immediately, as Shapley (who it seemed had attached himself to me, to the exclusion of the other guards) ordered me to halt as I made to take the staircase that led to my cell.

"You're moving home, Watson," he said, reaching forward to remove from my chest the badge showing my cell number. "Governor says we need your cell, so you're to be shifted somewhere less comfortable. Privileges are for those as deserve them, not rippers of old ladies like you. Now get moving!" He pushed me hard in the back, forcing me forward and to the side, where I stumbled and scraped my hand against the wall.

I knew that there was nothing to be gained by protest. I straightened up and, following his pointed finger, made my way down an unfamiliar staircase, along another identical corridor and into my new cell.

In truth, there was little on the surface to differentiate between my new home and the old one. The main difference was the addition of a second bed, on which sat a small, hunched figure. He greeted me with a nod as I entered.

"Brought you some company, Hardie," Shapley announced. "And he's a cold'un, this one. A killer, no less, so you best watch out for yourself. I'd be sleeping with one eye open if I was you." He laughed and slammed the door shut behind him.

Only once Shapley had left did my new cellmate speak. "And what do we have here then?" he said in a surprisingly friendly tone; there was no malice in his voice, and he smiled as he looked me up and down.

Unsure how best to respond, I settled for returning his nod, and sat on the edge of the unoccupied bed.

"What do they call you then?" he asked again, his scrutiny of me apparently over.

"Do–John Watson," I said. No need to advertise my professional status. "And you?"

He grinned widely. "Albert C. Hardie at your service, John, but me mates call me Bert."

I bristled a little at "John", but recalling where I was, did my best to repress my discomfort. I did not intend to be in prison for long, but while I was, it would be in my interests to make friends if I could. "Bert it is then," I said, and offered him my hand. He stared at it briefly then, a decision seemingly made, he extended his own and we shook. His handshake was firm, almost too much so, and he held my gaze for a long moment before releasing my hand. I took the opportunity thus presented to study his face in detail. He could not have been much more than fourteen or fifteen, thin but robust, with a pale, pockmarked face from which two small unblinking blue eyes peered out.

He was obviously as interested in me as I was in him. "Is that right what he said? Are you a murderer?"

"It is all a misunderstanding."

"A poisoner, I expect," he said, thoughtfully. "That's how your sort like to do it, ain't it?"

"I am no poisoner, I assure you," I said stiffly. "Nor a murderer of any other stripe. There was—" I hesitated. Was it wise to speak of my case with a stranger? I had heard of spies being placed in prison cells, men desperate for commutation of their sentence and willing to report on their fellow prisoners to that end. I was aware the boy was staring at me and that I was taking too long to respond. In the end, I simply repeated myself, "—a misunderstanding," though I knew how inadequate I sounded.

Hardie, though, seemed to find it an acceptable reply. "Me too. I misunderstood that you're better not to dip the pockets of off-duty police."

He laughed and, to my surprise, I found myself joining in. "Is that what brings you here?" I asked.

"This time it is, yeah. I got a bit too cocky, to tell the truth, John, and tried my hand at something which ain't really my game. Saw this swell; he'd taken a drop more than was good for him. Leaning against the wall, he was, eyes closed and singing to himself, with a nice little lump in his jacket front. I was on my way home – I'd had a drop as well, and I said to meself, just let it go, Bert. But I never listen, not even to meself, so I slid over, acting like I'm going to help him up, and slips me hand inside his coat. Next thing I know, I'm lying on me face and he's standing there, waving his card at me, telling me what's what. And so here I am. Just arrived yesterday."

He grinned again, arrest and imprisonment obviously little more than an unpleasant occupational hazard to one such as he.

"This is not your first time in prison then?"

"Not by a long chalk. I've been nabbed three times – no, four, now I think on it – but never sent down for long. I'm too tricky for that, John. I know how to play the game. Give the judge a sad tale, rip me clothes a bit, knock a year or two off my age. Six weeks is the most I've ever got."

I shook my head, but his cocksure self-belief was strangely comforting and buoyed my flagging spirits once more. If a child like Bert could face imprisonment with such fortitude, surely I could too?

"This is your first time though, ain't it?" he continued, still smiling.

I nodded. "It is. As I said, it is a misunderstanding. One that will shortly be cleared up."

I remembered the upsurge in hope I had felt on leaving Holmes's presence and told myself that though everyone in positions of authority seemed determined to make my current situation as unpleasant as possible, I had on my side the finest investigative mind in the country. Holmes would uncover the truth, I was sure.

"Thought it was," declared my new friend with satisfaction. "But you've got the right idea. Keep your chin up. And don't tell the guards a thing. That's the surest way to a slit throat and a quicklime grave."

"I'll certainly keep that in mind," I replied, and settled myself as comfortably as I could on the hard bed. The room was cold, the bare bricks leaching away what little heat there was. I pulled a thin blanket over my knees, and asked Hardie what I could expect from the remainder of the day.

"Well, there's services in a bit. Always handy for passing

a note if there's someone you want to talk to." He paused in consideration. "Not much else, though. Not before your trial. You get an hour in the yard and a bite to eat after, but you missed that today. Best to stay here, get your head down if you can, and keep yourself to yourself."

It seemed sound advice. Holmes had made a similar suggestion, in fact. "I intend to do exactly that, actually. But at the moment I can't imagine how I'm going to pass the time. Are we allowed reading materials? Books, perhaps?"

Hardie shook his head. "Don't know about books. You can get a newspaper if you can pay for it, though."

That was something, at least. I filed the information away for later, then sat in awkward silence for several minutes, as our conversation faltered and failed. Hardie sat opposite me, legs crossed at the knee, one eyebrow raised as though amused by my discomfiture, obviously unconcerned that we seemed to have no common ground on which to base so much as a single conversation. Finally, in fear that I would spend the remainder of my time in Holloway in silence, I asked him about his life outside prison.

I wondered how he would react to what I felt sure was a breach of prison etiquette, but to my surprise, he appeared completely unconcerned.

"Dunno where me father is. Left me mother when I was a babe. She used to say he'd been murdered down Chinatown, but I heard he'd taken up with a barmaid and moved somewhere Highgate way. Didn't make any difference to me. Not really. Mother had a touch of the morbs now and then about the old feller, but not me. Never knew him, did I?"

It was a familiar tale. "So you were brought up by your mother? That must have been hard on the poor woman."

"I reckon it was. Not that she was much use, but there was a neighbour or two who'd make sure we was fed when they could manage it. And when they couldn't, well, there's always ways to make a penny or two, if you're willing to take a risk."

"By theft, you mean?"

"A bit o' that, I s'pose, but I did me share of mudlarking too, until I were chased off by them as thinks they own the mud itself. I were in a gang for a while, me and some other lads. We looked out for each other, but that didn't last neither. Police grabbed a couple of 'em and some wanted to try their luck up north. So I were back on me own, wasn't I? Could have been the making of me, that. Allowed me to spread my wings. That's what I told meself, anyway. But no mates means no lookout, and nobody to help you get away when a copper grabs your collar."

He shook his head, but the smile never left his face, as though he found his own ill luck humorous. I found myself warming to Albert Hardie, a child condemned more by the fact of his birth than any innate wrongness in his character. I could see no evil in him as we talked of the London he knew, and I told him a little of my own life, though missing out any mention of Holmes or my role in his investigations.

By the time the lights were extinguished and the cell plunged into darkness, I had decided to do what I could for the boy upon my release. Perhaps it was the realisation that here was someone whom I might be able to help once the world returned to normal, or perhaps it was simply the company of a friendly soul, but I suddenly felt more positive than I had since I had found myself trapped in that terrible room.

I told Hardie some of this, and in return he beckoned to me in the dim light. "Here, have a drop," he whispered, and pressed a glass jar into my hand. Propping myself up on an elbow, I unscrewed the lid and cautiously sniffed at the contents. The smell of raw alcohol assaulted my senses, reminding me of long days spent in laboratories during my medical training.

"It's a bit rough," Hardie continued, "but it'll do you good."

Of course, I should not have been surprised at the presence of illicit alcohol inside a prison, but I admit that I had not realised it was so prevalent that even the likes of Hardie would have access to it. I had no great desire to pollute my body with such a poisonous brew – God knows what had been used to create it – but it would have been rude to reject so well-meant an offer and so I sipped a little, trying not grimace at the taste, then passed the jar back to Hardie with my thanks.

"It's all right," he said, lying back on his bed. "You got to look out for your mates when you're inside, don't yer?"

It had been a long and confusing thirty-six hours. The horrible death of Miss McLachlan and the night spent dozing in Scotland Yard already seemed a lifetime ago. Only as I lay in the dim light and sipped from Hardie's jar as we passed it back and forth did the full enormity of my predicament truly hit me, and I came close to being overwhelmed. I had complete faith in Holmes's abilities, of course, but the evidence against me was extensive, if mainly circumstantial, and Inspector Potter was not, I thought, inclined to try too hard to refute it. In addition, I had the new problem of a prison governor who, for some reason, had taken against me, and no means that I could see by which I could protest against his behaviour. Somehow, though, the peculiar kindness of Albert Hardie – and the warming glow of his illicit alcohol – provided me with a modicum of hope which I held to me and which allowed me, eventually, to fall asleep.

Chapter Six

O ver the next few days I was introduced to the strange rhythm of imprisonment. We rose early, to a breakfast of gruel-like porridge and stale bread, then washed ourselves in cold water and made our beds. That task completed, we had nothing to do but sit in our cells and amuse ourselves as well as we could.

I quickly realised that I preferred the extended periods of confinement in my cell to the occasional activities prescribed by the prison rulebook. Hardie was an engaging young man, with a plethora of stories to tell about his criminal life, and though I should perhaps have remonstrated with him regarding some of his tales, I never did so. His voice, often filled with joy at his own cleverness, brought a little light into our grim surroundings and lifted my spirits, which otherwise inevitably would have sagged as the long day wore on.

There was another reason for my preference for relative solitude. As Holmes had warned me, and Hardie reinforced, I would be safest if I could keep myself separate from the other prisoners. Besides the commonplace violence that plagued all such establishments, there was the very real possibility that one or other of the felons currently awaiting trial might have reason to remember without fondness the names of Holmes and Watson.

Even so, there were two points in the day when I had no choice other than to leave the security of my cell, and mingle with my fellow prisoners.

Religious services, which took place each morning at a quarter to nine, were the less worrisome of the two. We were herded to a rather impressive chapel, big enough to hold the entire prison population, arranged in long pews which faced a carved chaplain's lectern, on which lay open a heavy Bible, and a row of more plush seating for the governor and other senior prison staff. Indeed, all the guards were present at every service (Hardie later informed me that they were fined a shilling if they did not attend). They sat at the end of each row, presumably the better to observe the prisoners, but for the most part quickly dozed off or stared blankly at the ground. The devotions themselves were designed more to castigate prisoners for their failings than to remind those fallen low that there was a higher power who would never despair of them. In common with many of my fellow inmates my attention quickly wandered and, far from considering the condition of my eternal soul, I found myself watching notes and small packages slip from hand to hand. Eventually the chaplain brought the service to an end and we shuffled out the way we had come, and silently made our way back to our cells.

The stroke of ten, however, brought a more dangerous break in the monotony of the day. The heavy footfall of guards progressing along the corridor was followed by the creak of keys in rusty locks as cell doors were opened and we were led through the building to the grim rectangle of ground that served as the prison yard. Here we were left to exercise for an hour (though Hardie informed me that it was often longer, while guards searched for contraband inside). For one reason or another, I had contrived to miss exercise time on my first few mornings, but eventually, I had no choice but to take part. In all honesty, and in spite of my reluctance to mingle, I could not help but anticipate with pleasure the thought of time spent in the open air, no matter how enclosed the area or unappealing the surroundings.

Holloway Prison is laid out on the panopticon principle, with six wings arranged like the top half of a cartwheel, surrounding a central section, from which vantage point the entirety of the prison population can be observed by the guards. The front two wings house women and very youthful prisoners, but the remainder, at the time of my spell within its walls, held some four hundred men, the majority of them awaiting trial like myself. I had been placed in A Wing, the first of the male wings, situated to the left-hand side of the administrative quarters, and thus only a short walk downstairs and past some outbuildings to the courtyard.

I had taken Hardie's suggestion that I leave my jacket in our cell, and divest myself of my tie, lest I appear too obviously out of place, but in the event I need not have worried, for as I emerged into the dull light of an overcast day, I was confronted by a mass of humanity of all shapes and sizes, several of whom were dressed far better than I could have contrived.

The courtyard was an expanse of trampled ground ringed and criss-crossed by gravel pathways, along which prisoners were intended to walk in perpetual motion. In reality, groups of acquaintances came together in clumps between the paths and stopped to converse. My new friend and I took up a position within easy reach of the route back into the prison proper and while I looked around and wished for the hundredth time that smoking were allowed in Holloway, Hardie pointed out the various criminal types to me.

"You see the fellow in the top hat and the fancy coat? That's Christopher Stone, accused of swindling some Scotsman out of thousands. Sold him a gold mine in America, they say, only it turns out it wasn't his to sell. He'd have got away too, but he got greedy and sold it to another bloke too, and the second bloke knew the first bloke and they got to talking and by pure chance one of them mentioned the mine he'd just bought. That's what I heard anyway."

He shrugged indifferently and drew my attention to a group of grubby young men, thin, wiry types in dirty, stained jackets and flat caps. "And that lot there are all that's left of the Old Nichol gang. There was twice as many once, but they've all either swung or done a flit before the police felt their collars for them."

He shook his head ruefully. "Right nasty crowd, they are. You'd do well to keep away from 'em, John, especially if they take their caps off. I saw 'em kill a man once, with the razors they keep in the brims."

If I am entirely truthful, I was no longer listening to Hardie's excited chatter. Instead I was looking at a tall, broad-shouldered man who stood halfway across the courtyard from me. The yard was crowded with men, two wings' worth of prisoners poured into an area smaller than a rugby pitch, but somehow he had contrived to make a clear space for himself into which no other man, whether prisoner or guard, dared to tread. It was this isolation that had drawn my eye. Who could he be?

I turned to ask Hardie, but before I could do so I felt a hand grasp my shoulder and pull me backwards. What had been a steady stream of passing prisoners became a solid mass enclosing the two of us, pressing us back against the wall and cutting off our path to the safety of the prison interior. A meaty fist flashed towards me and connected hard with my cheek, snapping my head to one side and filling my mouth with the taste of blood. I had boxed a little in my younger days but the press of bodies made it impossible to bring my own fists to bear, so I lashed out with my feet, catching one man on the shin with a satisfying crack and leaving another on the ground clutching his stomach. Out of the corner of my eye I saw Hardie disappear beneath a crowd of bodies and pushed myself forward to his aid, struggling free for a second, only to feel rough hands grab my arms and pin them against my sides. Another blow to the cheek set my head ringing and caused my vision to blur. I shook my head and refocused my eyes just as a grotesque face swam into view, mouthing a curse, which I failed to make out in the sound and fury of the fight. I had a moment in which to register a mouthful of black teeth and a nose covered in angry boils before a flurry of blows sent me sagging to my knees. Above me, the black-toothed man pulled something that glinted metallically from his pocket and reached down, grabbing my hair and pulling my head back to expose my throat. There was nothing more I could do, and when I tried to push myself up from the ground my legs failed to respond and I knew that death was mere seconds away.

And then, just as quickly as it had begun, the attack came to an end. To my dazed senses it seemed that time had slowed down. The man who held my head fell backwards in a smooth motion, taking a clump of my hair with him, and vanished from view, while his associates appeared to fade away, disappearing into the throng of prisoners who were now running from our corner of the courtyard. My hearing cleared suddenly, and I was aware of whistles and shouts all around me while, as the press in front of me dissipated, guards ran in my direction, their clubs swinging indiscriminately at any passing inmate.

Above the tumult, however, I was aware of one voice. The broad-shouldered man I had spotted immediately prior to the attack held out a hand to pull me up and repeated his words, loud enough for everyone in the vicinity to hear.

"This man is under my protection. Anyone who touches him answers to me."

He steadied me against the wall then, with a half-smile and a nod, turned on his heel and slipped back inside the prison just as the first of the guards reached our position. I fancied I heard him murmur, "I always pay my debts, Dr. Watson," but my head had begun to spin once more and as I slid back down the wall, I could be sure of nothing except the fact that I would meet this man again.

When I came to, I was lying in a strange bed, enclosed by curtains on rails that had been pulled round in three sides of a square. A small table to my right-hand side was the only other furnishing. A hospital bed, obviously. I struggled to sit up, wincing at the sharp pain that blossomed in my chest. A cracked rib, perhaps. Gingerly, I pulled up the top part of my pyjamas. Yes, the tightly wrapped bandage that circled my midriff indicated some such injury, though I was pleased to note that the material was clean and free of blood. Nothing worse, then.

Moving from a seated position to standing was a painful experience, and as my feet found the cold floor, I felt twinges in my back and legs, which suggested further, hopefully minor, damage. There was no sign of my clothing but the tips of my shoes peeped out from under the table, and I pulled them on my bare feet before slipping through the curtain and looking out at the room in which I found myself.

The ward – for such was clearly its function – was brightly lit by daylight streaming through large, unbarred windows. Facing me were six beds, all but one of which was hidden by curtains similar to those that had enclosed my own. The final, unconcealed bed was empty, but turning to look behind me, I saw a similar arrangement on my side of the room, save for the fact that only my own curtains were closed. Five other men, it seemed, were currently enjoying the hospitality of the medical ward. I hoped that Bert Hardie, whom I had last seen engulfed by my attackers, was among them.

There was one quick way to find out.

"Hardie," I said loudly. "Bert Hardie, are you here?" It was not quite a shout, for I had no wish to bring any staff running, but loud enough to carry across the room. For a moment, silence prevailed. Then, to my delight, the already familiar, confident tones of my cellmate rang out in reply.

"John? Is that you?"

The voice had come from the bed directly in front of me. I hobbled over as quickly as I could in my untied shoes and pulled back the curtain. Hardie sat, propped up on a pillow folded in half, with his hands behind his head. His face was bruised from just below the left eye socket to the chin, and the right was closed completely in a puffy, purple bruise, but otherwise he appeared in no worse health than normal.

"I bet I look a pretty sight," he grinned. "Better than you, though, I hope."

Up until that point I had not considered the blows I had taken to my cheek, but now I reached up and touched the tenderest part, swiftly pulling my hand away with a wince as I felt the bone beneath the skin shift painfully.

"Yeah, best not to touch," Hardie said sympathetically. "I asked the doctor about you when we got here, and he said we'd got off lucky. Just bruises for me, and a bust cheekbone and bashed ribs for you. I can tell you, I was glad to hear that."

I was touched, I admit, that he had thought to enquire after me, especially since his own wounds were the result of our new friendship and thus, if only inadvertently, my fault.

He waved a hand at the base of his bed and I gratefully lowered myself onto it, ignoring the sharp pains brought on by the movement. I suspected we would not have long to talk before the doctor or, more probably, a guard, discovered I had left my own bed and escorted me back there.

"What happened?" I asked. I could remember nothing beyond the end of the attack, and the broad-shouldered prisoner who had come to our assistance. "How did we get here?"

"Another bit of luck," said Hardie. "If you weren't pals with Matty Galloway, I reckon things would've gone a damn sight worse."

"Matty Galloway?"

"The big bloke who pulled Ikey Collins off you and sent his boys running." He squinted up at me with his one good eye. "You telling me you don't even know who it was saved us? You don't know Matty Galloway?"

The name was naggingly familiar, but my head was heavy and sore, and I could bring no details to mind. Hardie caught my look of uncertainty and shook his head with a smile, evidently amused by my ignorance.

"Matty Galloway is the boss of the biggest gang of crooks in the country! The most dangerous man in London, I heard. And you say you've never heard his name?"

As he spoke my memory began to clear, and I realised that I did know something about Galloway after all. Any man with access to a newspaper would at least have heard of Matty Galloway in those days, and if his name is forgotten now, well, that is no cause for complaint. I called to mind the reports I had read of his exploits. He was suspected of ordering the deaths of over a dozen men, and of committing half as many murders again with his own hands. But why had so large a fish been deposited in so small a pond as Holloway Prison? And why had he come to my aid? I put both questions to Hardie, speaking quickly, for I could hear footsteps approaching our little nook.

"He's to go on trial soon, I heard. Caught red-handed, they say. Not that that matters a jot."

"But why would such a man help me – us? I'm certain I've never met him, and no criminal in London would be inclined to lift a finger to assist me."

As soon as I spoke I realised I had said too much. The smile faded from Hardie's face and, for the first time since we had met, he frowned.

"What makes you say that? Here, wait a mo. You're not a lawyer, are you?"

With no good answer to hand, I grasped Hardie's suggestion with enthusiasm.

"Something like that. I worked with the police on a few cases, at least. Let's leave it at that."

Hardie's expression made it clear that he was not completely satisfied, but any further questions would have to wait. Hearing the footsteps stop outside the curtains, I pushed myself to my feet with a groan just as they were drawn back, revealing the guard Shapley.

"What do you think you're up to, Watson? Who said you was allowed to go wandering about?"

He grabbed me by the arm and roughly pushed me back towards my own bed, taking no notice of the moan I was unable to suppress as my damaged ribs banged against his elbow.

"This ain't one of your cosy Knightsbridge clinics, Watson. Now get back in that bed before I tell the doctor that there's nothing wrong with you that a night in a punishment cell wouldn't cure." He grinned with pleasure at the thought, exposing his large yellow teeth. "Might come to that anyway, if I know the governor. He don't care for prisoners starting fights, not at all. If I was you I'd keep my head down and do exactly as I was told for the foreseeable. Maybe that way he'll turn a blind eye. And maybe he won't."

With that he shoved me against my bed and, reaching down, pulled the shoes from my feet. He tucked them under his arm, with a final wide grin. "I'll keep hold of these for now, shall I? Give them to the doctor to keep an eye on, just in case you take a fancy to another stroll."

He stepped backwards, and pulled the curtains closed behind him. I was left alone again, but now there were several new mysteries to occupy my mind. Who was Ikey Collins, and why had he tried to kill me? And why had an infamous criminal saved my life? I wished that Holmes were beside me. More than ever, I had need of his great intellect.

Chapter Seven

❧

My sojourn in the hospital was, unfortunately, all too brief. Within a few hours, Shapley reappeared alongside a man in a white coat, whom I assumed was a doctor, though as he spoke not a word in my direction, I could not be sure. Whoever he was, it seemed he had deemed Hardie and myself fit enough to return to our cell. Shapley took great delight in rousing us from our beds and, with a wicked grin that never left his face, attached shackles to our wrists (though, thankfully, not to our ankles). Thus encumbered, we passed out of the hospital building, which stood separate from the main buildings, and by a convoluted route made our way back to the cramped cell which was our home. We had missed dinner. Shapley ignored my request that some sustenance be found for us, and locked us in, still hungry. I saw his face in the glass door panel for a second, then he was gone. Hardie muttered a curse under his breath, and reached down to the hiding place he had made beneath his bunk.

"I don't think he likes you," he said.

"You may be right." I pressed a hand against my aching ribs, and smiled weakly at the youngster. "Though he is by no means unique in that respect."

"Never mind, eh? A drop of this'll help."

I received the offered jar gratefully, and took a long sip of the rough alcohol. My taste buds had been sufficiently numbed, so that it slipped down far better than I expected, and its warming glow was enough to dull both the pain in my chest and the hunger pangs in my stomach. I passed the half-empty jar back to Hardie and lay back on the hard bed, considering recent events.

"You said that our attacker's name is Collins. Is that right?"

"That's him. Waiting to be tried for fencing stolen watches down Whitechapel, I hear."

The name was unfamiliar and, rack my brain as I might, I could think of no occasion when our paths had crossed. I was sure that I would have remembered so distinct a face, even had his name never come up. So why had he attacked me?

I said as much to Hardie, expecting no reply, but once again the boy surprised me.

"Paid to do it, as like as not," he said with a peculiar look on his face, part concerned frown and part puzzled amusement. "Though who'd pay to knock off you, John? What with you being but an unfortunate fellow, innocent as the day is long and with a grudge against no man, and no man with a grudge against you?"

As he spoke, his ever-present smile grew wider and wider. I confess I was becoming irritated by his attitude. What was there to smile about? Whatever the motive of Mr. Collins, it was clear that I would be in danger every moment I was outside my cell. Hardie, though, was not finished.

"But the famous Dr. Watson, though – now there's a man who

might have an enemy or two behind bars, eh? I bet him and his great pal Sherlock Holmes have placed a man or two behind these walls? And some of them might be willing to pay to have him knocked off, I reckon."

Finally, he could contain his mirth no longer and a laugh, louder and deeper than I would have thought possible in such a young man, burst from his lips.

"You must think us all real fools, if you thought you could keep that hid for long. I knew as soon as you said about working with the police. Haven't I seen your likeness in *The Strand* often enough?"

"You read *The Strand?*" The doubt in my voice would have been insulting in other circumstances, but Hardie seemed to take no offence, and instead laughed all the louder.

"You think a guttersnipe like me wouldn't be able to read at all, don't you? And even if I could, I'd stick to the penny dreadfuls and leave the rest to my betters. That's the way of it, isn't it, John?"

I half shook my head and half nodded, uncertain what to say. "Not at all," I ventured at last. "In fact, I had noticed that you are quite well spoken for a…" I hesitated, for I had no wish to insult further the only friend I had in this benighted place.

"…a guttersnipe, like I said," Hardie concluded for me, but I was relieved to see the smile never left his battered face. "And I reckon I am, too. Well spoken, that is. Or can be, when I need to be, which is as good as. Didn't I tell you that I spread my wings after my pals all got locked up or left town?" He took a fresh sip from the jar, then handed it across to me. "One of the neighbours taught me to read when I was a kid, and it wasn't hard to pick up the way the likes of you speak. I was going to go into the confidence game, like that Stone. Swell clothes and as much food and drink as you want, that's the game for me. But," he concluded with a shrug, "that copper put paid to that, didn't he?"

There was no self-pity in Hardie's voice, I was pleased to note. More than ever, I resolved to do what I could for the boy once my life had returned to normal. "I would not grieve that particular lost opportunity too much," I said.

"Perhaps not," he replied, the matter apparently of no genuine concern. "Either way, let's figure out who in here would be most interested in having the famous Dr. Watson killed."

"Who can say? I doubt there is a list of other prisoners readily available to us, but I shall definitely ask Holmes" – my voice dropped to a whisper as I mentioned his name – "to see if he can obtain one. Though if, as you suggest, Collins was hired to do the deed, then I must needs be cautious at all times and in all places."

The thought was an unpleasant one, and I brooded in silence, considering how easily I had fallen from grace, and how little weight had been given to my good character and the assistance I had provided the authorities over the years.

Hardie's voice interrupted these dark thoughts.

"I can ask around. Be the Watson to your Holmes."

The offer was sincerely made, and the comparison made me smile, but it was one I knew I could never accept. Bad enough that someone wished me harm, far worse if Hardie too became a target. I said so to the youngster and he took the rebuff well enough, grumbling only a little before agreeing to be guided by me in the matter.

"With some luck – and the assistance of Holmes – I hope to be free of this place within a few days at most," I reassured him. "In the meantime, I will keep to this cell as much as I can, and ensure that I am in sight of a warder at all times when I must be outside."

He seemed to accept this, though I could tell he was not entirely happy. The night was drawing in and it was becoming difficult to make out even the approximate figure of my cellmate, not six feet distant. And so, wincing a little at my various aches, I lay back and waited for sleep to come.

Chapter Eight

The regulations of the prison were clear, and it was they that allowed me to speak with such confidence of staying clear of trouble. Prisoners were confined to their cells except at those times when they were engaged in official prison activities, which in reality meant time spent in the exercise area, the chapel or at interview. On every such occasion, a guard was detailed to escort the prisoner to the activity in question, and then to bring him back again. Hardie had hinted that there were ways around these strictures, but I had no intention of testing the limits of my freedom, or lack of it, and had resigned myself to spending the greater part of every day locked in the same small room.

When our cell door opened on the morning of the following day, therefore, I was a little surprised, but assumed I was to be taken to see the governor again, or something of that nature. I looked up as the door swung back, but in place of the guard I expected, there stood two men in prison uniform. Hardie gave a strangled cry and jumped to his feet, the empty bottle from the night before gripped in his hand like a club, but before he could so much as raise it in anger, one of the men – a tall, heavy-set individual with a tattoo of a dragon curling from his collar along the nape of his neck – took a step inside and twisted it from his grasp. He stood over the boy as the other came inside, to be followed by the unmistakable figure of Matty Galloway.

Precisely, Galloway half-turned and pressed the door closed.

He smiled at me coldly and indicated with a nod that I should be brought to my feet. The silent pair who held me obeyed unhurriedly but effectively, twisting my arms across my back as they levered me up.

"Good day, Dr. Watson," Galloway said. His voice was quiet, almost reserved, as though he were speaking in a church or a library, but there was nothing timorous about him. He held himself with the confidence of a leader, secure in a place of his choosing and under his control, without arrogance but also without undue humility. This prison was his kingdom and I was an outsider. I knew that I was in greater danger at that moment than I had been at any point since the commencement of this whole nightmarish affair.

"Good morning," I replied, after a moment. "Mr… Galloway?"

"You phrase that as a question, Dr. Watson," he said. "Would you have me believe you don't know my identity? Have I so misjudged my own fame, would you say, that I expect my name at least to be known to all inside this establishment?"

He leaned forward, until his face was mere inches from my own. "Is my delusion so great, Doctor?" he asked, his breath hot on my cheek.

There was nothing I could think to say, and the silence grew uncomfortably long. I tensed the muscles in my arms and rocked backwards as I had been taught, determined to give some account of myself at least, when Galloway broke the tension by laughing.

He straightened and nodded once more at the men who held me. I felt the pressure on my arms slacken. I relaxed a little, but remained vigilant.

"You have pluck, I'll give you that," Galloway smiled, with genuine warmth, I fancied. "Intended to go down swinging, did you? I admire that in a man; ask anyone here. Give me pluck in the face of certain doom over brains or cunning any day. You always know where you stand with a plucky man."

He reached into his jacket pocket and pulled out a silver cigarette case. He lit two gaspers and handed me one, indicating to my two minders that I might now be released entirely.

"Sit down, Dr. Watson. You and I, we need to have a chat. Thing is, it seems to me that I've reason to thank you, and because of that, in return you might say, I'm going to explain some things to you. Things which might come in handy, if you hope to survive in this place."

Oddly, he reminded me now of Holmes at a crime scene, intent only on the matter at hand, but aware of everything around him – every breath of air, every discarded object, every human being – which might prove of importance. The two men who had held me might as well not have been there at all. At that moment, in that place, there was only Matty Galloway and myself.

"The problem you have, Doctor, is a certain blindness when it comes to the criminal classes. I've followed your cases, you see, read every edition of *The Strand*, every newspaper report, even had my lads outside ferret out bits and pieces which don't ever get written down. And it seems to me that you and your Mr. Sherlock Holmes only recognise two types of criminals. Just two. First, you've got your thug, your lumpish brute, straight out the rookeries and the slums, cosh in one hand and knife in the other. No brains, only brawn, so not often of interest to gents such as yourselves, but at least you recognise their existence. That sort's your muggers and your bug-hunters, your lurkers and your bludgers. Second are the ones you do take an interest in. Gents – or near as, from where I'm standing. Educated fellows, with nice houses and nicer manners, but with something missing inside, something that stops the others from turning bad. That's your blackmailers and your magsmen, Dr. Watson, your fraudsters and confidence men – the sort that Mr. Holmes eats up for breakfast and again for tea."

I tried to interject, to ask what he was leading up to, but he held up a hand and his companions again gripped my arms painfully.

"Let me finish, if you don't mind, Doctor. You will have your chance to ask questions. Indeed, I hope you shall, for as I say, I do feel that I owe you a good turn, and I'd like to give you all the information you need." He inhaled deeply from his cigarette then flicked the half-smoked remnant into a dark corner. "Don't get me wrong, though. I say you only admit of two types of criminal but there are other… singular souls out there who, I'm sure, must have crossed your path. I do not speak of them, for each of those must be judged on his own specific talents – and besides, there are none such in here, nor ever likely to be. Men like that don't allow themselves to be imprisoned." He sighed, and seemed to lapse into meditation for a period. Then, "No, what you need to know, what you need to recognise, is a final class of criminal, one you *will* most likely meet in this place. Indeed, one you are meeting at this very moment. For that matter, our paths have crossed before now, though you didn't know it. I am of that type, Dr. Watson. For me, crime is neither a thuggish display of strength, nor a matter of cruelty and deception. For me crime's a business. There's no anger in what I do, just a desire to do what's best for me and those who work for me. If a label is needed, then think of me as a... shopkeeper."

Again, he smiled, and as he fell silent, I remembered what Holmes had asked of me, and did my level best to gauge the man. His clothes, of course, told me nothing, for he was dressed exactly as we all were. There was the silver cigarette case, which argued for comparative wealth, but I knew Holmes would expect more from me, and I found myself considering just how he had contrived to maintain possession of so valuable and conspicuous an item. If the search I had undergone on my arrival were standard, it would have been impossible to smuggle so much as a hairpin into the prison. The cigarette he had given me was of high quality and Turkish, but again that was evidence only of his wealth, which was never in doubt, according to Hardie. What else would I be able to tell Holmes?

I had no time to draw further conclusions in any case, for Galloway spoke up once again. "You may be wondering why I tell you all this, Doctor," he said. "It is so you may understand why I acknowledged you as I did in the yard earlier. You have done me a good turn–" Again, my attempts at protest came to nothing as he pressed on regardless. "Now, now, no need to say a word. Of course, you did no such thing. You are an innocent man, guilty of no crime, as are so many souls in this place. But even so, the belief in the world at large is that you have – how shall I put it? – done me a right good turn. And as a businessman, I know that good work must be rewarded, and rewarded publicly, so that everyone can see the benefits of such. So think of that handshake as your payment. There's more than one of the other types of criminal in here who bears you terrible ill will, Doctor, and might, left unchecked, have done you a mischief. Now they know that you're under my protection, and to harm you would be to cross me.

"And they'd be very foolhardy to cross me. Very foolhardy indeed."

With that, he turned on his heel and left the cell. The two thugs who held me released their grip and followed a moment later, leaving me slumped, a cold chill settling on my spine. I heard Hardie's voice as though he were some distance away but could make out nothing of what he said. All my attention was focused on one solitary, unpleasant truth.

Whether what had just occurred placed me in greater or lesser immediate jeopardy I could not say, but one thing was eminently clear. By placing myself, however unwillingly, under Galloway's protection, I had allied myself in the eyes of the world at large with a known criminal. I could see no way in which that was a development to be welcomed.

Hardie, however, insisted that Galloway's visit was a positive one.

"Stands to reason, if you ask me," he said, once the immediate effect of our rough handling had abated. "Bloke like Galloway, he don't care to be in anybody's debt, so he pays you back in protection, and makes sure everyone knows it too. I tell you, John, it's no more than him keeping things even."

"Balancing the books, you mean?" I interposed, recalling Galloway's description of himself as a shopkeeper.

"Something like," agreed Hardie. "In his line of work, it don't do to be seen to be owing favours."

It was at least a possible explanation for Galloway's otherwise inexplicable amity – such as it was – but I could not rid myself of the faint feeling that there was more to recent events than met the eye. Galloway was a gang leader, I must never forget, and would benefit from a curtailment of Major McLachlan's investigations as much as any man. It seemed far-fetched, but could he be in some way responsible for Miss McLachlan's death, and was his protection nothing but a ruse designed to cast further suspicion on me? Holmes was due to visit later in the day, and I would mention the possibility to him then.

In the meantime, the day continued along already familiar lines, though I was excused the daily exercise period on account of the previous morning's fracas. Hardie, however, refused to stay inside, and returned, once his hour was complete, with news.

"You're the talk of the yard, John. Nobody's talking about anything else but your run-ins with Ikey Collins and Matty Galloway. Collins is in a punishment cell, of course, and won't be out for a day or two, but I managed to get close enough to some of Galloway's lads to hear them talking."

I protested at the risk he had taken, and reminded him of his promise of the night before, but he waved away my worries as he threw himself on his bed.

"Calm yourself, John! I was just sitting nearby, enjoying the fresh air, wasn't I? No reason why anyone should look at me twice. And besides, you'll be pleased I did, once you hear what they were saying."

In spite of myself, I had to admit the truth of his words. The more information we had, the more likely that we would be able to discern a motive for Galloway's unexpected largesse. Perhaps it would have nothing to do with my own case, but even if it did not directly do so, the mystery of Matthew Galloway was one that required thought on its own merits. Grudgingly, therefore, I settled back to listen, and Hardie described the scene in the yard.

"There was three of them. Two I don't know, and one who's

always at Galloway's side. Don't know his name, but he was here earlier, the one with the dragon tattoo on his neck. He was the one doing most of the talking too. 'We'll find out soon enough,' he was saying when I managed to get near enough to hear. 'Galloway always has his reasons, you know that,' he says, and the other two, they nodded but they didn't look convinced. 'He's called a meeting,' says Dragon Tattoo, 'in the usual place, and he says he's got something to tell everyone.' One of the others pipes up then, and asks if it's about the doctor – that'd be you – or about the other swine, but Dragon Tattoo says how would he know, he's not Galloway's keeper, and after a bit of grumbling, they moved off. Dragon Tattoo gave me a bit of a look first, but he didn't say nothing, so I reckon he's just not the friendly sort."

I was less confident about that, but there was no denying that the boy had unearthed valuable information. Clearly, it would be in my interests to eavesdrop on the forthcoming meeting, though I could not for the life of me see how that could be managed. The identity of the "other bloke" was a new wrinkle to a mystery which, increasingly, I felt intersected with my wider difficulties. I quizzed Hardie about the possible location of Galloway's meeting, but he knew nothing for certain and almost as little as conjecture.

"Galloway's got a few of the warders in his pocket, that's for sure. He comes and goes as he pleases, and his men too, so they could be meeting anywhere. It'll have to be either during exercise or at chapel, for even a bought guard couldn't ignore a dozen men not in their cells at any other time."

"They can hardly hold a secret meeting in the chapel," I noted, after a moment's thought, "but there would be nothing unusual in a group of friends standing together in the yard, would there?"

Hardie agreed, but reluctantly, and I could see that he harboured doubts about my theory. I was about to quiz him further, when the cell door swung open, and Shapley growled that I had a visitor. Briefly I wondered whether this was not a trap and Shapley one of Galloway's bought guards, then recognised that there was no need to go to such lengths. He had already proved he could enter my cell with impunity.

Consequently, I pushed myself to my feet, wincing at the sharp pain in my ribs, and followed Shapley down the corridor outside.

Chapter Nine

In my writings, I have occasionally been guilty of portraying Sherlock Holmes as a cold-blooded, emotionless man, more concerned with the intellectual challenge of a case than the human beings it affected. The injustice of such a portrayal was never more clearly seen than that day, when I found myself once again sitting opposite him, in a private visitors' room on this occasion. To my relief, Inspector Potter was not in attendance. Instead, Lestrade accompanied my friend, his face twisted in concern as I made my way across the room.

"I've seen you look better, Doctor," he said by way of greeting.

"I've definitely felt better, Inspector," I replied.

Holmes said nothing. He sat, his fingers intertwined on the table before him, eyes hooded and dark, glowering at the knotted wood as though somehow it offended him. Without looking up, he spoke quietly, but with force and a passion which I did not recall hearing in his voice before.

"You will be released as soon as is humanly possible,

Watson. You have my word on it."

He glanced up, with what I can only describe as a look of guilt on his face, then flicked his eyes back to the table top. I knew what troubled him, and hurried to reassure him.

"This is not your doing, Holmes. Nothing you might have done could have prevented it, nor could anyone blame you for your lack of progress, given how short a time has passed." I smiled as best I could, endeavouring to lighten the mood. "And besides, I have received worse injuries on the rugby field."

Holmes, however, was not to be placated. "Perhaps you have, Watson, but that is hardly pertinent. I should have worked harder to bring about your release before now, but I made the decision to follow a promising line of enquiry instead. And you have paid painfully for my misjudgement."

"But I am to be released?" In my haste to reassure Holmes I almost let the most important of his words pass me by. "Double reason to consign recent events to the unmourned past! Come now, Holmes, enough moping. Tell me how you came to secure my freedom!"

Lestrade filled the brief silence that followed by pulling a folded sheet of paper from his jacket pocket and laying it on the table before him. A warder barked my name in warning as I reached a hand out to take the paper, so the inspector explained what it contained.

"I'm afraid you're not in the clear yet, Dr. Watson, but Mr. Holmes, it turns out, has friends in very high places. This morning Scotland Yard received this telegram, direct from the Prime Minister's office, ordering that, in light of the cowardly attack perpetrated on you yesterday, and in view of the services you have rendered the Crown in the past, you are to be released immediately into the recognisance of Sherlock Holmes and allowed to aid him in his investigations into the murder. There is no suggestion that the charges against you will be dropped, or that we – that is, Inspector Potter and his team – have any fresh suspect in mind, however. Mr. Holmes asked me to look into the girl who led you into the trap, but there is no sign of her, and Inspector Potter has dismissed her as just a gutter urchin paid a shilling to lure you inside, if she exists at all, which he makes plain he doubts. I'm afraid that you are merely to be released on licence, and will still face trial in due course."

It was less than I might have hoped for, but more than I expected. I would remain under a cloud of suspicion for the moment, but I would at least be free of Holloway and able to assist Holmes in uncovering the true killer.

"Thank you, Inspector," I said. "I won't forget the faith you have shown in me, nor the assistance you have provided."

Lestrade gave an embarrassed cough and nodded an awkward acknowledgement in my general direction. "There's nothing to thank me for, Doctor," he muttered. "Mr. Holmes is the one with the ear of the highest in the land, not me. All I'll be doing is the paperwork."

"Not at all, Lestrade," I demurred. "But perhaps you can do one more thing for me?"

I quickly described Galloway's visit to my cell. Holmes sat silently throughout my account, but Lestrade gave out a distinct grunt when I mentioned Galloway's name, and another when I admitted that I was now under his protection.

"Matthew Galloway is not a man you would want laying claim to you, Dr. Watson," he warned. "I'll see what detail I can ferret out regarding his most recent activities, but you want to avoid him if you can. 'The dark prince' some call him, but it's no compliment.

Actually," he added, rising to his feet, "I'll make a start on that now. If you'll excuse me, gentlemen…"

Once Lestrade had left us, we sat and smoked a cigarette apiece. I think Holmes recognised that I needed a moment of silent companionship before discussing my wider predicament. Only when I stubbed out my cigarette did he bring up the subject of my recent assault and my unlikely champion.

"You are right, of course, Watson, that Galloway is a man of means, even within these prison walls. The silver cigarette case, the Turkish cigarettes – each points to a man able to manipulate the system, to bend it to his will. There are only three ways that I know of, by which a prisoner may obtain contraband of such an expensive nature. Smuggling by way of prison visitor is the most obvious method, naturally, but we can rule that out immediately, at least in its most common form. Even a small item, once smuggled in, must remain hidden, lest the authorities confiscate it. But you say that Galloway is bold and makes no effort to conceal his contraband. Indeed, if he discarded a cigarette barely half smoked, we can safely surmise that he has no concerns regarding their replacement. Cigarettes are, strictly speaking, forbidden here, but he has no worries that such restrictions apply to him. So… a shopkeeper he calls himself, but I think a more apposite description might be a wholesaler. An importer and exporter. And his imports at least are no secret. Indeed, he as good as advertises his wares, which indicates recourse to one of the other two options. Bribery or threat… or both."

Holmes's voice tailed off as he fell into a reverie. I saw his eyes lose focus as he turned his mind inward, considering Galloway. I lit another of the cigarettes he had placed on the table between us and waited, as content as I could be in this malign building.

"We must, I think, discover the extent of his influence. He may not be directly involved in your case, but he remains the one who stands to benefit most from the crime of which you are accused. In choosing to acknowledge you he has, perversely, both made you safer in the short term and placed you in greater danger in the long. It plainly serves his interests to have you hanged, even as he is seen to comfort you on every step to the noose."

I glanced sharply at Holmes. "I had considered whether Galloway's actions in the yard today would have any bearing on my own perceived guilt or innocence. But why should anyone outside these walls even know anything has occurred?"

I thought I saw pity, or at least compassion, in Holmes's eyes as he replied in a low voice. "News of today's meeting will not stay contained for long, Watson. Prison guards are not well paid and thus cheaply hired, if not bought outright. Someone will pass on the information to a newspaperman in exchange for a shilling or two before the day is out. I have no doubt that the news will make the morning editions if I cannot once more oblige Mycroft to intervene. Even if he does, men of importance will need to be consulted, and they may be less sympathetic once they hear of your new protector. There is only so much even Mycroft can do."

"Of course, the news that I have been publicly thanked by the man most likely to benefit from McLachlan's recusal will not aid me," I said, suddenly tired once more.

Holmes offered no false succour. "Matthew Galloway is one of the rats who infest this city, Watson, though a somewhat more successful rat than most. In Inspector Lestrade's colourful description, he is a dark prince of the underworld, almost untouchable so far as the police are concerned. He has fingers in every illicit pie, and an interest in every gambling den, opium stew and disorderly house in London. And yet the constabulary have thus far been unable to convict him of so much as a breach of the peace."

"Yet here he is in Holloway," I pointed out. "Perhaps his luck has come to an end?"

"I very much doubt that, I'm afraid," Holmes replied. "If my memory serves, each of his incarcerations in the past has come to nothing. Witnesses change their stories, alibis are established, and the Crown finds itself unable to proceed."

"Obviously Galloway can apply pressure in every direction," I suggested, but I knew as I said it that I was simply stating the obvious.

It was a sign of Holmes's concern for me that he allowed my words to pass unremarked. "It would certainly seem that way."

"Can the police do nothing?"

"Galloway is a rich man. He runs a coach and pair, employs two dozen servants and owns racing horses and fine art, even has a small estate in the country. Those whom he is unable to terrify into silence, he can buy outright. There is little the police can do to stop him."

"Strange that he has never crossed our path before now." I was more concerned with Galloway's interest in me, but the thought did occur that I would be in a far less perilous position now had we had cause to investigate him at an earlier date.

Holmes was dismissive. "Not at all! Galloway is a very common sort of street thug. Not without resource or wit in his own sphere, I grant you, but hardly likely ever to present the type of involved conundrum I find of interest. A fact that perversely appears to have offended the man, rather than relieving him as one might expect."

He crossed the room and peered out of the small window.

"No," he said after a minute. "Our concern is not with Mr.

Galloway's past activities outside this prison, but his current ones inside. Why did he come to your aid, and why did he proclaim his sponsorship of you so publicly?"

The obvious answer did not bode well for my chances of an acquittal in court. If even a vicious criminal like Galloway believed me guilty, what chance had I of convincing a jury of my innocence? I mentioned my theory that he might be using me as a cover for his own foul deeds, but Holmes was not reassuring. "That is, of course, one possible explanation, but not the only one. Galloway may well be entirely sincere in his belief that he is in your debt. At the moment it is impossible to say which is true."

Holmes stepped away from the window and looked down at me. "Whatever his motivation, you would do well to avoid him if you can. Word will undoubtedly spread regarding his involvement with you, and it will certainly not be to your benefit for there to be a repeat."

Holmes's logic was sound. I had no desire to speak to Galloway again and, besides, I would be free of the prison within a matter of hours. I reminded Holmes of that fact, though he had clearly not forgotten.

"True, Watson, but I would advise you to remain in your cell until someone returns with your official release papers. I have already completed such paperwork as is required from me, but the wheels of prison administration move slowly, and you are not likely to be free until this evening. In the meantime," he concluded briskly, retrieving his hat from the table, "there are one or two small errands which I can profitably carry out. Rest assured, I will return in time to collect you and accompany you home to Baker Street, but for now I shall take my leave."

Without another word, he rapped upon the door. There was

a clatter as the guard outside found the correct key on his chain, then the door swung open and Holmes strode out, leaving me to consider my approaching freedom with heartfelt relief.

Chapter Ten

True to his word, Holmes was waiting for me at the prison gates, standing beside a four-seater in which Lestrade already sat.

"Come along, Watson," he chided, with a rare attempt at humour. "If you delay too long, the authorities might decide you wish to continue enjoying their hospitality!"

There was no need to tell me twice. I hurried across the cobbles and into the carriage, dropping into the seat with an exhausted sigh. Lestrade gave a crooked smile of greeting and handed me a small hip flask.

"A drop of this will do you good, Doctor," he said, and I was reminded that Bert Hardie had used the same words when sharing his drink with me. I had been moved to another cell soon after Holmes left, a holding cell for prisoners about to be released, and had not had a chance to say goodbye to the boy, but I had no intention of forgetting the promise I had made to myself. As soon as this nightmare was behind me, I would do whatever I could for him.

In the meantime, a long draught of surprisingly decent whisky was just what the doctor ordered, followed by a short trip across the city to Baker Street. While we travelled, Lestrade filled in the details of his most recent investigations.

"I was able to find out a little more about our Matty Galloway, you'll be happy to hear, Mr. Holmes. For one thing, how he comes to be inside Holloway at all. It seems that he and his boys were caught red-handed, holding bags of coin which definitely didn't belong to them." Lestrade grinned, showing his small teeth. "Potter was furious. It wasn't him who caught them, see. He'd been tipped the wink by one of his narks that Galloway was planning to rob a jeweller's in Hatton Garden." Lestrade chuckled at the memory. "Instead, he was collared breaking into a bank in Piccadilly. Tobias Gregson got the credit, though the rumour has it that it was one of Galloway's rivals informed on him. But you'd think the gangs were Potter's by right, the way they say he carried on. That's the sort he is, though, Mr. Holmes. Too ambitious by a long shot. He'd rather Galloway had escaped, so he could arrest him himself, later on. Sheer idiocy, if you ask me."

I had never heard Lestrade talk so slightingly of one of his colleagues before. It was entirely out of character for the little detective, and I caught Holmes's eye with a question in my own, but he gave an almost imperceptible shake of the head. Better to let Lestrade tell his story without interruption.

"Go on, Lestrade," he said quietly.

"There's little enough more to tell, Mr. Holmes, sad to say. I cannot fault Inspector Potter for his industry, I'll say that. I think I mentioned that he had men out to track the girl who tricked you into following her, but there is no sign of her, nor can anyone vouch for her existence, saving yourself. And to be fair, these street urchins come and go and nobody is any the wiser."

To hear that the girl – the best possible suspect other than myself – had disappeared as though she had never existed was a serious blow to my defence.

I slumped back in my seat, prey once more to the rapid changes in mood that had plagued me since the case had begun. Lestrade continued to talk, but I admit I was only half listening. Instead, I watched London pass by the carriage windows, and wondered how long I would be free to enjoy this glorious city I called home.

"…as might be. And that's about it. So, what do you think, Doctor?"

I was aware that Lestrade had just asked me a question, but I had no idea what it could have been. I looked across at Holmes, but his attention was elsewhere and he gave no indication that he had been listening to Lestrade either. Blushing with embarrassment, I asked the inspector to repeat what he had just said.

"Hmm, very well, Doctor, if I must," he replied testily. "I said that the only other point of interest according to Inspector Potter is that a chap across the street thinks that he saw someone at the window of the room at one point. Waving a white handkerchief, he said, though he could not be exactly sure of the time."

"A signal to an accomplice, perhaps?" I ventured.

"Potter thinks so, though I am afraid that he believes you were the man signalling," answered Lestrade sorrowfully.

"But that is ludicrous!" I protested. "There has been no suggestion of my having an accomplice before now. Is Potter so determined to convict me of this crime that he will bend any new piece of evidence to fit his own prejudice?"

"I am sorry, Doctor, but he currently works on the theory that you noticed Constable Howie and realised that you would be unable to escape undetected, and so alerted an unknown lookout to make himself scarce, while you concocted the tale of being locked in the room by a phantom girl."

We pulled up outside 221B before I could respond, but Lestrade remained in the carriage, pleading pressure of work at the Yard. In truth I was not unhappy to be left alone with Holmes in our familiar rooms. The pleasure of a return to the normal and the everyday filled me as I pushed open the door to be greeted by a smiling Mrs. Hudson.

Standing there, it was hard to believe that it was less than a week since I had followed the girl into the trap that had ensnared me, but equally it felt like months since I had last sat peacefully in my own home.

Mrs. Hudson would have fussed round me, I'm sure, but Holmes ushered her out almost as soon as she had laid out a light supper, and again I was not unhappy. I ate a little, then filled my pipe and settled myself contentedly in my chair by the fire.

"Very well, Holmes," I said, as soon as my pipe was lit, "now that I am free, it is time for you to tell me how matters stand exactly."

Holmes nodded through a cloud of pipe smoke. "There is good news and bad, as you would expect," he said. "The good is that the police have been unable to provide any sort of motive for you to kill Miss McLachlan. Mycroft was able to have reporting of the case suppressed but one of the more salacious rags published an apparently unrelated piece which suggested that you have large debts and a gambling problem."

"What! How dare they!" All contentment was forgotten as I leapt to my feet in fury. "I am not as busy in my practice as I could wish, but I can assure you that I have no debts of any significance! And I hardly think my occasional speculation on a horse or two could be termed a gambling problem!"

"Calm yourself, my dear fellow," Holmes soothed. "Nobody gives the accusation credence, excepting that idiot Potter, who scrambles after evidence like a dog snapping at moths. The editor of the 'paper in question has been spoken to, and reminded of his civic responsibilities."

I was aware that my face was flushed and my fists clenched tightly at my sides – what a ludicrous figure I must make. But the news that Potter was so actively seeking my downfall was, perversely, sufficiently enraging to have a sobering effect on my temper. If he were convinced I was guilty, he would not rest until he could prove it.

"Potter is determined that I am a murderer," I said dejectedly.

"As I said, he is idiotic, even by the low standards of Scotland Yard. Having seen Potter at work, the only surprise to me is that Lestrade is not already Chief Constable. Compared to Potter, he is the ideal detective."

This unexpected praise for Lestrade was enough to puncture my anger entirely. I laughed, then laughed again at my friend's confused expression.

"Your sense of humour astonishes me at times, Watson," he grumbled. "Potter's behaviour is no laughing matter. He has refused me access to the murder room. Worse, he has already released Miss McLachlan's body to the family, thereby preventing me from examining it."

This was a serious setback, designed to deflate my spirits. I noted with appreciation that Holmes had not shared this news while I remained incarcerated.

"That is preposterous!" I exclaimed. "Can Lestrade not intervene, in the matter of the room at least?"

"He is attempting to do so at this very moment," Holmes replied evenly. "That is the business at Scotland Yard of which he spoke. And there is a possibility, no more, that several photographs were taken of the deceased woman, which may be of some use to us. I have impressed upon him the need to obtain both permission to examine the scene of the crime, and copies of these photographic images of the victim."

That was something, I supposed, but I could not deny that my contented mood had taken a heavy blow. So much of Holmes's work relied on his ability to sift through the detritus of a crime. To have that opportunity taken from him could only hinder his investigation.

In suddenly sombre mood, I looked around the room, taking in the familiar fixtures, and wondered how long I would remain a free man. True, I had been released for now, but only at the behest of Mycroft Holmes, and the odds that I would continue in that happy state seemed to be lengthening by the moment. I glanced over at my friend, but he had closed his eyes in thought, and it seemed wisest to allow him to remain so.

Chapter Eleven

After a fitful night's sleep, the morning found me more hopeful. Before retiring, Holmes had expressed confidence that pressure from Lestrade would soon allow him access to the murder room, and had claimed to be intrigued by the quality of the photographs taken there. I wondered if he were simply attempting to allay my fears, but he assured me that he had initially been too negative and that Lestrade would find a way to circumvent Potter's interference. I could only hope that was true.

We breakfasted while we waited for word. Rarely have bacon and eggs tasted so perfect, or *The Times* been so fascinating. Once or twice I caught Holmes looking at me thoughtfully, but he said nothing, and though I wondered if he had something to ask me, I could not bring myself to shatter the companionable silence by checking. The weather outside had taken a turn for the worse, and rain spattered hard against the window panes, but even that – and the heavy grey clouds visible above the opposite roofs – I welcomed. Every touch of normality was something to be savoured.

As this thought passed across my idling mind, Mrs. Hudson knocked at the door, and handed a telegram to Holmes, who tossed it unread onto the floor.

"Excellent," he said, rubbing his hands together. "Now that we have confirmation from Lestrade, we can examine the room in which Miss McLachlan met her doom. If I can uncover nothing there which the police missed, then I shall give serious thought to retirement!"

He was full of sudden vigour, and obviously eager to be on the move, but my eyes had not left the discarded telegram. "Should you not check that Lestrade has obtained permission?" I asked, reaching down and picking up the telegram.

"There is no need, Watson. The telegram comes from Scotland Yard, so can only have been sent by Potter or Lestrade. The former sees me as a competitor, and has obstructed and blocked me at every turn. Had he good news for us, he would delay sending it as long as possible, not speed it to us like this. Were the news bad, he would deliver it in person, savouring the victory.

"The telegram, therefore, is from Lestrade. He would take the opposite tack, and deliver any negative report in person, hoping thereby to soften the blow. Which means that this is positive news. Now, take hold of your hat and coat and we can be on our way. The longer we delay, the more chance there is of Potter interfering and the decision being reversed."

I needed no encouragement, for as Holmes spoke I felt new stirrings of hope in my breast. I had allowed the travails of the previous days to cloud my judgement and cause me to forget the brilliance of my friend. Now, though, I remembered.

If there was anything to be found, I knew Holmes would find it.

* * *

Lestrade was waiting for us at the entrance to Linhope Street, sheltering underneath a jutting door lintel. He adjusted his hat and pulled his coat tight around him as he stepped out into the rain to greet us.

"Finally!" he said with exasperation. "I thought I'd catch my death in this downpour."

Without waiting for a reply, he strode off down the street, Holmes and I trailing in his wake.

Constable Howie stood in the doorway to number 16. He straightened his back as Lestrade approached, then held the door open for us to enter. I followed Lestrade and Holmes upstairs, hesitating for a moment as we turned the bend in the staircase and the room we were there to see came into view.

The door was closed but unlocked. Lestrade pushed it open, and I saw that the lock had not been replaced since being forced open at my request. I paused on the threshold, and peered inside.

The interior was as I remembered it, except that the stench of violent death had been partially overlaid with that of lavender, the bed had been stripped and the bedding disposed of. Streaks of dried blood could still be made out on the floor beneath, but other than that there was no sign of the events of a few days previously. Even so, I wished that I were somewhere else.

Holmes stood at my side, facing the window. He turned to Lestrade with a scowl on his face.

"It is insufferable that Potter denied me access to this room until now, when who knows how many feet have trampled over the evidence. Much that might have been of interest will have been destroyed, and whatever is left will, at best, be severely contaminated."

The inspector had the grace to look embarrassed, but attempted to defend his colleague nonetheless. "It is his right, Mr. Holmes, as you have been told more than once. Inspector Potter is no believer in amateur detection, and made that very clear to me when I spoke to him on your behalf."

I could well imagine the reception Lestrade would have received from the belligerent Potter, and thought it good of him to have made the effort. Holmes must have had the same thought, for though he grunted in annoyance, he let the matter drop, and even highlighted a positive aspect to Potter's actions.

"At least when Potter arrives I shall be able to examine the photographs which were taken on the evening of the murder. Bertillon in Paris has had some success with the process, but this will be the first time I myself have made use of such images. It is our good fortune that Major McLachlan has sufficient influence to insist that they were taken, before the scene of the crime was too badly disturbed."

I feared that Holmes was placing too much faith in these photographs. I had of course seen the facial images which the police now often took of criminals, the better to identify them at a later date, but this latest innovation – capturing the aftermath of a crime in situ, as it were – seemed to me unlikely to prove of very much merit. Even photographic images taken in ideal conditions tended to be imprecise and inexact in nature, and precision and exactitude were of prime importance in any criminal investigation.

I had no time for further thoughts on the matter, for Lestrade was impatient and invited us to enter.

Holmes, however, was not to be rushed. He knelt by the broken lock and examined the splintered wood with his magnifying glass. Next, he strode into the room, counting his steps out loud, then dropped to his knees and, ignoring the dirt on the floor, peered under the bed and the wardrobe. At several points he picked up tiny fragments of mysterious origin from the floorboards and dropped them into a small bag, which he held in his left hand.

Only twice did he address either myself or Lestrade directly.

"The building has gas laid in?" he asked first, as he toyed with the stump of one of the many candles which had illuminated the room when last I had been there. Lestrade confirmed that it did, but Holmes had already discarded the candle and seemed to have lost all interest in his own question.

Another minute passed in silence, then, "And the bed linen which was removed? Was it of good quality?"

Lestrade consulted his notebook. "That it was," he agreed. "Good cotton sheets, a cotton pillow case and bed cover."

"Any markings on the cover? Embroidery, for example?"

"Not according to this. Good quality but plain, it says. Is it important?"

Holmes nodded sharply. "Perhaps," he muttered. He took one final turn round the room, stopping in front of the window and then again by the cheap print which hung from one wall.

Finally, he focused his attention on the inspector and myself. "We have made definite progress, gentlemen. This room may have more secrets to reveal, but they will, I fear, require the images that Inspector Potter has promised to bring with him. For now, we must be content with knowing how the victim was convinced to remain in this room, one so far below her usual station."

"Are you claiming to have discovered something, Mr. Holmes?" Lestrade asked doubtfully. "Potter and his men have gone over every inch of this room, and found nothing at all."

"I am *claiming* nothing, Inspector," Holmes responded irritably. "I would have thought that any fool could draw the same conclusion from a brief examination of this room, but given what you have just told me, it seems there is at least one who has already failed to do even that."

So saying, he opened the bag he held and tipped its meagre contents into his hand. Several tiny white fragments adhered to the skin of his palm. "Crumbs from a meringue, if I am not mistaken. An expensive confection to find in a rundown single room, would you not agree?"

"Perhaps the lady brought it with her?" Lestrade offered.

"A meringue is a fragile object, Inspector. It has scarcely survived the passage from hand to mouth; how do you imagine an infirm old woman in her night things would transport it across London? No, it is but one part of a larger enterprise, the elements of which are clear as day to anyone who cares truly to observe."

He waited less than a second for a response from either Lestrade or myself then, getting none, continued his explanation.

"Watson? You have been exposed to my methods more than anyone. I refuse to believe that no good habits have rubbed off on you in all that time. Come – look about you. What do you see?"

I slowly turned in a full circle, studying every aspect of my surroundings. The bed was as I have described it, comprised of rusted and stained metal, and surmounted by two thin pillows. The wardrobe, table and water jug were as I had seen them previously. I walked over to the picture on the wall. It was a poor copy of what I thought was probably a garish original, and showed a young man tying a bag to the horns of a deer, with a castle gatehouse in the background. I could see nothing in the picture that might aid us in our investigation and, glancing out of the corner of my eye at Lestrade, I could tell that he was similarly baffled.

Something Holmes had said nagged at my mind, however, and it was only as I turned back to the bed that I realised what it was.

"The bed linen was of good quality, Lestrade said. Too good to belong to this hovel. Therefore, the killer brought it with him!"

"Very good! We will make a detective of you yet. But why? High quality bed linen is as alien to this place as the meringue, yet both are here – or were, in any case. Why should that be?"

Here I stuttered to a halt, and was forced to admit that I was at a loss.

"No?" said Holmes. "You disappoint me, Watson, but very well, if I must explain every little thing…" He rubbed his hands together, and allowed the meringue dust to fall to the floor. "The meringue and the linen serve the same purpose, as do the execrable print on the wall and the candles which were preferred to the gas light. Someone prepared the room in advance for Miss McLachlan, like a stagehand placing props before a performance.

"Consider this room as it must have looked to that unfortunate lady. Elderly and infirm, with failing eyesight – the lorgnette, you remember? – and a wandering mind, she cleaves to the familiar as a drowning man would to a lifebelt, and is disturbed by anything which deviates from that. With her eyeglasses removed, however, and in the flickering candlelight, tucked beneath good, clean sheets, she will feel comfortable, at home even. I suspect you will find that meringue was the late Miss McLachlan's favourite sweet, incidentally, Lestrade. And of course there is the print…"

"What about it, Mr. Holmes? Perhaps you're making sense to Dr. Watson, but I admit, you've lost me."

Holmes glared at Lestrade, irritated anew by the interruption.

"Obviously," he replied, dryly. "But it is a vital part of the charade constructed for Miss McLachlan. There is an old – and, I must say, improbable – legend that when the Scottish king Alexander III ascended the throne in 1249, he ordered every clan chief to send him tribute by the fastest messenger possible. Lachlan Mor, chieftain of the McLachlans, angered by this peremptory command, tied his money bags to the horns of a roebuck, literally the fastest messenger on his lands. For that reason, the crest of the clan remains, to this day, that of two bucks holding the clan coat of arms. Major McLachlan is known to be proud of his family history, and there is no reason to suspect that his aunt was any less so. The presence of such a print would help to reassure her that all was well, and that she was among friends."

I marvelled again at my friend's ability to retain the most trivial and arcane knowledge, but Lestrade was less impressed.

"That's all well and good, Mr. Holmes, but how does it advance our investigation, or bring Dr. Watson any closer to the restoration of his good name?"

"Try to use your mind, Lestrade, such as it is! We know – and more importantly can prove – that Watson was with a patient not half an hour before Constable Howie discovered him, at an address approximately fifteen minutes' walk from Linhope Street. That barely leaves enough time to create this tableau and carry out the murder."

"It does leave just enough time though, Mr. Holmes," Lestrade corrected him. "Fifteen minutes plus seven minutes taken for Howie to break down the room door. That still leaves eight minutes to kill the victim."

"I did say 'barely', Inspector," Holmes snapped. "The alternative is to assume that Watson brought Miss McLachlan here, having arranged the room in advance, then killed her. Far more likely that whoever added these decorations did so because they needed the lady quiescent and amenable for a period of time prior to her murder. While they waited for Watson to pass and then be lured into their trap, for instance."

Lestrade responded with a grunt, admitting the sense in Holmes's words but reluctant to give them too much weight. "An interesting theory, Mr. Holmes, but at the Yard we prefer hard evidence."

"And you shall have it," Holmes replied confidently. "But in order that I may provide you with proof I must have facts to build upon, and at the moment—" He stopped suddenly, and cocked his head to one side. "But here is Inspector Potter, if I am not mistaken. Perhaps the package he carries will smooth the path from conjecture to certainty."

Chapter Twelve

It took no great analytical powers to recognise that Potter was displeased with Holmes's presence at what I am certain he considered *his* murder scene. He stormed through the open door, trailed by a harassed-looking police constable, and came to a halt in the centre of the room, where he stood, silently glaring at the three of us.

Lestrade broke the ensuing silence by asking whether Potter had brought the photographs.

"I have," the inspector replied, addressing his remarks to Holmes rather than his fellow policeman. "Though what good they will do you, I cannot say. My men and I had access to this room when it was still splattered in gore, and we were unable to discover anything of a specific nature. What hope have you of achieving more with only three blurred photographic images to aid you? Schell," he barked at the waiting constable. "Give it to him then, man!"

If Potter's attitude concerned Holmes, he gave no sign of it. He reached out a hand to accept the folder proffered by the young policeman, then spread the contents out on the battered table. Lestrade hurried forward to observe, but I hesitated, unwilling to revisit a horror I had already experienced once. I knew I had no choice, however, and so – after a moment's pause – I too stepped alongside Holmes and stared down at the images laid out below me.

There were, as Potter had said, three images in total. The first had been taken from the door, I suspected, and encompassed the entirety of the room. Whether thanks to the size of the area thus included or because of some flaw in the photographic process of which I had no knowledge, the photograph was grainy almost to the point of inscrutability. The bulk of the bed could be made out as a dark rectangle to the right-hand side of the frame, and the window as a smaller, lighter square directly facing the camera, but otherwise all I could discern were clumps of grey and black which could as well be flaws on the lens as the specific contents of the room.

My heart sank. If the other images were of the same poor quality, what chance had we of uncovering the new evidence Scotland Yard required?

Holmes obviously agreed. "Useless," he muttered and pushed the photograph angrily off the table.

The image underneath was fortunately far clearer, though that only made its subject more upsetting.

Taken close to, it showed the late Miss McLachlan's injuries. I was grateful to see that the technician who had created the image had taken the time to cover much of the poor woman, including her face, but the stab wounds were crisp and surprisingly clear. Too clear for my liking, in fact.

Somehow, the permanence which the photograph bestowed upon the grisly scene rendered it more repellent than it had been in life. Obscene was the word that came to mind.

Not so Holmes, who gave a grunt of obvious satisfaction. "This is splendid," he murmured, bending low to examine the detail of the wounds with his glass.

Not for the first time I marvelled at my friend's ability to set to one side any extraneous emotional response. There was little doubt that it made him a more effective investigator, but his lack of feeling could be difficult to appreciate at times like these.

"Splendid in what way?" I asked, more sharply than I intended.

"The shape of the wounds, Watson!" He pointed to several narrow incisions. "A common kitchen knife leaves a distinctive pattern at its point of entry, with a noticeably pointed edge on one side where the blade is sharp, and a square edge on the other, from the blunt flat of the blade. But these wounds have pointed edges on both sides. They were made by a two-sided knife – or perhaps a bayonet. Certainly not by any blade one would expect to find in the average household."

"A bayonet?" Lestrade murmured thoughtfully. "I'd advise keeping that to yourself, Mr. Holmes, what with Dr. Watson being an ex-army man."

"He was an army medic, Lestrade," Holmes replied firmly. "He is hardly likely to have brought an old bayonet home as a souvenir. Besides," he continued more evenly, "Watson is not the only military man intimately involved in this case."

Lestrade shook his head in confusion, but Potter was quicker off the mark. "You don't mean Major McLachlan?" he exclaimed. "Can you actually be about to suggest that Sir Campbell McLachlan murdered his own aunt? For what possible reason? And how? If that is the best you can do to save your friend, Holmes, then he might be better dispensing with your services altogether!"

Holmes ignored Potter altogether, and addressed his reply to Lestrade. "Naturally, I am not saying that Major McLachlan is the killer. That would be preposterous, and the very suggestion is idiotic. However, the major is well known as a collector of military memorabilia. I would be interested to know if he has a weapon in his collection whose blade matches these wounds. Though he may not have killed his aunt, the knife used to do so may have originated in his home."

"Brought along by the killer, you mean?"

"Quite so. Clearly, the killer brought Miss McLachlan to this room somehow. Why should the murder weapon not have come from the same location?"

Potter had listened patiently enough to this exchange, but now interrupted to point out that the police had been unable to find a single witness to the abduction of Miss McLachlan, or her presumed passage across London to Linhope Street.

Holmes waved a hand dismissively in Potter's direction. "Do not berate yourself too much, Inspector. It does no good to dwell upon such failures. For that matter, it may be that there simply were no witnesses to be found. Even so, I would be grateful if you would send one of your men to speak to the major, to establish whether he has recently lost a suitably sized bayonet or knife." He did not wait on a response, but quickly turned his attention back to the table in front of him. "In the meantime, let us turn our attention to the final image."

The third photograph fell somewhere between the preceding two in terms of scope. In an image taken from the foot of the bed, the photographer had captured the full length of the body, demonstrating the position in which it had been discovered. My heart sank as Holmes bent over it; like the first it was blurred and heavily grained, and I could scarcely imagine even Holmes uncovering some vital clue from it. I fancied I saw the hint of a smile on Potter's face as Holmes picked it up and tilted it in the light.

Suddenly Holmes gave a strangled cry and darted to the bed, the photograph gripped in his hand.

"The bedding, Lestrade!" he exclaimed. "The list that you had. Read from it again, if you would be so kind."

The two inspectors stared at him as though he had taken leave of his senses, but I felt a surge of hope at Holmes's obvious excitement. Evidently he had spotted something.

Lestrade fished his notebook from his pocket, and flicked to the appropriate page. "Good cotton sheets, a cotton pillow case and a bed cover," he said, casting a puzzled look in my direction. "Does that help you at all?"

Holmes gave no reply. He crossed to the window and peered closely through the glass, then pulled it open and stretched his head out into the drizzling air. A moment, no more, passed, then he withdrew his head and turned to Potter.

"I believe that a witness across the street saw a man signalling from this window some fifteen minutes before the police arrived?" he asked.

"He did."

"Thereby further constricting the possible time available for Watson to commit murder! But let us put that to one side for now. This man's view – is it from a window directly opposite, or one set at an angle?"

"His home is six doors down the road."

"So, an oblique angle?"

"I suppose so." Potter was becoming more irritated by every question, I could tell, even if Holmes appeared oblivious.

"Do you wish to speak to the witness, Mr. Holmes?" Lestrade asked, obviously as aware as I of the tensions in the room and wishing to defuse them if he could.

"Hmm?" Holmes was distracted, lost in thought, and took a moment to consider the inspector's question. "No thank you. The man is plainly unreliable, and it is more important that we retrieve the murder weapon than waste time on his half-glimpsed misunderstandings."

"Indeed, Mr. Holmes," Potter sneered, "that would be most helpful. Unfortunately, we have no idea where the murder weapon might be. If," he concluded maliciously, "it is not one of the knives found in Dr. Watson's bag."

Holmes shook his head and tutted, as though he were a teacher chiding a disappointing pupil who he knew could do better. "If you will be so good as to follow me, Inspector Potter, I shall demonstrate that the victim was not killed by one of the tools of Watson's trade."

"And how will you do that?"

"Why, by presenting you with the actual murder weapon, of course!"

He spun on his heel and headed for the stairs. A moment later, we three observers came to our senses and hurried after him.

Holmes was already in the street by the time we caught up with him. The rain had turned into a mist of tiny wet drops which seemed to hang in the air like spider's silk, dampening my face even as Holmes came to an unexpected stop in front of the house next door, the one shrouded in scaffolding. Seen from the front, little of the building itself was visible, with only occasional glimpses showing through the heavy cloths that covered the poles, ropes, boards and ladders which otherwise obscured the brickwork. An overgrown garden to one side, and a heap of abandoned and rotting glass and wood, which might once have been a potting shed, added to a general feeling of long-term neglect.

"This house has stood empty for a decade at least," Lestrade said, as though confirming my unspoken question. "It was bought by a builder six months ago. He started work on it only two weeks past, but we've had his men stood down since... well, since the incident."

I took a step towards Holmes, who had paused at the base of the scaffolding. Evenly spaced ladders led from the ground into the cloth-covered gloom at three spots, and as I reached out to tap him on the shoulder, he moved to the furthest one and began to climb.

"Here!" Potter shouted. "Where do you think you're going? That house is private property and you've no right to enter it!"

"I am not entering it," Holmes shouted back over his shoulder. "I am simply inspecting the space directly in front of it."

He disappeared beneath the nearest cloth, and could be heard moving about above us. A full minute passed, in which all I could make out was a series of muffled thumps, then he descended the ladder again, a look of satisfaction on his face.

"As I thought," he muttered to himself then, without a word to any of us, he ascended the middle ladder.

Again, a minute passed, then another. I thought at one point I heard Holmes jumping and at another a bulky shape appeared in one of the cloths as he pressed against it, but soon after we all heard him give a cry of triumph, and scant seconds later he was back on the ground, clutching a dirty, wet, grey bag in his hands.

His hands and face were filthy, his trousers soaked through at the knees, and he had a small cut above his right eyebrow, but even so, he paused to open the bag and reveal the wicked-looking, curved dagger hidden in its folds, before walking past us and back into number sixteen.

Holmes had tipped the knife onto the table, and tossed the sack in which it had been hidden onto the bed. Alongside the knife he placed the third photograph and, with a long finger, tapped the pillows at the top of the image.

There was a pair of them, thin-looking objects, one darker than the other where blood had soaked into the material. I glanced at the bed, where the same two pillows still lay, one again darkly stained, and the other relatively untouched. As to what Holmes had seen in them, and how that had enabled him to recover the murder weapon, I was at a loss, and said as much.

"Every part of the bedding is of high quality, Watson," he explained with exaggerated patience. "Cotton sheets, and a cotton pillow case. An expensive bed cover. Care was taken to make Miss McLachlan's final repose as comfortable – and as comforting – as possible. Why then was there but a single pillow case?"

I heard Potter snort behind me, but I knew Holmes did not often ask idle questions. Lestrade too knew enough to take Holmes seriously.

"Perhaps the killer did not know there would be a second pillow requiring a case?" he said.

"No, I knew it could not be that," Holmes replied with a frown. "Whoever did the killing, they were meticulous in laying out the room. Had they been short of a pillow case, they would have removed the pillow and made do with only one."

He bent over the bed and carefully examined each of the

pillows. "The cleaner of the two cases was removed," he said, "and the pillow replaced. Note in the photograph that the right edge of the lower one is dark with blood, then there is a white, unbloodied gap before the top pillow overlaps it. Initially, the lower pillow was more closely aligned with the top, meaning that blood could only stain the small, exposed section. The killer did not replace it exactly after removing the case, however, leaving a portion of unstained material on display."

Even Potter could not help but look down at the photograph and then at the bed in front of us. It was exactly as Holmes had said, though the import of his discovery eluded me.

"What of it?" Potter growled. "I am still waiting for an explanation regarding your suspiciously swift discovery of this dagger. If you hope to deflect attention by means of this pointless distraction, you will be disappointed, I warn you."

In reply, Holmes scooped up the sack he had just discarded and carefully smoothed it out on top of the less stained pillow. Laid flat, it was obviously a perfect fit. Any remaining doubts that the filthy object was also the missing pillow case were allayed by a dark slash of colour at one end, which exactly matched the bloodstain on the pillow.

Lestrade lifted one corner and let it fall again, his thin face a mask of confusion. "So, the killer hid the knife in the pillow case?" he asked slowly.

"In a manner of speaking," Holmes replied. "It is possible that the murderer concealed the knife inside the pillow case, intending to carry it away with him, but he would, I think, swiftly have become aware that a sharp knife will easily tear a hole in even good quality linen." He turned slightly to address me. "I assume the girl who accosted you had no such item on her person, Watson?"

I shook my head. I had almost forgotten the girl, but Holmes obviously had not.

"Of course not," he said briskly. "But the knife is with the pillow case, even so." He mimed picking something up from the bed. "The lady lies dead, her killer standing over her, bloody knife still in his hand. It is a substantial weapon, and so cannot be tucked into a belt or dropped into a jacket pocket. The girl is long gone, was perhaps never in the room, and now he is alone. He crosses to the window and crouches down, fearing someone will see him framed against the candlelight. He presses his fingers against the glass – you can see two full sets of fingerprints at chest height, here and here – and peers as best he can down the street. If there is nobody about, he might be able temporarily to conceal the knife about himself, and drop it down a drain somewhere nearby.

"But there are people in the street. He might be seen! The girl will be meeting with Watson soon, and the killer knows he must be gone before he arrives, but he cannot leave the knife, not if he wishes Watson to take the blame. He presses his face more closely against the glass, and remembers the scaffolding next door. It hides him from view for now, but he must act quickly. He pulls the cleaner pillow case from the bed and drops the knife in its bottom. A few tiny drops of blood escape the blade as he does so, falling here" – he pointed to a spot a foot or so from the bed – "and here," indicating another spot nearer the window. "He opens the window carefully and leans out as far as he dares. Whirling the now weighted pillow case about him–" he leaned out of the window and matched his actions to his words "–he lets it go, and watches it land among the builders' detritus next door. He closes the window and slips away, observed only by a neighbour who thinks he has witnessed a handkerchief being waved."

"That's a fine story, Mr. Holmes; one worthy of Dr. Watson himself. But there is no proof that anyone other than Dr. Watson was in the room that night. He could as easily have done as you suggested."

The burgeoning hope I had felt stir in me during Holmes's recital was crushed at once by Potter's insistence that I was the guilty party. He was right in what he said, of course. Nothing that Holmes had said so far exonerated me in the slightest.

"He could," Holmes admitted, breaking into my gloomy thoughts. "But Watson has never owned a knife such as this, and I would lay even money that Major McLachlan is missing a kukri from his collection of military paraphernalia."

"A koo-kree, Mr. Holmes?" In Lestrade's mouth the foreign word was stretched out and pronounced with the exaggerated care of a man who has never spoken any language but English.

"A sort of everyday curved dagger, popular in Nepal, but found throughout south Asia." I had seen several of them in Afghanistan, where they were popular souvenirs among our soldiers. "Holmes is right. I've never owned one, but Major McLachlan's would be a strange collection if it did not contain at least one."

"Exactly so, Watson," Holmes added. "You will note the small nick in the hilt, however. A serious collector, such as the major is reputed to be, would not keep a flawed item such as this on show, so it may not have been missed yet." He eyed Potter in a sidelong fashion, weighing something up before he spoke. "Perhaps you could make enquiries at the major's household, Inspector, and ascertain whether he is missing a kukri?"

"There is no need to remind me of the fundamentals of my job, Mr. Holmes," Potter snapped. "I will make such enquiries – and other enquiries into any knick-knacks which the doctor here might have brought back from his time in the army."

Holmes was unabashed. "You might also usefully make enquiry of the landlady whether she heard anything at the time. I know she claims to have known nothing of the murder, but the thump of the knife landing among the scaffolding next door would have made a substantial noise."

"There I must disappoint you, Mr. Holmes," Potter smiled. "The lady has gone to stay with family in the country while we sequester her house. She may never return, apparently."

"You do not know where she has gone?" The anger in Holmes's voice was unmistakable as Potter shrugged his shoulders. "Just as you cannot find the girl."

"We only have Dr. Watson's word that *she* even exists," Potter countered, and it was all I could do to restrain myself from knocking some of the discourtesy out of him. But I was in trouble enough without adding the assault of a police officer to my list of charges.

Holmes too was silent, but Lestrade spoke up suddenly. "There are the fellows who helped Constable Howie break in the door," he suggested. "Perhaps they might have heard something or seen the knife being thrown?"

"A capital idea, Lestrade! You are definitely improving! I had almost forgotten those gentlemen as I concentrated on other avenues, but you are quite right; I should speak to them at once."

"As they committed no crime, they are not in custody, so that may prove difficult," Potter replied on Lestrade's behalf, glaring at his colleague. "Or will you blame the police for failing to hold them too?"

"Not at all. But they can presumably be found?"

"Howie is on duty in the area," Lestrade offered, crossing to the door. "Shall I send Constable Schell to find him? He may be able to shed some light on these three gentlemen."

He sent the constable scurrying down the stairs before anyone could reply, and a matter of minutes later, Constable Howie entered, breathless from running.

Chapter Thirteen

❧

A t our previous meeting, I had — understandably, I think —
failed to take much notice of Constable Howie, but now
that he stood before us, helmet under his arm, it was clear that he
was a reliable and sensible man. A little over six foot tall, he was
about thirty years of age, slim and broad shouldered, and already
showing signs of a receding hairline.

He spoke slowly, but not dully, obviously meticulous in his
work and keen to make no missteps in front of two senior Scotland
Yard inspectors.

"The street, and surrounding areas, were all but deserted
that night, sir," he said in reply to Holmes's enquiry. "As I said
previously, the only people I had seen in the preceding period
were the three souls who assisted me in breaking down the door."

"You had seen them before then?" asked Holmes, with interest.

"A few minutes earlier, yes, sir. They were standing drinking
on the corner of the street. I would have moved them on, but they
were doing no real harm, so I made sure they saw me watching

them instead. Giving them a chance to be on their way before I came back down the street."

"Admirable, Constable," Holmes commented approvingly. He crossed to the little table and poured the dregs of the water from the jug over his dirty hands, then dried them on his handkerchief. "If you could tell me everything you can recall about the men as we take a short stroll down to the street corner, I shall be in your debt."

Howie glanced across at Lestrade and Potter. I distinctly saw Potter's mouth begin to form an objection, but fortunately Lestrade was the quicker and he barked, "On you go then," before his fellow inspector could say a word.

Linhope Street came to an end where it met Ivor Place. A thin sliver of grass had grown in a slice of muddy ground that ran alongside the wall of the last house in the street, and it was there that Constable Howie led us.

"They were standing here, sir," he said, indicating the grassy area. "The taller two were leaning back against the wall, and the smaller one was facing them. The bottle was getting passed back and forward a fair bit, but they were talking quietly and laughing friendly enough."

"One of the men was noticeably smaller than the others?" asked Holmes. "Did you get a good look at him? The man with his back to you?"

"I did, sir." I stood across the street from them for about a minute, letting them know I had my eye on them. The two facing me soon stopped talking, and the little one turned round to see why. He turned away sharpish, but I'd know the three of them again, even without having them help me out with the door."

Holmes clapped his hands together. "Splendid! I foresee a long and successful career in the police for you, Howie, if this is the usual standard of your work. But," he went on, his eyes narrowing in concentration, "perhaps you could describe the smaller man for me? In as much detail as you can recall, if you please."

I was puzzled by Holmes's concentration on this one man, and doubted whether Howie's description would be of use in any case. Five foot five at most, clean-shaven with brown hair, and wearing a brown suit and battered bowler hat, it could be any of a thousand men in the surrounding streets, and a hundred thousand in London as whole.

"Would you like a description of the other two, Mr. Holmes?" Howie asked, but Holmes shook his head distractedly and crouched down by the grassy strip.

"There was definitely no one else in the area who should not have been, Constable?" he asked after a minute. "Nobody acting suspiciously, or who seemed out of place?"

"Nobody, sir. The streets were quiet as the grave."

I winced inwardly at Howie's unfortunate choice of words, but Holmes seemed satisfied.

"And had you seen any of these men before?"

"The taller two, yes, sir. I can't say that I know their names, but they live in the area. One of them works as a rat catcher now and again. The other used to be a sailor, if I remember right. Doesn't do much of anything now. The little one's new in the area though. I'd never laid eyes on him before."

Holmes rose to his feet and brushed some dirt from his hands. "Thank you, Constable," he said. "You have been very useful."

"I think we have seen all we need here," he said, addressing himself to the two inspectors. "If you would make the finding of these three gentlemen, particularly the smallest one, your priority, I believe it entirely possible that I can demonstrate Watson's innocence even to Scotland Yard's satisfaction."

Of course, Holmes's words were music to my ears, but I knew from previous experience that he would not explain himself prematurely. I had to be content with a sidelong glance and the merest hint of a smile.

Potter, however, was not so sanguine. "Are we permitted to ask why it is so important that we turn up these three tramps? Is your contention now that one of them murdered Miss McLachlan, then waited around afterwards in order to be present when the body was discovered?" He laughed, without warmth. "Did one of them perhaps also dress himself as a young girl and lure Watson away with his blandishments?"

Holmes simply ignored Potter and, turning to Lestrade, repeated his belief that he might be able to present a solution to the case, should the three tramps be found.

The inspector's face twisted and coloured at Holmes's request. "It is not actually my case, Mr. Holmes," he began apologetically. "I'm only here in an unofficial capacity, remember. But," he continued, looking directly at Potter, "I am certain that Inspector Potter wouldn't dream of allowing any potential lead in the case to be missed. Isn't that right, Inspector?"

Potter glared between the three of us. "I don't need you telling me my job any more than I need him," he said, flicking his hand at Holmes. "If I can spare a man, I'll put him on the job, don't worry."

"We will endeavour not to," Holmes replied dryly. "Perhaps Howie here could be the man you spare? He seems an observant fellow, and already knows two of the men."

Potter's eyes narrowed in irritation, but in the end he nodded his agreement. "As you wish. Constable Howie, tomorrow your job will be to seek out these three vagrants. I would hate Dr. Watson to feel he was not given every possible assistance in his attempts to escape the noose."

He did not appear happy to make the concession, but succeeded in turning the grimace on his face into a tight smile before bidding us a collective good day. I watched him walk away from us, back towards his carriage. In spite of the rain, which had increased in strength throughout the morning, he strode along with a straight back and his head held high. I could picture the water dripping steadily from the brim of his hat, and imagine his refusal to allow anything so inconsequential as the weather to influence him.

It would be no simple task to convince a man such as he to change his opinion, I reflected unhappily. Even with the murder weapon now discovered, and Holmes apparently convinced a solution lay with the missing tramps, I struggled to convince myself that all would be well in the end. Not with Inspector Potter's intransigence between me and that happy conclusion.

My thoughts mirrored by the downpour which had turned London grey and sodden, I watched Potter disappear into the gloom, and wished futilely that I had never entered Linhope Street at all.

Chapter Fourteen

Holmes had seen all he wished in the murder room, and so we left Lestrade and Howie to close up, while we walked in the steady rain towards Baker Street, each of us lost in our own thoughts.

We had covered only half the distance when Holmes came to a sudden stop. I thought at first he had spotted a hansom or growler for hire, the road having been conspicuously free of them, and indeed one trotted round the corner just at that moment. Marvelling at my friend's ability to deduce even when a horse might come into view, I signalled to the driver to halt and gratefully bundled myself inside, with Holmes on my heels.

"Baker Street first, then Chesham Place please, driver."

Holmes had spoken before I could give any directions. I looked across at him and he explained.

"Chesham Place is the London address of Major Sir Campbell McLachlan. Having set the bloodhounds of Scotland Yard on the trail of three members of the lowest class of people, I thought it more fitting that you and I interview one of the highest."

He grinned and drummed his fingers quickly on the left leg of his trousers, then leaned forward and explained his plan.

By the time we arrived at McLachlan's house Holmes had finished his explanation. He intended to pose as Inspector Alexander, brought in from the country to assist Potter in this vitally important case. Naturally, I was to play the part of his devoted sergeant.

"Flattery, Watson, is meat and drink to the politician," he concluded with a smile. "But remember at all times that McLachlan is renowned for two things. First, he is ferociously jealous of any perceived slight to his family name. He is rumoured to have killed a fellow officer in a duel after he was overheard disparaging the military capabilities of a distant cousin of McLachlan's. Secondly, though it is perhaps linked to the first, he is famously intolerant of uninvited visitors. It is said of him that he is at any man's bidding while sitting in Parliament – where he is applauded as an industrious and approachable MP – and no man's while sitting at home. We must tread carefully with him."

McLachlan's home was a distinguished town house on several floors, surprisingly modern in style. Our carriage came to a stop behind another, on which were emblazoned the horns of a roebuck. Holmes brushed the top of the bowler hat he had collected from Baker Street and, adopting a slightly hangdog expression, knocked diffidently on the front door.

After a delay just long enough for me to wonder if anybody was at home, the door opened and an elderly, stooped butler enquired after our business in a weak, reedy voice. Holmes explained our fictitious police errand and we followed the butler inside.

Major Sir Campbell J. McLachlan stood with his back to the embers of a dying fire as we were shown into an unusually decorated reception room. Every inch of the walls was decorated either with the mounted head of an animal, or one of a selection of swords, knives and pistols. The jumbled mass of dead-eyed faces and shining blades was unappealing and in questionable taste, in my opinion.

The same could, in truth, be said of the major himself. He stood a good six foot five, with luxuriant whiskers and the final remnants of what must surely once have been a full head of curly red hair, now dotted here and there in clumps on an otherwise bald scalp, like haystacks in a field of scythed wheat. He wore the full regalia of a Highland major of fifty years before, complete with tartan trews, and red jacket decorated with gold brocade. He also affected a monocle, through which he viewed us with ill-concealed contempt. It was as though a caricature from *Punch* had sprung to life.

"Well then?" he barked before either of us could speak. "Country bumpkins come up to the big city for a bit of a jolly? Is that it? Hmm? Hmm?"

Without waiting for a reply he switched his attention from us to his butler, who stood to one side and slightly behind us, shuffling from foot to foot, and clearly keen to be elsewhere.

"And you, Murray! What're you doing, inviting country plodders into my house! Get out of my sight before I take a whip to you!"

To my astonishment, he picked up an old inkwell from the mantelpiece and hurled it at the butler, who swiftly turned on his heel and disappeared down the hallway as it crashed against the doorframe by my side. It was an extraordinary performance.

Holmes, however, was unperturbed. He glanced momentarily at the doorframe and the dented inkwell then brought his hands together in a slow, loud clap.

"Quite right, Sir Campbell!" he exclaimed. "It's the only way to treat them. Give a servant an inch and he'll take the family silver!"

McLachlan frowned, his belligerence giving way to uncertainty. "You think so, do you, Inspector? Have much experience with servants, do you, out there in Little Chipping by the Marsh, or whatever stinking hamlet you call home? Hmm? Hmm?"

"Enough to know that you have enacted the little tableau to which my sergeant and I have just borne witness many times before, and that you had no intention of harming your butler, as he well knew. I should not be surprised to learn he is within earshot, in fact."

McLachlan's habit of ending every sentence with a pair of heavy nasal breaths was distracting, but in spite of the insolence in his words, his tone when next he spoke was more respectful.

"You think so, do you? And do you also expect me to be impressed by your party tricks? I've seen men in India run swords through their own bodies and eat supper afterwards, and holy men sleep on blazing coals as easily as you or I would on a feather bed. What are your childish games compared to that? Hmm? Hmm?"

"Neither tricks nor games, I assure you, sir. Merely the ability to take note of what surrounds us all and extrapolate truths from there. For instance, there are at least seventeen individual dents in a one-foot length of this doorframe and none anywhere else. Murray made certain of his position between the doorframe and ourselves when entering the room, and stood ready to shift to one side as soon as you launched the inkwell. Which," he concluded, picking up the object and holding it out before him, "shows undeniable signs of being used as a projectile several times in the past. A performance, designed to unnerve and wrong-foot unwelcome visitors, in other words."

McLachlan considered Holmes for a long moment, then smiled and said, "Murray," in a normal voice.

Behind us, the old butler stepped into the room and took up position just inside the door. "Yes, sir?" he asked. There was no trace of the thin-voiced, near hunchback who had led us to the room. In his place was a slim man of medium height, with short-cropped fair hair, turning grey at the temples, and a back as straight as my own. A passing examination of his face confirmed that they were one and the same man, but it was difficult even so to reconcile one with the other.

"Whisky, Corporal. One for myself and the inspector – and will beer suit you, Sergeant?"

"I'm afraid we cannot drink while on duty, Sir Campbell," Holmes replied smoothly. "Though the sergeant is, I believe, fond of a glass or two."

There being nothing I could say, I said nothing, and instead reminded myself that it was vital Holmes gain McLachlan's trust in order to find answers to his questions. It appeared he had made a good start, for the major was as affable now as he had been antagonistic before.

"I thought he might be," McLachlan was saying as I refocused my attention on him. "He has the look about him. Saw a lot of it in the army, of course. Just a whisky for me in that case, Murray," he dismissed the butler, then, "So you're here to assist Potter, are you? A good man, but he can't seem to get anywhere with poor Aunt Sarah. And he knows more about the gangs who stalk these streets than any man other, perhaps, than myself."

"Corporal Murray served under you for some time?" Holmes asked at an apparent tangent.

"Murray? He certainly did. Twenty-two years in the regiment, eight of them as my batman. Saved my life near Peshawar, and when the army turned us both out to pasture, I asked him to continue keeping an eye on me. Brave as a lion, loyal as a hunting dog – and I believe loyalty is a lane best travelled in both directions. I would trust Murray with my life – or those of any member of my family," he concluded firmly, leaving us in no doubt that he had understood the purpose of Holmes's question.

"Regarding your family, Major," Holmes continued, unabashed. "The only other relation now staying at the house is your brother, Alistair? Is that correct?"

If McLachlan had been prompt and certain when describing Corporal Murray, he was anything but when considering his own brother. Even confirming that he was resident seemed an effort, the words almost needing to be dragged from the major.

"Yes," he said finally, then fell silent while Murray brought in his whisky, added soda and presented it to him on a polished silver tray. Once the corporal had left, he sipped at his drink before asking whether Holmes was certain that I would not like a glass of beer. "In the kitchen, perhaps? We have lost a servant or two recently for... well, for one reason or other, but Cook can still rustle up something to satisfy a man of good appetite like your sergeant, I'm sure."

Had Holmes laughed, I might well have walked out, regardless of the consequences, but instead he simply shook his head gravely. "The sergeant is needed to confirm my own memory of our conversation, Sir Campbell. Far more reliable than the old method of one man scribbling in a notebook."

McLachlan was less than completely mollified but, left with no choice, he acquiesced with reasonably good grace.

"Very well, Inspector. I have always believed that the expert should be given his head." He gestured across to a pair of matched sofas in one corner of the room. "We should take a seat if my brother is to be the topic of conversation, I would suggest."

Once we were seated – myself included, to my satisfaction – McLachlan began to speak in a low but steady voice.

"Alistair lost his way when he was a young man, Inspector, and he has never been able to find himself again." He raised a hand as though forestalling a protest that did not come. "I am not being poetic, believe me. I am not by nature a poetic man. When I say Alistair lost his way, I mean it quite literally.

"You see, Alistair was a late birth, born long after our parents had ceased to expect any further addition to their family. I was already a young subaltern by then, stationed near Kabul, and by the time Alistair came to adulthood I had made a good career for myself in the army and had no time – nor inclination, I admit – to return to England, even when my father died.

"Alistair was sixteen at that point and, with my father gone, the absolute focus of my mother's attention. She spoiled him in every meaning of the word, Inspector, indulging his every whim; funding, however unknowingly, his every vice, and telling him at all times that he was destined for a special fate.

"Perhaps if I had come home, things would have been different? Perhaps Alistair would have been different? But there is nothing to be gained by posing unanswerable questions, and the fact is that Alistair went quickly to the bad. By eighteen he was consorting with young men far beneath his own class, ruffians and criminals, and by twenty he had left the country entirely, with at least two outraged fathers on his heels.

"I heard none of this until years later when I retired from the army and returned to the family home. Nor did I hear of Alistair's years on the continent, one of a group of well-known debauchees, infamous even in the fleshpots and drug dens of Italy and France. My mother denied any wrongdoing on the part of her beloved younger son and died secure in the belief that he was a successful continental businessman."

McLachlan's voice fell away and his gaze seemed to pass through Holmes and myself, to focus on some distant, sorrowful part of his own past. I would not have intruded on this private grief but Holmes felt no such compunction.

"Your brother returned home after your mother's death?" he asked.

McLachlan blinked heavily and nodded. "Somewhat earlier, in fact. It seems even the continent had become a little too 'hot' for him. But with my mother gone, he had no choice but to come, cap in hand, to me. Without the generous stipend she allowed him, he had, at that point, no income at all. As the elder son, I had inherited everything from my father on his demise, and though I had been content to live on my army pay and leave all the capital with my mother while she lived, I had no intention of extending the same courtesy to my brother, word of whose dissolution reached me as soon as I arrived in England. I ordered him home, and informed him that his previous sybaritic existence was at an end."

"And he has remained under your control since then?"

"Control is not how I would put it, Inspector. 'Influence' is perhaps a better word."

"The word is immaterial. Has his behaviour improved?"

I could see McLachlan's back stiffen at Holmes's dismissive attitude, and wondered that Holmes himself could not. Even if he had not, McLachlan's reply should have warned him to show more circumspection in his questioning.

"I fail to see what my brother's behaviour at home has to do with the murder of my aunt," the major said frostily. "Is that not what you are supposed to be investigating?"

"He has forced a maid or two to resign her position, though?"

McLachlan's face flushed with genuine anger. "How can you possibly know that?"

"I did not until now. But you mentioned a recent problem retaining servants. The connection between that fact and the presence of a notorious rake in the house is an obvious one."

McLachlan sagged at the shoulders and placed his empty glass on the table between us. "There have been one or two... incidents," he admitted quietly. "I was forced to have Murray dismiss a maid."

"Was violence involved?"

The reluctance in McLachlan's voice was palpable. "The allegations were that Alistair had made improper suggestions to certain of the younger female servants," he muttered, almost too quietly to hear. "But suggestions were the whole of the matter, I am certain. Nothing more. And I have since taken steps to prevent any recurrence. My brother is a changed man, I can assure you, Inspector."

"Hmm," was all that Holmes said in reply. He rested his hand on his crossed legs and tapped one long finger against his knee, apparently lost in thought.

"Did the late Miss McLachlan have a favourite painting?" he asked unexpectedly.

McLachlan frowned in confusion, but replied readily. "Why, yes, Inspector, she did. A gift from my father. He painted it himself, and she cherished it. It is a rather fine watercolour, and popular enough in the local area to be available as a print. There are several copies in this house, in fact."

"And did your brother know of the painting?"

"He did, though he was not alone in that."

"Of course," Holmes murmured, half to himself. "You said that your brother had no income at the time your mother died. The implication being that his fortunes have improved recently?"

McLachlan seemed increasingly confused by Holmes's rapid changes in tack, which was obviously my friend's intention.

"He... that is... well, yes, they have. Alistair was the sole beneficiary of Aunt Sarah's will and has inherited a goodly fortune on her demise. As I said, she had no children of her own, and made no secret of the fact that he was to inherit on her death. She moved into this house when her faculties began to deteriorate – sadly, she became ever less lucid and I was forced to constrain her to remain within the house at all times. Still, she was the older sister and in her right mind when she made her will – and she remained a woman of substantial means. Those means have now fallen to Alistair, who tells me he will be moving out within the week. But why are you so fascinated by my brother, Inspector? I have already told you that he is a changed man. Would you not be better served focusing your attention on this disgusting creature, Watson? Potter tells me he is certainly the killer. A gambling sort, apparently, who killed my aunt to pay off his debts to one of the gangs who would like nothing better than to force me to cease my investigations into their activities."

I could not help but stiffen at this description, but fortunately Major McLachlan had long since forgotten my presence, and gave no sign of noticing anything amiss. In any case, Holmes barely let him finish before continuing his interrogation.

"You place a great deal of trust in Inspector Potter, it would seem."

"I do. He has proven himself to be a truly moral man."

"Morality is important to you, of course."

"As it should be to every man!"

"Of course. And Inspector Potter is a moral man, in your opinion?"

"Have I not just said so? And that is not mere opinion, I might add. His bona-fides are irrefutable."

Holmes considered this last comment for a moment, then continued on a fresh path of enquiry.

"Regarding your work with Inspector Potter, Sir Campbell. You have been responsible for the passage through the Commons of several bills concerning gang activities?"

"I have."

"I have not, I fear, been able to keep up with news from the capital as well as I might. Am I correct in saying that you have thus far concentrated your efforts primarily on the continental gangs?"

"That is indeed the case. In speaking to senior policemen, it was made clear to me that we must first eradicate the criminal fraternity who hail from outside our own shores, before moving on to what I would term the home-grown troublemakers."

"Because the methods they bring with them are alien to us, and so more difficult for the police to curtail?"

"Exactly so." This sort of questioning was clearly more to McLachlan's taste and he had settled once more into his earlier amiability, exactly, I suspected, as Holmes intended.

"And has this approach proven successful?"

"I wonder you have to ask, Inspector. Surely news of our successes has reached even your country parish?"

"Quite so, Sir Campbell, quite so. I ask merely for clarification. But now, if we might return to the matter of the assaulted maids, I wonder–"

"HOLMES! What on earth are you doing here?"

Potter's voice resounded about the room. He stood in the doorway, red in the face, his fists clenched in fury, with a police constable beside him.

"Holmes…?" Major McLachlan glanced from Potter to the two of us, confusion writ large on his face. "What is the meaning of this, Potter? This is Inspector Alexander and his sergeant – or so they led me to believe!"

I stood quickly, feeling every inch a villain, and suffused with embarrassment. Strange to say, I had all but forgotten that we were guests in this house under false pretences, and had almost begun to believe myself Inspector Alexander's trusty colleague. No excuse came to mind, and I suspect I would still be standing there in mute shame, had Holmes not similarly risen and given McLachlan a tiny bow.

"I apologise for the deception, Sir Campbell, but it was vital that I had the opportunity to speak to you. As you just said, Inspector Potter has already closed his mind to alternatives to his own flawed theory. In doing so, I very much fear that he will allow the real killer of your aunt to go free, and send a good and innocent man to the gallows."

"Innocent man–" McLachlan might like to present himself as an eccentric to his visitors, but he had not risen to the rank of major in the British Army, and survived as a parliamentarian in the adversarial atmosphere of the House of Commons, without a fair degree of natural intelligence. He whipped round towards me. "You! You are Watson! How dare you, sir! Murray! Murray!"

No sooner had the words left his mouth than his former batman appeared at Potter's side. "Sir?" he asked calmly.

"Escort these two blackguards out at once, and do not worry yourself to be too gentle. They are never to be allowed within these walls again! And you," he exclaimed to Holmes, "may consider yourself lucky that I do not pull one of the weapons from these walls and take the flat of a blade to your miserable hide!"

Potter had watched developments with a smile, but now stepped forward to add his own views. "I would have you arrested for impersonating a police officer, were it not for your willingness to call upon certain influential people at the first sign of difficulties. Genuine policemen do not have time to waste on foolish play acting, Mr. Holmes, no matter how malicious."

Murray closed on us, but before he could lay hands on either of us, Holmes quickly asked a question. "Do you have a kukri knife in your collection, Sir Campbell?"

McLachlan, surprised I think by the question, answered automatically. "I have several, though only one in pristine condition."

Murray was but a step away as McLachlan frowned in irritation, and it was plain that we needed to leave immediately. Potter's self-satisfied smile followed us as we made our way from the room with as much dignity as we could muster. It was, in truth, little enough.

I was full of nervous excitement as we travelled back to Baker Street.

"Finally, we have a suspect, Holmes! Alistair McLachlan had both the means and the motive to murder his aunt. He had access to the knife used to kill her – you noticed that the major said that only one of the examples he owns is unblemished? – and moreover there is the large legacy he has inherited on her death."

"That is true, and we shall certainly present such a theory to

Inspector Potter in due course," Holmes replied laconically, and with less enthusiasm than I had hoped. "But does it not strike you as odd that Mr. McLachlan should choose to drag his elderly aunt across the city to kill her, rather than doing so in her own bedroom, even if he was so desperate to escape the shackles of his brother's keeping that he could not wait a year or two for nature to take its inevitable course? And what motive do you assign him for implicating you in the murder? Is he perhaps a particularly dissatisfied patient?"

These were good questions. The first was of lesser significance, for had not Holmes and I many times found the plans of murderers to be convoluted and illogical? But I could conceive of no reason why any member of the McLachlan family should wish me harm, far less my disgrace and death. I had given the matter some thought while imprisoned, but had been unable to bring to mind a single occasion when our paths might have crossed.

"That said, he cannot be discounted altogether." Holmes had obviously noted my disappointment, and was at pains to reassure me. "Even if he is not the killer, he might at least serve to distract Potter from his vendetta against you."

Once more, what I had initially viewed as a breakthrough in the investigation seemed to be only a diversion, but I could not entirely convince myself that it meant nothing, and with that I would have to be satisfied for now. The next few days would, I hoped, see further and more concrete progress.

Chapter Fifteen

In fact, the next two days were wholly lacking in incident. Holmes set his legion of child helpers on the trail of the missing girl, and repeatedly took me over the events of that night, hoping to dislodge some new morsel from my tired mind, but with no success. Otherwise, we ate and drank, read, smoked and talked, just as we had always been wont to do. It was wonderfully relaxing, even if I could not always stop myself from worrying that the investigation had come to a halt.

On the morning of the third day, however, Mrs. Hudson appeared in the doorway of our rooms, with a small, grubby figure largely hidden behind her skirts.

"You have a visitor, Mr. Holmes," she announced disapprovingly, pulling the boy round by the collar and depositing him before us.

"Wiggins, come in," said Holmes, beckoning the lad forward and shifting his long legs to one side so as to allow the heat of the fire to warm him. "You have news for me?" he asked eagerly.

"That I do, guv'nor," agreed the little Arab, pulling himself up to his full height of, charitably, four foot ten. "The cove you're lookin' for? 'E'll be at the rat fighting tonight behind O'Rourke's pub."

"Splendid!" Holmes cried, clapping his hands together in delight. He fished in his pocket and pulled out a shilling, which he flicked towards Wiggins, who expertly snatched it from the air.

"I can tell you where 'e is now, if that'd 'elp more?" he asked, glancing hopefully at Holmes's waistcoat pocket.

"Somewhere in the depths of the worst part of London, I expect," Holmes replied. "Not the sort of address I would care to investigate without half of the city's constabulary behind me. No, Wiggins, your information regarding tonight's activities is invaluable enough."

He dismissed the boy, with a reminder to keep "the other matter" in mind, then reached for his pipe and settled himself comfortably in his chair. "We might as well take our ease for now, Watson, for we shall be doing nothing of note until this evening. Though if you would not mind sending a telegram to Lestrade, asking him to meet us at O'Rourke's public house at ten o'clock, I would be obliged. Oh, and ask him to bring along Howie. We may need his strength."

I needed to buy tobacco in any case – I had been smoking more than usual since my release, perhaps in reaction to the lack of nicotine in prison – so I shrugged on my jacket and headed out into the bright, cold street.

That night, Holmes and I approached O'Rourke's public house disguised as labouring men. I admit I was not entirely comfortable in the efficacy of our subterfuge, for though Holmes looked every inch the rough costermonger, I felt sure I would be unmasked the second we encountered any of the genuine spectators.

I need not have worried. Nobody spared us a second glance, as we followed a thin stream of people along the side of the building, down a passageway enclosed on the other side by a high wooden fence. Once we had cleared the walls of the public house, the space opened up in a large area of waste ground. In the centre, a large group had gathered.

The crowd was arranged around a shallow dirt pit, lined with an assortment of warped wooden boards. To one side several wicker cages – too small for dogs – had been stacked two high; they moved slightly as I watched, though the night was still. My curiosity aroused, I edged my way round and peered inside, where something stirred in the shadows. Suddenly, the wire mesh at the front of the cage bulged as a large brown rat slammed itself against the metal. I stumbled backwards in fright and stepped on a loose stone. My ankle turned on the rock and I fell to the filthy ground, grateful for the first time that I was disguised and unrecognisable.

"Fir Gawd's sake, if ye can't handle yer drink, Bill, then don't take none in the first place!"

A hand reached down and, grabbing the front of my jacket, pulled me to my feet. "It would be better, Watson, if you were to avoid drawing attention to yourself," Holmes hissed in my ear, then led me by the elbow across to the dirt pit.

The event was obviously about to begin, for the crowd pressed tight around us, forcing us to the very edge of the pit. While we waited, I examined the people around me. To my surprise, they were not the homogenous criminal mob I had expected, but instead represented a wide spectrum of London life. Surly costermongers in patched trousers rubbed shoulders with top-hatted gentlemen, shoeless children darted among small groups of professional men, dipping a silk handkerchief where they could, while the worst type of drunken drab glared with a mixture of contempt and envy at the occasional society lady who hung off the arm of her escort and congratulated herself on her terrible daring.

I was reminded of the fairs and circuses of my youth, though in corrupted form, a similarity only strengthened by a voice reminiscent of a ringmaster, which rang out across the yard from a position somewhere behind us. I turned to see who had issued this call for silence, but I need not have troubled myself as the crowd parted in front of a dark-skinned individual in a grease-stained jacket and grubby collarless shirt. He stepped over the wooden palisade that ringed the pit and moved to its centre.

"Ladies and gentlemen, welcome to tonight's entertainment," he shouted, waving a hand in the direction of two particularly disreputable-looking spectators. They pushed themselves away from the fence on which they had been leaning, and disappeared behind an outhouse. When they reappeared each was leading a dog on a length of rope.

The first dog was a grey-coated terrier, small and wiry in build, but with an inquisitive nature, which it demonstrated by sniffing at every person it passed and tugging eagerly on the rope. The other was a different sort of animal entirely. Jet black, with a single black eye through which it glared malevolently, it was of the bulldog breed, stocky and squat, with powerful jaws.

As they approached the pit, the crowd gave a cheer, and I took the opportunity to protest to Holmes.

"I must say, Holmes, I did not expect to be released from prison merely to spend my evenings watching dumb animals fight to the death. Should we not move around the crowd until we find our missing tramp, and then speak to him directly?"

Holmes tutted and shook his head. "Patience, Watson," he chided. "I have already identified our man. He is one of a group of similar unfortunates, cavorting with several women of dubious morality on the other side of the pit."

I looked across, but one group of drunken men appears identical to the next, and so I simply accepted that Holmes was correct. That being the case, our next step was obvious.

"Can we not speak to him now, then?"

"That would prove difficult. We are, as you can see, hemmed in by the crowd on this side, and our quarry is similarly held in place on the other. We shall have to wait until a gap between bouts before any confrontation can take place."

He had a point. I could barely move due to the crush of bodies around us, and as the little terrier was released into the pit, the spectators behind us pushed forward to see more clearly, further compacting us into the mob. There was no way for now that we could approach the tramp.

We did at least have an excellent view of the "sport" on offer, though in my opinion that was a distinctly mixed blessing. The terrier had been dropped into the sunken arena and had taken up a position in the exact centre, where it now stood, its head snapping back and forward as it waited for its prey to be released.

The little animal did not have long to wait. With a flourish, the "ringmaster" reached into one of the cages that I had examined earlier and pulled out a large brown rat, which he swiftly flicked into the pit alongside the dog. For a moment, the two animals eyed each other, then the rat (which was almost as large as the dog) rushed forward. The terrier sprang nimbly to one side in plenty of time, causing the rat to charge past and crash into a section of the wooden barrier. Again and again the terrier carried out the same manoeuvre, until the rat began to slow down under the weight of exhaustion and repeated self-inflicted blows. Suddenly, the terrier darted forward and, before the rat could react, grabbed it by the throat and began to worry it back and forth in its jaws. No more than five seconds elapsed before the little dog released its prey, now quite dead.

The same sequence of events was repeated half a dozen times, to a melody composed in equal parts of triumph and defeat from the gambling fraternity around us, before the dog was removed from the ring and the black bulldog deposited in its stead.

In the commotion that accompanied this change, Holmes tugged at my jacket and we pushed our way through the crowd, Holmes in character cursing loudly at anyone who stood in his way while I followed in his wake. We had travelled about a third of the way to our target when the "ringmaster" called again for silence and released the first rat. Unable to progress any further, we stopped and watched as the stocky bulldog, forbearing the trickery of the far nimbler terrier, simply allowed the rat to attack then, as soon as it came within range, snapped its massive jaws on the rodent's head, cracking it like an egg.

"Too easy?" roared the ringmaster. "Let's make it more exciting, shall we?" With that, he threw first one, then several more, handfuls of rats into the ring. A roar went up from the mob, who again surged forward, pressing so closely together in their excitement as to leave small gaps behind them, into which Holmes and I gratefully slipped.

We had closed to within ten feet of the tramp when he chanced to look directly at us pushing against the crowd and, alerted by some sixth sense, turned and dived among his nearest neighbours.

"He's making a run for it!" I shouted to Holmes, but he had

already spotted the movement. With a mighty heave, he pushed aside everyone who stood before him and emerged from the back of the crowd only a few feet from our quarry. I extracted myself a few moments later, just in time to see Holmes grab and miss the tramp's collar. The miss caused him to overbalance and he slipped to one knee in the mud. He immediately righted himself, but the delay had allowed the tramp to stretch the gap between them to fifteen feet and as Holmes started off in pursuit again, he had only a short distance before he would be out of sight round the corner and free to hide himself in the surrounding rookeries. I quickened my pace, but a small group of spectators, losing interest in the sport on offer, crossed my path at the most inopportune moment and he was hidden from view until they passed.

As the crowd before me dispersed, I could see that Holmes would fail to lay hands on his quarry and I was quietly cursing our miserable luck when Constable Howie stepped into the tramp's path and, with one quick blow, sent him sprawling on his back. Directly behind, Inspector Lestrade came running up and stopped, panting slightly, above the recumbent and groaning figure on the ground.

"Up you get, you," he said as I reached the spot a step behind Holmes. Howie grabbed the tramp by the collar and heaved him to his feet. He was a little unsteady, which was to be expected, but I wondered if his senses had been addled by the blow, as he swayed from side to side and grinned at us like a fool.

"Martin Chilton-Smith, at your service, your honours," he said with a bow, having first taken an unsteady look at each of us. "Once of the respectable classes, now brought low through drink and low living. Although you now have me at a disadvantage, Mister...?"

"*Inspector* Lestrade. And this gentleman is Mr. Sherlock Holmes."

The effect was astonishing. Previously the little vagrant had been shuffling from foot to foot and grinning drunkenly, but as soon as Holmes's name was spoken he stopped in his tracks and soberly extended a hand.

"I'd be honoured to provide any service I can to the famous Sherlock Holmes," said he, ingratiatingly, but I could see Holmes was not fooled.

He stared at the tramp until he dropped his hand, unshaken. "You have already been of considerable disservice to me, Chilton-Smith," he said coldly. "A disservice which, should it lead to any harm befalling my friend, will prove to be the worst day's work you have done in your miserable life."

Holmes had never explained in any detail why he was so interested in the disreputable figure who stood before us, but it was now clear that he believed him somehow to be involved in the plot which had led me to my current precarious position. The specific role he had played came as a surprise, however.

"You are the reporter who scribbled the scurrilous lies about my friend here, are you not?" he said, and Chilton-Smith visibly paled even through the filth ingrained on his face.

"What...?" he said, all the foolishness knocked out of him. "What?" he said again, then, in an entirely more cultured voice, "How the devil did you know I was a reporter?"

Rather than reply directly, Holmes suddenly grabbed the tramp by the collar and turned him round where he stood. As the little man struggled in his grip, he reached down and pulled his right ankle upwards, exposing the well-shod sole of his shoe.

"In my experience a man may coat his face in grime, rip his clothes and put up with the most horrific stench if he feels a disguise is necessary, but invariably that same man will baulk at wearing shoes with soles which let in water. Earlier, I was able to examine the ground where you and your two companions loitered the night Watson was falsely accused of murder. Two of the boot prints I discovered were as expected, holed and tattered and leaking scraps of cardboard where poor-quality patching had come to naught, but the smallest boots showed soles without a blemish. No genuine vagrant could ever afford such footwear.

"Additionally, while on the surface your jacket is as soiled as one would expect, the gin you have so carefully spilled on the arm and collar is an expensive one.

"Finally, I have always known that a newspaperman must have been in the vicinity at the time. I was able to quash all reporting of Watson's arrest, and yet one report did appear, complete with details which could only have been known to someone with first-hand knowledge of events. The article was unattributed, but I'd happily wager that had there been, the name Martin Chilton-Smith would have appeared beside the text."

"Enough, enough," the little man said, waving one hand at Holmes. "So I wrote a piece on an arrest I happened to see. Is that a crime?"

"Not exactly a crime, but definitely unwise, I'd say," Lestrade piped up. "It places you in the vicinity of a brutal murder, for one thing."

"Now, wait a minute..." Chilton-Smith protested. "You can't seriously be suggesting that I had anything to do with it. I was just there and saw what happened. I never set foot in the house before the constable asked for my assistance, I swear."

"You saw what happened?" Holmes's voice betrayed no eagerness, but I could tell from the way he leaned forward slightly as he spoke that he believed the reporter had information which would be of assistance to him. "Describe it to us, if you please."

"Well, there's not that much to tell. I've been working this area for a month or so, as background for a series of articles on the wicked failure of the government to do anything to help the London poor. It's a decade since Booth created his maps, but still the lords and ladies who run the country spend more time setting their police dogs on the working man than–"

"Get to the point!" Lestrade interrupted angrily. "We've no interest in your socialist claptrap here. Just tell us what you saw."

Chilton-Smith frowned, and seemed about to protest, but a glance at Holmes's cold expression caused him to think better of it. With a cough, he went on in a quieter tone.

"Well, I was standing on the corner, chatting to a couple of unemployed men whose acquaintance I'd made, when I saw the constable here break into a run and disappear into one of the houses on the street, the one next to the scaffolding–"

This time it was Holmes who interrupted. "Earlier than that, if you would, Mr. Chilton-Smith. Tell us what you saw from the moment you took up position at the end of the street."

"Earlier?" the reporter repeated, confusion obvious on his face. "Well, I saw the constable, for one thing. He slowed down and made sure we saw him as he passed on the other side of the road. That's what I mean about the police harassing... but never mind that," he trailed off, as Lestrade grunted in warning. "Like I said, the constable passed by on the other side and began to walk down the street. He was about halfway down when something caught his attention and he ran into the house. I reckoned there was something going on that I might be interested in, so my friends and I strolled after him, wanting to see what was occurring, if you see what I mean."

"Earlier than that," Holmes insisted. "Before the police officer arrived."

"Before? Well, we played a little pitch and toss and shared a rather unpleasant drink. Nothing else I can think of."

"You did not see this gentleman?"

Holmes pointed to me, and the little man peered in my direction, as though seeing me for the first time.

"Well, it's possible I did. I couldn't say for sure, on account of the poor light, but someone very like your friend did pass by on the other side about five minutes before the constable. He was following a young girl, in a hurry from the look of things. I assumed it was a father and daughter making their way home and didn't pay them much attention."

It was not much, but I felt my heart skip a beat as he fell silent and took a step closer to me, staring up at my face.

"Yes, it could be the man," he said finally. "I can't say for sure, but yes, it could be him. Wait though," he went on, "isn't this Dr. Watson himself?" He shook his head ruefully, the beginnings of a smile on his face. "I should have realised straight away. Where Sherlock Holmes goes, Dr. Watson follows, eh?" A crafty look stole over his face, and with it a return of his confidence. "But you weren't there that night, were you?" he continued, addressing Holmes. "Not when Dr. Watson was being led away, charged with murder."

"No, unfortunately I was not. But what you can tell us may go a great way to clearing his name. For, if the window of time between Watson first entering the street and the constable hearing his cry has narrowed from thirty minutes to a mere five, how could he possibly have had sufficient time to kill Sarah McLachlan, far less prepare the scene?"

All signs of diffidence gone now, the reporter straightened

his filthy coat and spoke in a more confident tone. "I can't say I know what preparing the scene signifies, but it's possible I can help. Or perhaps I can't. Perhaps my memory's improved, now I get a better look at your friend's face. Maybe I didn't see him at all, except when he came out of the house, covered in that poor woman's blood."

The implication was clear. Chilton-Smith cocked an eyebrow at us, and grinned. "It could be that my memory would improve even more – and in a way more to your liking – if Sherlock Holmes would agree to an interview. My readers would be fascinated to hear the great detective's views on the cruel poverty in which his fellow Londoners are forced to exist."

"Why–" Lestrade lunged at the reporter, but Holmes held out an arm and brought him to a premature halt.

"Control yourself, Lestrade," he ordered, then turned his attention back to Chilton-Smith. "It would seem that now you have my friends and I at a disadvantage. If I understand you correctly, you are willing to give a truthful account of events only if I agree to speak to you for the purposes of publication. Is that correct?"

"That's about the strength of it. A bit colder than I'd put it myself, but correct in the essentials."

"And you would be willing to sign your name to any statement you make?"

"Of course. It'd hardly be worth your while if I didn't, would it?"

It pained me to have my prospects of freedom in the hands of this odious little man, but at the same time I rejoiced that at last someone could corroborate my version of events, even if that would not be enough to establish my innocence completely. Selfishly, I hoped that Holmes would agree to his terms, but said nothing, for I knew how jealously my friend guarded his privacy.

Holmes, in fact, seemed unperturbed, and indeed almost distracted. Casually, he reached into his pocket and pulled out a coin. "Very well," he said, "and let us seal the bargain properly, with silver." He flipped the coin towards Chilton-Smith, but his aim was awry and it fell to the ground at the feet of the newspaperman, who bent down to pick it up. As he did so, Holmes murmured, "You are a married man, I see, Mr. Chilton-Smith?"

"I am," the reporter responded uncertainly. "Though what that's to do with our current business, I don't know."

"Newly wed, too."

At this, Chilton-Smith stiffened, rightly wary that something had changed in Holmes's demeanour. "Six months past," he agreed. "But how could you possibly know that?"

"A simple enough deduction," Holmes replied. "I fancied that I had caught a glimpse of a silver chain round your neck earlier, and when you bent down just now I was able to confirm that fact. In the role you currently play, a chain such as that would long since have been sold for drink, or worse. One glimpse of it and you would be revealed as a fake.

"Why would you risk exposure in such a manner, unless the chain – or something hanging from it – was of particular value to you? A wedding ring seemed the most likely answer. There is also the very faintest of indentations on your left ring finger, such as might be made by a ring not long worn. Men who have been married for some time have a far more pronounced indentation – and besides, what man married twenty years would be sufficiently sentimental as to wear their wedding ring close to their heart, regardless of the risk?"

Chilton-Smith frowned suspiciously at Holmes. "Well, so I'm newly wed, what of it?"

"Just this," said Holmes evenly. "I wonder how your new wife would react if Inspector Lestrade were to pay her a visit, and make mention of the disreputable company you have been keeping lately? Disreputable *female* company, that is."

Chilton-Smith erupted in furious protestations. "What the devil are you suggesting?" he demanded. His hands balled into fists, and I took a step closer to Holmes, in case matters became violent, but for the moment the little man seemed content to bluster. "Standing in the company of any number of women is no crime, you know!" he insisted, which prompted Lestrade to respond, with a sly smile on his rat-like face.

"Right again, sir. You do know your law, I see. Obviously I would have no call to come to your door in pursuit of yourself. But how would it be if I were to visit your good lady wife, not looking for you, but for a common prostitute with whom, I have reason to believe, you are very good friends?"

Chilton-Smith glared at the inspector for an uncomfortably long time, then he shrugged in defeat and turned back to Holmes.

"Definitely no interview, then?" he smiled, and I had the sudden sense that he was a resilient sort, quick to recover from any setback. He probably had to be, in his line of work. Evidently, he had realised that he had no leverage in the current situation, and decided to make the best of it.

"In that case, here's exactly what I saw that night. I cannot be certain beyond doubt, but I am almost sure that the man I saw walk along Linhope Street in the company of a young girl was the same gentleman whom I later saw in a locked room at number sixteen in the same street. That gentleman is Dr. John Watson, who now stands before me.

"I first saw Dr. Watson around five minutes before a police

constable entered the street. Now, does that satisfy you?"

"Not quite," said Holmes. "I have a few more questions. Did you see the girl leave either house or street?"

"No," admitted the newspaperman, "but until the constable ran into the house, I wasn't paying much attention. The street is open at both ends, too. She could have walked straight out, and I would never have noticed."

"You did not see a white cloth at one of the house windows?"

"A white cloth? No, nothing of that sort."

"And no other men entered or left the house or street, excepting Watson, the police constable and your companions and yourself, so far as you are aware?"

"Well, I can't be certain, as I said, but I don't believe so. Is that enough to satisfy you?"

Holmes nodded. "It is a beginning, certainly. But I have one further task for you, which will pay your debt off completely. Write a piece for your newspaper, following up the first, in which you state that evidence – *strong* evidence – has been uncovered which will lead to the exoneration of Watson."

Chilton-Smith recoiled as though struck. "That is a disgraceful suggestion!" he exclaimed. "The press in this country has a duty–"

Lestrade cut him off before he could launch into another speech. "Howie, you go on ahead to the Yard, and ascertain the home address of Mr. Chilton-Smith. It looks as if we may have need of it after all."

The implication could hardly be missed. Chilton-Smith blanched and stammered a protest, then thought better of it and subsided into unwilling agreement. "Very well," he muttered, "but I warn you that my editor is unlikely to print any such article."

"That is your affair," Holmes replied coldly. "But if I were you, I would do all I could to persuade him that publication is in everyone's interests. Now," he said more warmly, turning his back on the newspaperman, "I think we are finished here. A bath and a pipe are the order of the day, Watson, wouldn't you say?"

I nodded, well pleased with the progress we had made. We bade the policemen good night, and made our way back to the street, in search of a hansom cab.

Chapter Sixteen

True to his word, Chilton-Smith's article appeared in the evening edition of the following day's newspaper. As Holmes had requested, it alluded to new evidence uncovered by the police which, it stated, would undoubtedly soon lead to my full exoneration and a thoroughgoing apology from the authorities. I read it with the curious mix of pleasure and embarrassment that comes from seeing one's name in print, though leavened with a degree of caution, for I could not for the life of me see what Holmes actually hoped to achieve by it.

I said as much, but Holmes had an answer.

"Someone went to great pains to place your neck in the noose, Watson, and until now they have gone without serious challenge. This little article will, I hope, force their hands and bring them out into the open. Whoever they might be."

It was a sensible plan, though not one designed to provoke an immediate response. I folded the newspaper and laid it to one side, then prodded the fire into greater activity, for it was a cold morning, the coldest of the year so far.

"What of Alistair McLachlan, Holmes? Have your street Arabs turned up anything useful concerning his activities?" I enquired, remembering Holmes's mention of "the other matter".

"Alistair McLachlan?" he replied with a puzzled look. "Wiggins and his motley crew have not been checking on McLachlan, Watson. I did, however, make enquiries of my own while I was out yesterday afternoon. Mr. McLachlan was at home on the night of the murder, according to a footman who was happy to share his memories in exchange for a half crown. Of course, that does not of itself prove his innocence, and I have sent a telegram to Potter, requesting that he should be investigated thoroughly.

"I have other news, however. I met a messenger from Lestrade as I returned with the newspaper, and he passed on the information that a kukri knife has indeed been found to be missing from Major McLachlan's collection. An old and damaged specimen, kept in a drawer, apparently, and so not missed until now. It has been identified as the same weapon that killed Miss McLachlan."

"Taken from a house I had never visited before now!"

"True, but we cannot prove it. At the moment, we are not in a position to provide certain proof of your innocence. But each new doubt that we cast, each new fact that we uncover; these are bricks in the wall we are constructing between you and the gallows."

"Will it be enough, though, Holmes?"

"By itself, no. But this single brick does not stand alone. We have an alternative suspect – Alistair McLachlan – with motive for the killing, if not for the attempt to place you on the gallows. We have the sworn testimony of Chilton-Smith that you arrived in tandem with a girl, at a time that makes it all but impossible for you to have carried out the murder in the manner we know it was performed.

We have your own lack of motive. And we have the fact that we know you to be innocent."

I appreciated the closing sentiment, but I could not help but wonder if Holmes's wall would prove sturdy enough.

Perhaps as a result of these continuing doubts, a desire for fresh air and activity stole over me. By late morning, the weak, wintry sun had given way to a cloudy but dry sky, which served to take some of the chill from the air, and removed any excuse I had for staying indoors. As I pulled on my jacket and wrapped a long scarf round my neck, I asked Holmes if he wished to join me in a walk, but he demurred and returned his attention to the slim volume on his lap.

I had only walked as far as the crossroads with Marylebone Road, wondering if it was too early for lunch, when a voice hailed me from a passing growler. Inspector Potter leaned out of the cab window and beckoned me across as the horse pulled into the side of the road.

"Dr. Watson! The very man I hoped to find at home. Would you have any objection to returning to 221B with me? There has been a new development in your case, and I would prefer to discuss it somewhere other than a public street."

Initially I thought to refuse on principle, but something in Potter's voice, a certain tone of triumph, inclined me to accede to his request lest he decide to make it a command.

"Very well," I said. "Holmes is at home and Mrs. Hudson will show you up. I shall be there shortly behind you."

I watched the carriage make the short journey along Baker Street and slowly made my own way back, taking the few minutes required to marshal my thoughts and consider what news the inspector might bring. It seemed implausible that the newspaper article had already borne fruit, but other than that the only fresh evidence I could bring to mind concerned the damaged kukri. Had the identification of the murder weapon proven key? Surely, Potter's news concerned one or other.

I climbed the stairs to our rooms with an optimistic tread, therefore, and was in consequence unpleasantly surprised to find Holmes standing before the fire, scowling down at a sheet of paper he held in his hand. Inspector Potter, accompanied by a constable I did not recognise, stood with his back to me, but as I entered he turned quickly and gestured to the constable to stand by the door.

"Dr. John Watson," he announced solemnly, "it is my duty to inform you that, in light of new evidence which was delivered to Scotland Yard not half an hour since, it is my duty to take you into custody and return you to Holloway Prison. There you will await trial for the murder of Miss Sarah McLachlan."

My stomach twisted inside me as he nodded to the waiting constable, who immediately took up a position directly behind me. The suddenness, the unexpected nausea, and the confusion I felt caused me to recall the moment I had been wounded in the army, so severe was the shock.

"What on earth are you talking about, Potter?" I managed to say from a mouth now bone dry.

Holmes answered my question. He held out the paper in his hand and I seized it from him, quickly reading the few lines that comprised the entirety of its message.

In words created by the artifice of cutting individual letters from a magazine or newspaper, the message was short and to the point.

EVERY MAN HAS HIS PRICE. iF YOu DON'T WANT

oFFed AS oUr man wAtson dId THe oLd lAdy, yOu bEst bAck oFf at oNce.

Clipped to this extraordinary missive was another, smaller piece of paper, obviously but a single part of a greater whole, for one edge was ragged and torn. It appeared to be part of a letter, missing its top half, but what remained was damning in the extreme.

It was an IOU for two hundred pounds, made out to persons unknown, but clearly signed at the bottom "John H. Watson".

"I have never seen this letter before! That is not my signature!" I insisted, and I fear I may have shouted, for Holmes laid a hand on my arm and assured me that he had already told Potter the same thing.

"He has, Doctor," Potter confirmed calmly, "but I have here a copy of your signature, provided by Inspector Lestrade, and I must say that the two seem almost identical to me."

He pulled a scrap of paper from his jacket pocket and handed it to me. There seemed no point in examining it – I knew what my signature looked like and had already realised that the forged version on the IOU was similar to my own – and I let it drop to the floor, unread. My head spun and I braced myself against the back of my chair, hoping that Potter did not notice my weakness.

"Almost identical?" Holmes put in scornfully. "I fear that in your haste to convict my friend, Inspector, you have allowed yourself to be convinced too easily that it is the genuine article."

He took the IOU from my frozen hands, and spread it out on the table before him. "See here, the bar on the capital 'H' is slanted to the left, whereas Watson's–" he stooped and retrieved the scrap of paper from the floor "–is completely horizontal. The small 'n' is also entirely different in construction, as is the manner in which the two 'o's are joined to the letters which follow them."

"Minor variations, Mr. Holmes," Potter retorted, though without rancour. "Such as might be expected from a man finding himself facing financial ruin."

"Preposterous!" Holmes began, but Potter was not finished.

"Regardless of the verisimilitude of the signature, the IOU is hardly the more troubling of the two documents, is it? Have you anything to say regarding the letter, Doctor? I should tell you that it was delivered to Major McLachlan less than an hour ago. The butler, Murray, found it in an envelope pinned to the major's front door and, at his instigation, at once carried it to me at the Yard. As you can see, it is unequivocal in naming you as the killer of Miss McLachlan."

The initial shock had begun to wear off and I had recovered enough of my voice to reply, though I knew that whatever I said would be discounted by Potter. Still, I had no intention of returning to confinement without at least stating the truth.

"I have nothing to say except that it is a mystery to me, both in its content and its appearance at Major McLachlan's home. I have never been indebted to any man for a sum as large as two hundred pounds – indeed, I cannot conceive of a way in which I could possibly owe so monstrous a sum – nor was I involved in the murder of Miss McLachlan."

"Never for so large a sum?" Potter interrupted. "But you have other debts?"

"No more than any man in business," I answered uncomfortably. "My practice has been less busy than I could wish, and I have been forced to borrow a little now and again. But always from my bank!" I concluded, and for the first time since the nightmare had begun I felt genuine rage swell inside me.

I realised I had allowed myself to become numb as a protection from the unbelievable events which had overtaken me. I had seen similar behaviour in Afghanistan; soldiers who had experienced too much bloodshed, who found themselves in a world they could never have imagined, retreated within themselves, turned cold and distant, capable of little, if any, human emotion. But in that moment my mind cleared of the peculiar fog which had shrouded it and I recognised that I had allowed myself to be quiescent for too long; that the official sanction of arrest and imprisonment had, at some level, caused me to accept whatever happened as my due, as a just punishment for an offence I must, somehow, have committed. But I had not, and it was not.

In a sudden fury, I barked questions at Potter. Why, if I had killed McLachlan to settle a debt, did my creditor still have my IOU? How could I possibly have run up a debt so large? Why would my unknown controller send a threat that named me, and thus condemned me, when it was at the same time insinuated that I had carried out my side of some hellish bargain? In such a situation, what guarantee did he have that I would not now save myself by giving his name to the police?

"Are you ready to do so now, Doctor?"

Potter's calm voice seemed to come from nowhere. Dimly, I became aware that I was standing a mere foot away from the inspector, so that our faces were uncomfortably close, and I could see my spittle on his face. Only with an effort of will did I manage to bite off my next question, as I belatedly realised the impression I was making.

"No, Inspector, I am not," I said in a more normal tone. "For the simple reason that there is nothing to tell. I did not kill Sarah McLachlan, nor am I in the thrall of some mysterious killer to whom I owe a small fortune."

I straightened my waistcoat and ran a hand through my hair, then resettled the scarf, which I had not yet removed, more snugly round my neck.

"Now, if you would be so kind as to lead the way, I believe you mentioned a return to Holloway."

I turned to Holmes, who had stood in silent contemplation throughout.

"I am relying on you, Holmes. I know you will not fail me."

He held my gaze for a moment, then nodded once, sharply.

Nothing more need be said. I gestured towards the door.

"After you, gentlemen," I said and pulled it open.

Chapter Seventeen

The sound of the cell door closing behind me once again filled me with something approaching despair. It was far harder to begin a second spell inside prison walls. I felt as though I had been given an opportunity, a chance to forge the path to my own freedom, but that I had lost that the moment Potter arrived with news of the letter to McLachlan. Worst of all, I had no idea how it could have happened. Someone was determined that I should hang, it seemed, and though Holmes had turned all his great powers towards a solution, and Lestrade was busy tracking down every ne'er-do-well whose path we had crossed, as I sat on my grey bed in that grey cell and stared at the tiny window and the scrap of cloud-covered sky beyond, I believed that their efforts were in vain, and that I would soon enough face a humiliating trial and an ignominious death. I curled up on the bed like a small child, and lay there, my mind empty of thought, until I drifted off into an uneasy sleep.

Hardie had not been in the cell when I was brought in, but it was he who shook me awake sometime later. It was not yet dark outside, but I could hear the noise of keys jangling further along the corridor and knew that the lights would soon be doused for the night. Even so, my spirits were lifted by the sight of the youngster, who greeted me as casually as if I had only been away on a short holiday, from which he had always expected me to return.

"I knew you'd be back," he grinned, confirming my suspicions. He dropped down onto his own bed and, propping himself up on one arm, reached beneath it for his bottle. It was only a quarter full, but he shared it readily enough and, as the lamps were switched off and we were plunged into the half-light of evening, I described my brief period of liberty.

"You were out and you didn't make a run for it," he said with mock scorn. "You must be addled in the brain, John, really you must. You should have been off as soon as your pal the inspector turned his back. A man like you can always make a bit o' money, writing and doctoring and what have you, and if you were somewhere a bit uncivilised – Africa, maybe, or Scotland – you could live like a king for pennies. Least that's what they used to tell us."

He shook his head and took a long pull at the bottle. "I'd have been gone so quick, I'd have left my shadow behind on the ground."

I smiled at the idea of myself on the run in deepest Africa and accepted the bottle that Hardie now passed across.

"So what now then?" he asked eagerly. "I nosed about a bit while you were away, but everyone's tight as a drum and nobody'll say a word about Collins or why he's got it in for you."

I considered how much to tell him, and decided that the less he knew the better. "I doubt Collins's attack was anything more than opportunism. I've never crossed his path that I know of, but perhaps he was working for someone else. There is no shortage of people who wish me harm, when all's said and done." I passed the bottle back to Hardie, along with a gentle warning. "Stay away from Collins, Albert. Don't forget that his men put you in the hospital too."

I heard Hardie snort derisively in the rapidly encroaching dark, and twisted round on my bed so that I could reach out and tap his arm. "Don't underestimate these people, Albert. Collins would have killed you without a second thought after he'd done with me, and don't ever think otherwise."

"What about Galloway, then? He's been asking about you, wanting to know if I'd heard from you."

This was worrying news. "What did you tell him?"

"Nothing. Wasn't nothing to tell. I'd no more idea than he had what you were up to."

I heard a justified note of recrimination in the boy's voice. I had not given Albert Hardie a second thought in the days of my freedom. Still, I could minimise any further risk to his safety.

"Stay away from Galloway too," I ordered. "He's a dangerous man."

"I don't need you to tell me that, John!" Hardie's voice was scathing. "Fine turn up that'd be, you telling me how to stay safe inside!"

"I'm serious, Albert," I insisted. "Stay away from him."

Grudgingly, he acquiesced to my wishes. I feared he might take our disagreement to heart, but fortunately the alcohol had set a warmth aglow in my stomach, and the effect was obviously the same for Hardie, who soon shrugged off any irritation he might have felt. I heard the bottle clink softly on the floor as he placed it back beneath his bed, but I was already half asleep and it was all

I could do to return my young friend's goodnight before I fell into a deep slumber.

The next morning was another of the cold, dry days that dominated that winter. A banging upon the cell door woke us at the usual early hour and the day proceeded along familiar lines. I had resolved to keep to my cell as much as possible, and with the exception of chapel and one unexpected interview, I did so.

The first notice I had that I was required was a hand on my shoulder as I shuffled along the chapel pews before the day's services began. Shapley breathed in my ear, ordering me to follow him, which I did eagerly. Perhaps Holmes had already demonstrated the IOU letter to be a forgery, or the journalist Chilton-Smith had recalled something of importance?

The man who sat in the room to which I was shown was a stranger, however, though one I felt I knew from somewhere. It was impossible to gauge his height accurately but he was not a short man, though he was slim of build. A sparse growth of fine, fair hair was carefully stretched across his scalp and held in place by a noticeable quantity of hair pomade. A slackness about his mouth caused it to hang slightly open so that I could hear him breathing before he spoke.

"Please take a seat, Doctor," he said, in a soft, sibilant voice which seemed well suited to his appearance. "Cigarette?" he asked, pushing a silver case towards me. I glanced at Shapley, but he gave no indication of having seen or heard anything, and so I lit one and inhaled deeply, examining my host while he did the same to me.

I smoked the entire cigarette in silence, waiting for the man to speak further, but he was evidently content simply to observe and so, after discarding it, I was forced to take the initiative.

"You have the advantage of me, Mister...?"

"McLachlan," he smiled, though not warmly. "Alistair McLachlan. I believe you know my family?"

He posed this as a question, but it was plainly an accusation. This then was the younger brother of Sir Campbell, the nephew of the woman I was accused of killing. The man who we suspected, even hoped, might be the actual killer.

Now that I knew, I could not mistake the familial connection. The shape of his nose was nearly identical and his chin but a weaker version of the one I had seen on the major. In temperament, however, he was clearly altogether different.

He fitted a fresh cigarette into a jet-black holder and eyed me through the smoke.

"You are not as I expected, Doctor," he said with a hint of amusement.

"Really," I replied carefully. "What did you expect?"

He laughed, and it seemed out of place, almost joyful. "Oh, a monster, of course. A slavering beast, with my aunt's blood still fresh on his terrible hairy hands." He sighed. "Isn't that the popular image?"

"And you do not perceive that in me? I am relieved."

More than relieved in fact, for as much as he saw no monster in me, I saw none in him. Even on so short an acquaintance, I could not imagine this languid character committing the atrocity I had seen in Linhope Street.

"I was fond of my aunt, but not overly so," McLachlan replied, disregarding my question. "She kept me short of money, which is not an action designed to promote affection in any breast, and so forced me to endure the company of my pompous, puritan older brother. But she was a decent enough sort in her own way. Her servants were devoted to her, which says something, I always think." He laughed again. "Unlike my dear brother! With the exception of that odd little chap he brought back from the wars, he's universally despised below stairs, you know. Hardly surprising. He treats the servants like natives from his campaigns, and dismisses them without a reference for the slightest infraction. He'd do the same to me, if he could, I shouldn't wonder."

I stared at him, sitting smirking before me, but said nothing, which obviously suited him, for he was clearly a man who liked to talk.

"And that dreadful hypocrite wonders that I fell for one of the maids? A common enemy can bring the most disparate personalities together, you know, Doctor. Grievance makes far stronger glue than favour, I find. But that creature Murray discovered our love, and out Mary went. Mustn't risk a blemish on the family name! Can't have a McLachlan taking up with one of the staff!"

For the first time his voice betrayed an emotion beyond minor amusement. He lit yet another cigarette while he spoke, but did not offer me one.

"But I digress shamefully. I did not wish my aunt dead, except in the normal way of things, when her withered old heart at last dried up completely. And I cannot deny that I owe her a debt. She has been far more generous to me in death than she was in life; her bequest has allowed me to rid myself of Campbell's oppressive superiority once and for all. So I have come to see the man accused of her murder expecting, as I said, a being less a man and more a beast. And what do I find but you! A commonplace soul in a commonplace frame, a man such as I might pass in the street any day of the week."

He pushed back his chair and walked around the table to stand behind me. I could hear his heavy breathing and smell his no doubt expensive cologne, but I did not turn to look up at him. His soft voice whispered above me.

"Do you know who killed my aunt, Dr. Watson?"

I found I had been holding my breath, and now let it out in a small gasp. "No," I said firmly. "Your aunt was already dead when I was lured into that infernal room. If she had not been, please believe me, I would have done all I could to save her."

It was the truth and it seemed to satisfy him. He returned to his seat and gathered up his cigarette case and matches. "I am a weak man, Doctor. Or perhaps I am a brave man who simply chooses to express his bravery in unconventional ways." He giggled and smoothed his hair with the palm of his hand. "But whatever I am, I am no idiot. For what it is worth, I am certain that you are an innocent man, to the extent that any of us can be."

He stood up again, and brushed invisible lint from his immaculate suit. "I leave for Paris in the morning, but I will send my card to your Mr. Holmes, with the address of my hotel written upon it. Should there be any way in which I can assist you, you may contact me there. For now, however, I shall bid you goodbye."

He held out a pale hand and I shook it, without standing. Our eyes met and then he let my hand fall and stalked from the room, so quickly that Shapley barely had time to open the door for him. In the vacuum created by his sudden absence, Shapley and I stared at one another, then he made an indistinct sound and jerked his head towards the door.

"Up you get then, Watson. The governor might bend over backwards for them McLachlans, but I've got work to do."

All the way back to my cell, I pondered Alistair McLachlan's behaviour. The more I did so, the less could I convince myself that he had slain his aunt.

Hardie was not in our cell when Shapley returned me there, but as services had not finished yet that was not unexpected. With nobody to distract me, I soon found myself dozing fitfully.

For the second time in twenty-four hours, Hardie shook me awake, excitement written across his face.

"I reckon Galloway's up to something, something big," he began without preamble.

My head was muddled by sleep, and I struggled to make sense of his words as he continued to speak.

"...followed one of his men to a room at the top of the building. I couldn't get any closer – there's a staircase that leads up to it, and someone's stood on guard there and warned me to clear out when he saw me – so I had to come back. But Galloway's definitely planning something."

"You were spying on Galloway? And one of his men saw you?" Anger flared inside me that the boy had so wilfully disobeyed my wishes, but I suppressed it for the moment. It was far more important for me to ensure that he had not been placed in danger, and that there would be no repeat. "Tell me exactly what transpired, Albert! Beginning with how you came to be in a position to spy on Galloway at all. How did you avoid services?"

Hardie grinned, not at all abashed. "It's easy done, John. You just wait until you've been counted in by one guard, then tell another you've been ordered to carry out some errand or other. Simple, see?"

"Very clever," I admitted, "but what possessed you to do

such a thing, when you agreed only last night to keep clear of Matthew Galloway?"

"And so I did!" This protest was accompanied by a wide smile, designed to take the sting from his admission. "I followed one of his men, not him, didn't I? Thing is, I saw a group of them speaking to Shapley and they passed him something, then they cut out of line and nipped up the stairs in the opposite way to their cells. I couldn't let that pass, could I?"

"You both could and should have," I insisted, but my desire for the information Hardie had gathered outweighed the need to chastise him for his foolish behaviour. "But laying that to one side for now, what did you discover?"

The boy shrugged, disappointment clear on his face. "Like I was saying, not much, but enough to know Galloway's up to no good. Him and his boys were holed up in a room up in the gods, with one left at the top of the stair as lookout. It was him that saw me and sent me on my way."

"Did he know you were spying on Galloway?" I asked.

"Never," Hardie responded with obvious pleasure. "I said I was exploring. He said he'd slit my throat if he saw me skulking round again. As if that great lump could ever catch me! I'm annoyed I didn't get a chance to listen at the door, though. There must have been a dozen men in there."

It was interesting news; there was no denying that. I had noticed that prison regulations were enforced less strictly than I would have expected, especially for the likes of Galloway, but even so, to be allowed to congregate in such large numbers indicated that more than an occasional blind eye was being turned in his direction. But Hardie had placed himself in enough danger, and it was time to reinforce my warning of the night before.

"Thank you, Albert," I said seriously. "This is very useful information, and it may be that Holmes is able to make use of it. But I need you to promise me that you will let the matter drop now."

Hardie's face fell, and he gave a half shrug, as though the matter were of complete indifference to him. My reaction had disappointed him, though, and his childlike attempts to hide that fact only reminded me of how young he was.

"You understand that I am grateful for your help, Albert," I continued in a conciliatory tone, "but I should never forgive myself if something were to happen to you on my account."

That was better. Hardie smiled and nodded and threw himself down on his own bunk. "If you say so, John. I'll not go within ten foot of him. But what about Ikey Collins?"

I shook my head firmly. "As I also said last night, I imagine that Mr. Collins was paid by someone else to attack me. I shall be on my guard now, but I doubt that he will attack me again, especially with Galloway's protection over me."

I could not help but laugh at the thought that the man I was investigating was also my protector. Hardie too was struck by the absurdity, and joined in the laughter. Even as I laughed, however, I could not rid myself of the thought that there was a finite amount of time to prove my innocence, and so far, Holmes and I had made little progress in doing so.

Chapter Eighteen

A date in late December was set for my trial, and with no indication of a significant breakthrough in my case, I arranged for my solicitor to visit to talk over my defence.

Osmont Marcum was a tall, saturnine Scot, who spoke little but listened intently as I described again the events that had led to my arrest and current incarceration. He sat opposite me with, open on his knee, a battered workbook in which he took copious notes in a small, tidy hand. In the main he contented himself with nods of encouragement as I spoke, but now and again he would ask for clarification of some point, transcribing my answers verbatim into his notes.

As I finished my narrative with a description of Potter's visit to Baker Street, he laid down his pencil, and looked across at me with a sombre look on his face.

"Well, Dr. Watson," he murmured in his soft Highland brogue, "that is quite a story." He flicked through the pages of his workbook, nodding to himself as he did so. "Yes, quite a story, but one which might be bent to our will, with the correct manipulation."

He stressed each syllable of the final word distinctly, as though creating time to decide what to say next.

"Naturally, we cannot directly suggest that Inspector Potter has been less than fair to you. No, that would not do at all. To accuse a policeman of fault plays no better to a London jury than it does to an Edinburgh one, you understand. But we can perhaps encourage a portion of those good men to come to such a conclusion unaided. The slant of your own statement, the evidence of the newspaper person, these are bound to cause any thoughtful man to pause, and wonder if the officer so often mentioned has been more idle than he should in his investigations.

"The name Sherlock Holmes will do us no harm, either. Your friend's name is known to the public, while the man himself is not, which – having spent an hour in his company yesterday morning – is certainly the best way round." He smiled thinly at his own jest. "Mr. Holmes is no doubt a great man, but his personality is somewhat... abrasive.

"In any case, Doctor, I would say that there are grounds for hope. I think I can make a decent fist of placing doubts in the jurors' minds, and that is the only requirement in law. A debauched younger brother, his eyes on the inheritance that will free him to continue his unspeakably vile practices – and in France, at that! – combined with the short time in which you could have killed the lady and your lack of a provable motive... if I cannot place the shadow of doubt in a man's mind with that as grist to my mill, well then, I should be ashamed to call myself a barrister."

It was exactly what I needed to hear, but at the same time I could not allow Marcum to proceed in the belief that Alistair McLachlan was a guilty man. I explained about our meeting, and my conviction that he was no more a killer than I was myself. The lawyer listened attentively while I recounted the conversation, then shook his head as a father might at a child.

"You are a fine, honest man, Doctor, and it speaks well to your character that you accept everyone else as the same, but if you will allow me to protect you from your own self, you should forget all that McLachlan said to you. Had I known that he wished to meet with you, I would have forbidden it, for the man is a proven reprobate and by his own mouth condemned as a rake who has ruined more than one young girl. Indeed, sir," he said, eyeing me critically, "I am surprised that you accepted his invitation to converse."

I was inclined to bridle at the idea that I was a hopeless naïf, but what would be the point? Marcum was right. It was his job to protect me even from myself, and I had nothing but my own intuition as evidence that McLachlan was innocent. I did, however, correct his assumption that my meeting with McLachlan had been voluntary.

"Do you say so, Doctor? You were marched to a meeting like a pig to slaughter? That is unusual enough to be worthy of comment. I shall take a note of that, I think."

This he did, then lapsed once more into contemplation of his workbook while I considered what he had said about my trial. Of course, I still had hopes that Holmes would somehow contrive to exonerate me before then, but I had not heard from my friend since passing back behind Holloway's walls, and besides, I was not so foolish as to assume a successful conclusion to the investigation as a certainty. There had been several cases in the past in which Holmes had been unsuccessful, though obviously I had never placed these before the eyes of my reading public.

In a moment of mawkish humour, I wondered if someone would write up my own downfall should this prove another of his rare failures. The Case of the Deadly Doctor, perhaps?

Marcum was regarding me quizzically, and I realised that I was smiling. "I'm sorry, Mr. Marcum," I apologised hurriedly. "You were saying...?"

"Merely that all is not as black as it may appear, Doctor," he repeated. "But it seems you have arrived at that conclusion already."

He rose and gave a small bow. "I shall take my leave of you now, and return in two days. By then I shall have a better idea of how best to present your case to the court."

I thanked him sincerely and watched him as he left, then followed the guard back along the now familiar corridors to my cell.

The following day was a special one in the prison. Detectives' Day was a regular occurrence in Holloway, if one I had until now managed to avoid. Several times a week, the police officers of London were invited into Holloway, where they were free to mix freely with the inmates, both to interrogate those suspected of a specific crime and, with luck, to spot among their number any man who, wanted for a more serious offence, found himself committed for a lesser one.

To the prisoners, Detectives' Day was a double-edged sword. For some, there was the risk of unwanted identification but for most it was an opportunity to mingle more freely, as restrictions on movement were relaxed, and exercise time unofficially extended.

Although it had apparently not always been the case, the current practice was to allow the prisoners to gather in the exercise yard, and for the visiting policemen to pass among the crowd, speaking to whomever they wished. Even with Galloway's dubious protection over me, I remained wary, and Hardie and I took up position at the edge of the yard, beneath two straggling, unhealthy trees. Like scientists watching competing protozoa swimming in a drop of water, we passed a half hour observing the detectives, visible in the mob only by the colour of their jackets, seek out their prey. Now and again, the winding progress of one would come to a sudden halt, a minute would pass, and then the colourful creature would move again, only now with a dully grey prisoner in tow.

I found the whole affair distracting, but Hardie soon grew bored, having witnessed the process many times before.

"I'm going to stretch my legs, John," he said as he rose to his feet, brushing dust from his trousers. "Will you be all right by yourself?"

"I think I should survive," I replied wryly. I mentally chided myself on my excessive caution as I watched him disappear into the crowd, which milled before me. I had been to war, had I not? The thought was a calming one. I resumed my observations, wishing I had my army revolver to hand.

The day was warmer than had been the case in recent weeks, and I actually felt myself struggle to stay awake. I had just decided that I had better take a turn around the yard before I fell asleep entirely, when an unwelcome voice interrupted my thoughts.

"I hope you're comfortable, Dr. Watson?"

Potter squatted beside me, a cigarette burning in his hand. He saw me glance at the forbidden luxury, and awkwardly reached inside his pocket to pull out a silver case.

"Take one," he offered. "Don't worry. The guards'll turn a blind eye to our little bit of rule breaking."

I shook my head and made to push myself to my feet, but Potter placed a hand on my shoulder and kept me seated.

"Don't rouse yourself for my benefit, Doctor," he smiled grimly. "I just stopped by to say hello and see how you were enjoying being back inside these walls."

I had always known that Potter disliked me and had, until that point, assumed it was because he was certain of my guilt. But at that moment, with his face close to mine and his hand upon me, I realised that there was more to it than that. More than anything, he seemed enormously tired, and even saddened by something.

"Are you sure you won't have a cigarette?" he offered again, and this time I took one, wondering at his manner. He pushed himself to his feet before awkwardly speaking again. "You know that there's no personal animus in any of this, Doctor? In my actions, I mean. I've got a job to do. I have my orders, same as the next man."

There was nothing to say to that, so I simply nodded and we smoked our cigarettes, then Potter shook himself and I thought he was going to say something else. Instead, he stared at me silently, before pressing several cigarettes into my hand. Then he turned on his heel and marched away without saying another word.

Shortly afterwards, the guards began to move we prisoners back to our cells, and Detectives' Day was over.

I mulled over Potter's strange behaviour as I walked in a group back to my cell, but could make no sense of it. As we climbed the stairs, the guard in charge held up a hand and we stumbled to a halt. Something was happening ahead, but from where we stood it was impossible to see which floor was involved. I pushed myself up on my toes but managed only to gain a decent view of another group of prisoners coming towards us from below, where my own cell lay.

Among the group was the unmistakable figure of Matthew

Galloway. He caught my eye and grimaced, then very slowly and precisely shook his head. It seemed the day was to be filled with people acting strangely.

As suddenly as we had stopped, we started moving again. We reached the entrance to my cell before any of the others, and so, following custom, I entered and waited for the other prisoners to be housed, at which point the guard would walk back along the corridor, locking each door as he passed. I glanced across at Hardie, lying on his bed – and rocked backwards, acid bile rising in my throat.

Albert Hardie lay face down on his bed, but it was clear how he had been killed. An arc of arterial blood across the back wall demonstrated that he had been standing when his attacker came up behind him and cut his throat. He must have stumbled forward and pitched onto the bed, causing the remainder of the blood which exited his open throat to pool beneath him. Experienced surgeon though I am, I felt my stomach heave as I pulled Hardie over by one arm, and propped his body up against the wall. The thick, ripping sound of his body pulling away from the congealed blood, combined with the sweetish smell, caused me to retch dryly.

I steeled myself, and bent over the corpse. Hardie's throat had been deeply cut, the incision extending from a point immediately below his left ear to another an inch in from his right. More chilling, however, was the cut made on his left cheek; a single bloody letter carved into the boy's flesh. Ragged and uneven it certainly was, but there was no mistaking the capital letter G.

Chapter Nineteen

For the next few minutes I believe I took leave of my senses. How else to explain the fact that at one moment I stood over the bloody corpse of poor Hardie and the next I had my hand on the shoulder of Matty Galloway in the corridor outside his cell?

All I knew for certain is that I had been running, for sweat trickled down my face as I pulled the gang leader round to face me. Behind me I could hear shouted orders and angry exclamations. One of Galloway's constant companions, quicker than the others, stepped forward with a growl and covered my hand with his, but his leader waved him off and took a step backwards, freeing himself from my grip.

"Dr. Watson," he said. "What can I do for you?"

Perhaps it was the mocking tone, or it may have been the half-smile that played about his mouth, but for whatever reason Galloway's question was enough to drive all caution from my mind. With no thought for the consequences – indeed, with no thought at all – I pushed myself forward and swung a fist at Galloway's face.

Had I considered the matter I would have realised the futility of such an attack. Men like Galloway do not survive long if they are unable to defend themselves. With something like contempt he moved his head back, allowing my wild blow to connect with nothing but air, then lashed out precisely, striking me in the solar plexus before connecting with my chin as I doubled over. Briefly my vision blurred as I gasped for breath, then I tumbled backwards, to land heavily on the tiled floor. By the time I had recovered sufficiently to rise to my knees, Galloway and his followers had vanished into their cells and I was alone, panting in frustration and impotent fury.

Unfortunately I did not remain so for long. No sooner had I pushed myself to my feet than Shapley appeared at the end of the corridor.

"What's this, Watson?" he snarled, making no effort to disguise his pleasure at seeing me brought so low. "Fighting again, is it? Don't bother to deny it either. I saw the whole thing. An unprovoked assault on another prisoner. No doubt about it." He smiled and moved to grab my arm.

"Unprovoked!" The injustice of the claim was more painful than any physical wound I had suffered. I batted his hand away and brought my face close to his. "Bert Hardie lies dead in my cell at this very moment and his killer walks away scot free, and you have the temerity—"

I should have expected that Shapley would not be alone. As I drew breath to continue my tirade I sensed a movement behind me, and half turned. I had a mere instant to register a figure stepping from a dark cell, and a truncheon swinging towards me, then I found myself deposited on the ground for the second time in as many minutes. This time, I had no energy or inclination to rise. I lay supine on the hard earth as Shapley leant over me and hissed, "Assaulting a prisoner *and* a guard, and now you tell me there's an intimate of yours dead in your cell! The governor won't look kindly on that, no matter what high and mighty pals you might have." He gestured to the man who had knocked me down. "Take him straight to the governor."

It took my befuddled mind a moment to take in the full horror of what he had said. Surely nobody could suggest I had killed Hardie? And yet, with my head still ringing and the sharp taste of blood in my mouth, I realised that was exactly what Shapley was suggesting.

When I arrived at his office, Keegan sat in his chair, engaged in muffled conversation with another of the guards, who bent low to make himself heard. Otherwise, the room was empty. Keegan glanced up at me quickly, then waved away the guard, who took up a position against the right-hand wall.

"Watson," the governor grunted finally. "I have this moment had it confirmed to me that the prisoner Albert Hardie lies dead in your cell. Clearly, he has been murdered." He glared at me across the desk. "Surely you can shed some light on Hardie's demise, Watson?" he asked, leaving little doubt that he expected me to do so.

"Matthew Galloway is the man you want!" I exclaimed with some heat. "His men warned the boy off, but clearly that was insufficient. Whoever actually wielded the knife, Galloway's is the hand behind it."

"Warned off?" Keegan's eyes lit up. "And why would Galloway need to warn the boy off? What had he been doing?"

There was no reason to prevaricate. "Hardie wished to help me and believed that he could best do so by observing Galloway and his confederates."

"He did this at your behest, I presume?"

"No, never," I protested. "In fact, I did all I could to dissuade him, but he is – was – an obstinate youngster, and would not be told." I recalled Hardie's earlier boredom, and in my mind's eye saw him walk away into the crowd of prisoners. It seemed certain that he had found the excitement he desired in spying once more on Galloway, and had paid the ultimate price for doing so.

"He would not be told," I repeated, "and Galloway killed him for it. He slit his throat, just as he said he would."

I heard Shapley enter the room behind me, but ignored him as best I could, preferring to focus on the governor, whose eyes I held unwaveringly. I was determined that he must be made to act against Galloway.

"In your cell?" he queried doubtfully. "And how did he manage to reach your cell unobserved, then return to his own, again without being seen?"

"No doubt he paid a guard to turn a blind eye. It would not be the first time."

"Have you any proof of this allegation?" Keegan asked after a short delay. "Did any other prisoner hear Galloway threaten Hardie? Or see him bribe one of my guards?"

"No," I admitted reluctantly. The room was warm and stuffy, and I struggled to marshal my thoughts. "Nobody else, but that makes it no less true."

It sounded weak, even to me, and Keegan brushed the accusation aside with contempt. "You sent this young boy in your stead, you claim, to spy upon a well-known and violent criminal, and that same criminal then, predictably, threatened to kill him. Only, nobody but you had any knowledge of either the spying or the threats? Have I summarised correctly?"

My head spun as I considered how best to respond. In my

place Holmes would have torn Keegan's apparent logic apart by noting some tiny detail that I had missed. Holmes would have spotted something–

But I had nothing. My head still rang from the recent blows I had received, and I wondered if I had a concussion. In the end, I shook my head impotently. There was no justice to be found here, I realised. Perhaps I would have to take matters into my own hands.

"I thought not," Keegan crowed, and ran a hand across his chin reflectively. "The allegations you have made against Galloway are common enough in an establishment such as this, and could be ignored, if that were the entirety of your poor behaviour. However, you have taken it upon yourself to make baseless allegations of far greater severity against my guards, and that I cannot brook! Shapley!"

He snapped his fingers without looking away from me, and Shapley stepped smartly forward.

"I think prisoner Watson needs to be reminded that actions have consequences, Shapley. Perhaps, while further investigation of Hardie's death takes place, you would see to that reminder?"

I could hear the anticipation in Shapley's voice as he answered in the affirmative and yanked me backwards. I was still facing into Keegan's office as the door swung shut. At my last glimpse of the governor he was staring straight ahead, a satisfied smile on his face.

In company with the other guard, Shapley half dragged and half pushed me down unfamiliar corridors and out into the fresh air. We crossed a patch of waste ground and proceeded until the squat shape of the prison pump house came into view. I knew then where we were going, for in earlier years water had been pumped through the prison by means of convict labour employed on a fearsome set of treadmills. We walked along the wall of the pump house, then passed through a doorway into the building which lay behind it. With one final kick, Shapley propelled me through and onto the tiled floor beyond.

He followed quickly, grabbing the front of my shirt and pulling me to my feet. "I always had my doubts about you, *Doctor Watson*," he sneered, "even before you ended up inside. Used to hear about you, following that Sherlock Holmes round like a dog, telling everyone how brilliant he was. No better than a dago slave flattering his dago king, if you ask me.

"Turned out to be just like one of them murderous foreigners, as well. But you're too much of a coward to admit what you done, ain't you? Killing the boy, him who looked on you as a friend? That's unnatural, is that."

He raised a fist in genuine rage and I cursed my befuddled condition as I weakly covered my head, prepared for the blow. But it failed to land. Shapley visibly controlled himself and lowered his arm. "Suppose I can't blame you for trying to get me and the lads involved. You don't owe me nothing, and the likes of you'll turn on anyone to save your own neck. Old ladies and little lads. That's about your limit. But Matt Galloway's been good to you. You'd think common decency would have held you back there at least."

I wanted to ask him what he knew about Galloway, but the words would not form and instead I watched in silence as he moved to the wall and turned on a light.

The room thus illuminated was long but relatively narrow, with stalls for the picking of oakum set on both sides and behind them, on the left, numbered sets of treadmill slots.

The wheel itself was difficult to make out, as it was hidden behind a row of slatted openings, each about one and a half feet wide, through which only a small section could be seen. I had read enough about other treadmills to know how they were constructed. Essentially a paddle wheel such as one might find by a country mill, only with extra wide slats on which a man might stand, the treadmill moved by dint of prisoner exertion. The example before me comprised twenty-four stalls, arranged in two groups of twelve, separated by a brick-enclosed space into which Shapley retreated.

"Put him in number thirteen, May," he called. "Take the seat out first though."

The guard reached into the nearest stall and pulled out a short plank, which he laid to one side. "In you go then," he said, prodding me forward.

"Dangerous things, treadmills," Shapley said, emerging from the brick enclosure. "A man used to get caught between the slats regular in the old days. Lost a leg, if he was lucky. Course, we don't use it nowadays and it ain't connected to the pump no more. More enlightened times, the governor says, but still... There's levers in there," he pointed back to the enclosed space he had just left, "lets me set different levels of what they call resistance. Comes in handy when there's someone needs to be taught a lesson that don't leave bruises. Best get you started," he said with a grin. "An hour or two treading the wind will soon have you minding your manners round Matty Galloway."

It was a strange thing to say, I thought, as I gingerly placed a foot on the slat in front of me. I expected it to sink beneath me but instead it simply trembled without otherwise moving. I turned as well as I could in the confined space and – with a burst of angry bravado – asked Shapley if the blasted machine was on.

"Other foot, Watson," he snarled. "They're steps, not a platform for you to rest on."

I lifted my foot and placed it on the next step, which

immediately sank beneath me as I had originally expected. Within half a minute, the wheel was moving steadily beneath me.

As I took one step after another, pushing each slat away from me as it appeared beneath my feet, I recalled Hardie's body on his bed and the look on his dead face. I heard Shapley call out to increase the resistance, but I was filled with energy, driven by anger and hate, and fuelled by the great wrong which had been done to the boy – and to me.

I pressed on, caring nothing for the guards or the governor, seeing only each step as it appeared beneath my feet.

Sweat ran down my forehead and into my eyes. The muscles in my calves burned and my breath came in great gulps, but still I pushed on. Dimly, I heard Shapley shout "More!" to his unseen confederate, but it signified nothing to me. I redoubled my efforts as spots swam lazily across my eyeline. My chest constricted as my heart rate increased until the pounding resembled a staccato drumbeat against my chest wall. Redness flooded my vision as Shapley gave some fresh instruction that I could not decipher – and then blackness replaced it and I knew nothing more.

Chapter Twenty

I slept little that night in the new cell into which Shapley and May had thrown me. Instead I lay curled up in a ball, gritting my teeth every time I moved, as my bruises and strains came into contact with the thin mattress. Occasionally, I rose and attempted to stretch my aching muscles, pacing the few steps from window to door and back again, before slumping back onto the bed with a stifled groan.

My mind was far more active. Just as I had when caught up by Potter at Baker Street, at some point on my pointless ascent of the treadmill, as my muscles burned like fire and Shapley's mocking laughter echoed behind me, I had remembered that I had done *nothing* wrong.

I reconsidered every second since my arrest, and slowly constructed a chain of events in my head, which I then mentally examined, looking for a weakness, an inconsistency, which could help me. Try as I might, I could identify nothing, and so I switched my attention from my own plight to that of my murdered cellmate.

I had pledged to help him when he was alive but having failed in that – worse, having been the cause of his death – perhaps I could do something to avenge his killing.

As dawn broke sullenly through the small window above my head, I found myself wishing fervently that Holmes had completed whatever errand had kept him from the prison for the past days. It would be a great boost to my spirits to discuss matters with him.

I was still lying on the bed when I heard a key turn and the cell door swung open. A new guard, a big black-bearded brute of a man with heavy eyebrows and narrow squinting eyes, barked an order to get up. After barely a moment's pause, he growled, "When I tells you to get up, you gets up!" and strode inside.

It seemed that there was to be no respite from yesterday's torment but, in my newfound spirit of defiance, I resolved that I would no longer accept brutality as my due. I climbed to my feet and balled my fists, prepared for whatever was to come.

"Is that any way to greet an old friend?" asked the guard as he closed the door behind him. "One would think you were displeased to see me, Watson!"

Holmes's face crinkled in a familiar half-smile as he gripped my hand in greeting.

"News of your young friend's death reached me at Baker Street late yesterday. I recognised at once that the risk to yourself in this place had become too great to be ignored. Fortunately, I had already considered the need to infiltrate the prison, and so had much of the preparations already in place. A telegram to the right person, and a meeting last night with one or two others, and I was as you see me now – Harry Andrews, freshly appointed guard at Holloway Prison."

In spite of myself, I could not help but laugh at Holmes's

obvious pleasure in his own cleverness, but the action aggravated the pain in the strained muscles of my chest, forcing a wince from me and instantly focusing the whole of Holmes's attention on my physical condition.

"But I see that I have arrived later than I should have." His brows furrowed as his eyes darted restlessly up and down my frame. "It is illegal to put any prisoner not yet convicted into a treadmill, Watson! Tell me, who ordered this?"

It was a measure of my relief and delight in seeing him that I laughed again at this demonstration of his powers of observation and, still laughing, asked for an explanation.

"There is no time for this, Watson," he replied severely then, perhaps recognising my desire for the familiar, relented sufficiently to provide an answer. "But if it will satisfy you…

"You have been a soldier, and taken a wound in battle; you would not groan in that manner unless you had in the recent past been extremely ill served physically. The manner in which you stood as I entered indicates several pulled muscles in your chest and upper thigh, reminiscent of those suffered by men labouring overlong on a treadmill, while the clenching of your fists at the sight of a guard provides a likely source for your discomfort. Additionally, you have a slight scuffing of your trousers caused by your knees brushing constantly against an object directly in front of you as you walked. I can think of seven different potential causes of such marks, but in a prison environment, a treadmill is by far the most likely culprit. Now if you are content, perhaps you will answer my original question. Who ordered you placed in the treadmill, and why?"

Quickly, I recounted the events of the previous days, including my meeting with McLachlan, while Holmes – or Andrews, as I must think of him for the foreseeable future – listened intently, nodding now and again, and frowning as I came to my interview with Governor Keegan.

As soon as my narrative was complete, Holmes filled in the details of his own recent activities.

"I feared that our visit to Major McLachlan had proven far less productive than I had hoped, but it has borne some unexpected fruit. Your lawyer is correct, however. Though I am willing to admit that you are a sound judge of character, I have little faith in anyone's intuition unless there are solid facts to support it. Still, I have not been to Baker Street for several days, and should his card await me there, that is something in his favour, I grant you. Rest assured, I am not so cold a creature as to accept the death of one innocent man in order to save the life of another. You have my word that I shall give due weight to what you have said.

"To return to his elder brother, however. Since we were expelled from his home, Sir Campbell has made of your case a great crusade, describing you in private conversation in the Commons as a gutter-press wordsmith for hire, and making great play of your alleged links to the criminal gangs who wish to bring him low. I have managed to keep the case unreported in the popular press, but I am sorry to say that political opinion is turning against you, Watson. It was all I could do to have myself placed here; there will be no further aid from those from whom I have previously sought assistance."

"What of the girl who began this? Have you had any luck in finding her?"

He shook his head. "It is as though she has disappeared completely from the face of the earth, Watson. I have had my irregulars scouring the rookeries and slums to no avail, and the offer of a reward for her location has thus far turned up only the unconnected and the addled."

"So we are no nearer a solution?" I enquired glumly.

"I did not say that," Holmes chided me softly. "There are times when no evidence is evidence in itself. But in the absence of anything which I could take to Scotland Yard, I would prefer not to raise your hopes prematurely. But do not despair. There is yet time."

A noise outside caused him to fall instantly silent. He gripped my shoulder lightly in his hand and guided me to the door. "My apologies, Watson, but I must play the part to some extent," he whispered as he hooked it open with a foot and shoved me into the corridor just as Shapley came into view from the central area.

"There you are, Andrews," he declared loudly. "I see you've met one of our most famous inmates – and one of our more troublesome too. Make haste, Watson," he addressed himself to me, "and get into line. You should know the routine by now."

It was as though the events of yesterday had not happened. No reference was made to Hardie's death, nor to my own punishment. I shuffled into my place in the queue of prisoners and wondered if Holmes were correct. Was there yet time?

Chapter Twenty-One

❦

From then on, Holmes was at hand whenever I left my cell.

It should not be supposed, of course, that Collins (or whoever he worked for – the question remained unresolved) and Galloway were the only prisoners who wished me ill. On two other occasions over the next week, attempts were made to harm me.

On the first, a skinny, scar-faced inmate took the space beside mine in the chapel, as we sang the hymn, and tried to slide an improvised knife into my ribs. Fortunately, I had wondered at his insistence on taking that specific seat and was ready for him. As he bent down to pull the knife from the ankle to which it was strapped, I mimicked the motion and savagely twisted his wrist before he could react, causing him to drop the weapon, which I then kicked away. An instant later, "Andrews" had reached us and bustled my attacker away to the punishment cells.

The second occasion was more serious. I was walking slowly around the exercise area, acutely aware of Hardie's absence, when a group of prisoners swiftly cut between the marked paths and rushed towards me. After Collins's attack I was prepared for such an approach, however, and as soon as the first man came within range I lashed out, catching him square on the chin and sending him sprawling in the dirt. The second man I incapacitated with a swift kick, but by then several hands were upon me. Guards who only a second before had been within a dozen yards of me melted away into the crowd of men, and things would have gone badly had it not been for the sound of Andrews' whistle and his sudden presence, swinging his truncheon with calculated efficiency. Two of the gang joined their compatriots on the ground, while the remainder scattered in fright. As with the scarred man in the chapel, I recognised none of my attackers. It was clear, however, that I was a marked man, even with Galloway's supposed protection.

I mentioned the paradox of Galloway's ineffectual protection to Holmes the next morning when, as had become customary, he opened my cell and we had a few minutes to talk.

"If Galloway's protection is supposed to keep Isaac Collins from my throat, how is it that it has had no similar effect on these other prisoners?"

"That is a puzzle which I have yet to decipher, Watson. Clearly, however, you can expect little assistance from the warders. Shapley has already sounded me out in my guise of Mr. Andrews. Yesterday evening, we completed our day's work at the same time. Quite naturally, he extended to me an invitation to the local public house, by way of a welcome to my new position. Once there, over several pints of abominable ale, he enquired, none too subtly, if I would be interested in supplementing my wages. 'All it needs is a blind eye now and again,' were his exact words. I affected to take the matter as a test of my honesty and laughed it off, which satisfied him for now, but it is a fact that certain guards cannot be trusted to act in the interests of every prisoner in their care. You are, I fear, one of those unfortunate prisoners."

I recalled the disappearing guards in the exercise yard, and shuddered inwardly. The message of the treadmill could not be clearer. My life had been judged expendable, and I could expect protection from no one.

"As to Collins, he has no link to you and has never crossed our path professionally, so we may safely conclude that he acted on behalf of someone else. However, the code of the criminal has so stoppered his lips that he has said no word other than to claim the attack as his own. The same attitude has been taken by those whose assaults on you are more recent. There, at least, it appears that each man is currently within these walls as a result, however indirectly, of our efforts. You may not have recognised him, but your chapel assailant was one of the thugs employed by Kavanagh, the Manchester arsonist, and the group in the yard were all at one time in the service of the blackmailer Jonathan Hoad, now safely locked away in Dartmoor."

"So Galloway's protection is worthless? Good. I have been in far more dangerous situations than I find myself in now, and I have no desire to owe the killer of Albert Hardie any favours."

"Well said, Watson! That is the stout-hearted fellow I know."

"Could Collins's employer be the same person who murdered Hardie?" I asked. "Could he be Galloway, playing some double bluff, his every move designed to increase my torment?"

Holmes glanced across at the cell door, but as yet there was no sign of any other guard and so we had a moment more unobserved.

"I fear you are becoming obsessed with Galloway, Watson. Why would Galloway wish to harm you? Besides, whether he was involved in the attacks on you and Hardie is not of paramount importance at the moment, when we are so close to your trial and, as yet, have no new suspect to offer Potter in your stead. I shall not be here for the next two days – I have certain matters to attend to outside the prison – but I beg of you, keep to your cell as much as possible and if you cannot, stay in plain sight of a guard at all times. Shapley and those like him are not above bribery and even assault, but they will baulk at murder, if I am any judge."

He smiled reassuringly. "I shall return no later than the evening after next, with good news I hope. Now, don't make me drag you out of your pit!" he concluded in a louder voice, for the benefit of anyone outside. "Get yourself into that corridor and ready to move!"

I hurried to do so, but my mind had already returned to Galloway and his involvement in Hardie's death.

Chapter Twenty-Two

The next day was one of the few that year in which the weather turned truly fearsome. Winds fit to uproot trees swept across London, and rain crashed against every exposed surface like a scour. As a result, exercise was cancelled and we remained in our cells all day, emerging only for services, during which I made sure to sit at the end of a row, beside a guard. Strangely, though there was no sign of Galloway or several of his closest companions during services, they were present in the corridor outside when it came time for the guards to escort us back to our cells.

The next day continued blustery, if less violent. I had spent the night considering Galloway's absence from the chapel and remembered Hardie's method of obtaining time at large inside the prison buildings. Holmes would return that evening and I was keen to have something to show him that might implicate Galloway in the boy's murder. Consequently, I resolved to slip the attention of my guard before services began, if I saw Galloway do likewise.

Events proceeded exactly as I hoped. I hung back a little in the line to enter the chapel; then, as soon as I saw Galloway in conversation with Shapley, I pushed my way forward and reported that Mr. May had asked me to fetch his belt, which he had left in the central office. With hundreds of prisoners to watch over, and no way for me actually to leave the building, none of the guards were much concerned with any single inmate, and I was irritably waved on my way. I walked towards the central doors; then, as soon as I was out of sight, I doubled back and cautiously followed Galloway and a group of almost a dozen other men as they moved upwards in the direction of the attic spaces at the top of the building.

Just as Hardie had described, the top floor ended in an archway that led to a set of metal stairs; these doubled back on themselves as they rose an additional level, terminating in a landing and a large wooden door. Crouched out of sight at the final bend of the stairs, I could with difficulty make out a single figure acting as a lookout and, to his left as he faced outwards, a smaller door half hidden in the shadows. I had just turned my mind to the question of getting past the lookout when a shout from inside the room behind him caught his attention and he swivelled on his heel to ascertain what was required of him.

As soon as he had fully turned his back, I raced up the stairs and slipped through the door to the right.

Narrow but deep, the room behind had, I presumed, originally been intended as a storage space but now lay largely empty. A haphazardly stacked collection of broken wooden crates was the only contents I could see. It was dark inside, which suited my purposes perfectly, for there was a small hole in the plaster above the crates through which I hoped I might spy on activities in the next room. Carefully, I clambered up and pressed my eye against the opening.

Exactly what the other room's intended function had been, it was impossible to say. In one corner were stacked mould-coated boxes, from which the sleeves of dust-covered prison jackets spilled out in untidy heaps across the floor. Equipment of some sort, long iron bars and cogs and wheels of various sizes, took up the length of the far wall, the whole lit by the dull light of the grey sky outside, struggling through three grime-encrusted windows. That still left plenty of room for the handful of prisoners gathered around Galloway, who stood on an upturned box in its centre.

From my vantage point I had a reasonable view of the men's backs, though the sound of their chatter was muffled and indistinct. There was no mistaking Galloway's voice when he spoke, however.

"Settle down, the lot of you," he commanded, and there was instant silence. "Right then, you all know why we're here. Adams has been a thorn in the side of our little community as long as I can remember. He might be high and mighty now, and bought himself respectability, but you all know as well as I that he's as much as villain as ever he was. It was his doing that brought me here, for one, but that's not why he's got to be croaked. If that were all he'd done, I'd wait 'til I was out and do him in myself. But he's guilty of a lot more than that, as all of you can attest."

There was a murmur of enthusiastic assent, and I shifted a little, hoping to see some of the faces in the mob. The crate moved beneath me, and for a second I thought I would fall, but thankfully it righted itself under me and I was able to maintain my balance. I looked again through my peephole, and was glad to see nobody in the other room had paid any attention to the noise.

In the meantime, Galloway had allowed the sounds of agreement to die down naturally, then recommenced his harangue.

"We all know about the words he has with the police, and

just today I heard from a man I trust that he's at his old business again, in spite of the warnings he's had. I say it's time to put a stop to him permanently!"

This time the murmur swelled in volume until I feared that the noise would bring the warders swarming upon the meeting. If that were to happen, I might well be swept up alongside the other prisoners, which would require some nimble explaining.

I wondered if now might be the time to leave. I had the name of the next man to die, after all, but at the same time I could think of no one named Adams, either inside Holloway or beyond its walls. A name was simply not enough. There was more to be learned, and I would not be responsible for another death that I might have prevented. I returned my attention to Galloway.

While I had been distracted, Galloway had proved himself wiser than his noisy confederates. "Keep it down, lads," he ordered, though without rancour. "What we need is someone to do the deed. Someone with access to Adams. But it'll need subtlety, don't forget. This isn't a warning, nor a public demonstration. Fatal but deniable, that's always the best way. A blade from nowhere, or a cosh to the head, then step away and leave a body behind, nothing taken. Quick and clean. Businesslike. I've someone in mind, but first, has anyone got any objection?"

To my surprise, he stepped down from the box and stood to one side, leaving the elevated position to any who wished to speak. It seemed there was more to Galloway's gang than met the eye. Never before had I heard of a gang leader willing to be swayed once he had made a decision, yet here was Galloway apparently encouraging genuine debate rather than imposing his will by force.

A minute passed, with clumps of prisoners talking among themselves and Galloway walking among them, exchanging a quiet word or two with every one of them. His voice was too quiet for me to make out any of the actual words. A shopkeeper he had called himself, but I was reminded of a politician on the campaign trail, passing among his constituents with words of comfort and reassurance. It was a most peculiar sight.

Finally, one prisoner, a hulking brute of a man with only one ear, the other a ragged stump, stepped forward and climbed onto the box. At once, the room fell quiet. Galloway, I noticed, gave the speaker his full attention.

"That's all well and good, Matty, but I bin thinkin' on it, and seems to me that what we needs is a bigger warnin', not a littler one. If Adams is still blabbin' to the coppers, then mebbe he ain't the only one. Mebbe a cut throat and left for all them others to see, in public like, that's the way."

His short speech done, he stepped down and resumed his place among his confederates. One or two were nodding their heads as he finished, but the general feeling appeared to be that he had spoken out of turn.

Galloway said nothing, but clapped the man on the back as he passed, then resumed his rounds of the room. Only once it had become clear that nobody else wished to challenge his plan, whatever it might be in detail, did he resume his position, a head above his fellows. Now I was reminded of the speakers at Hyde Park Corner, as he spoke a few general words of encouragement and reminded them of their loyalties.

"Mick's not wrong in one thing, I'll give him that. There'll be others like Adams, who might be foolhardy enough to speak against us. And perhaps a more public display would help dissuade them from their foolishness. But there'll always be folk like that and we can't go gutting them all. We get too public, and the authorities will come down on us hard. And we don't need that, do we? So long as we stand together, and don't make ourselves too visible, there's nobody can touch us. Remember that, and don't be fooled into believing that we can afford to be complacent. We can do a lot, but we can't do *exactly* what we want. No man can. We're protected just now because we keep it quiet, or make sure nothing can definitely be added to our account. If we get too *loud* though, well... that protection's likely to disappear. And we don't want that, do we?"

There was no doubt that his words had found favour with the men arranged before him. Many were nodding and one or two proclaimed their support more vocally. The one-eared man simply shrugged but made no attempt to regain the speakers' box, nor to speak out from the floor. Galloway slowly looked round the room, catching each man's eye in turn, and then answered his own question.

"No, we don't. We can't rely on loyalty from anyone but ourselves, so we need to tread carefully. Bear this in mind; even when we were kids, nobody gave us anything, but we survived and we prospered. Together. Right," he concluded, holding his hands out, palms down, above his men. "Time to get back to your cells. The warder's bought but he won't stay bought for ever. He's got a family to think of, and he can't afford to be losing his job. Off you go, and I'll set things in motion. Adams'll be breathing his last before the week's done."

A shuffling of feet and a final confused mass of conversations marked the end of the meeting, just as it might have done after a political gathering or a speech in a church hall.

It was time to leave. I guessed that services would be over very soon and I had learned more than I had expected. I had both a name to pass to Holmes, and the manner in which the man was to be killed. And I had gained an unexpected insight into the mind of Galloway. Callous and violent he undoubtedly was, as he had demonstrated with poor Hardie, but there was more to him than the common killer. He knew how to inspire his men and was willing, perhaps, to bend to their collective will. That nobody had seriously challenged him this night suggested either that his apparent democracy was a sham, or that his men knew that he could be trusted to do what was best for all of them. Was he too strong to be overruled, or too effective, I wondered?

I lowered myself down from my vantage point – and felt my stomach lurch as my boot slid on the dusty wood and I tumbled to the floor. I sprang to my feet and, acting entirely on instinct, ripped a section of wood from the smashed crate that had just betrayed me, and barrelled out of the door. So quickly had I moved that the lookout had barely begun to turn when I swung my makeshift club and fetched him a hard blow to the side of his head.

I did not wait for Galloway and his men to cross the brief distance to the door but hurdled the banister and fell the ten feet or so to the landing directly below. My ankle turned underneath me as I landed, but at least I was safely out of sight of the pursuers I could even then hear yanking open the door to the attic room. I stumbled away and half-ran, half-fell back towards the chapel, all too aware that there was no way in which I could slip back into the mass of prisoners without being noticed.

Not that it was likely to matter, for although I had given myself a small start, Galloway's men would be upon me long before I reached even the dubious safety of capture by those guarding the prisoners at worship. Either way, the information I had was doomed to prove worthless and I would have failed again.

I limped round one more bend, in full expectation that an

inmate's hand would soon descend on my collar, when I spotted a cell door lying slightly ajar. Unoccupied cells to be turned out prior to the residency of a new inhabitant were often left in such a manner, and I wasted no time in throwing myself into this one and pulling the door closed behind me.

I heard running footsteps pass by, and the sounds of men complaining that their quarry had evaded them. An instant later, another voice joined the cacophony.

"What are you up to, you damned fools?" Shapley's angry tone was unmistakable. "They're coming out of the chapel right now. They'll be here in a second. Quick, get in a line against the wall and let me do any talking that's needed."

I pressed my ear against the door, allowing my breathless panting to subside, as the throng of men did as ordered. I heard Galloway snarl at someone to keep quiet, then a new voice was added to the clamour outside.

"What's going on here, Shapley? Are these men with you?"

Of course, Governor Keegan was always first to leave the chapel. Whatever he said next was lost amid the murmuring throng of voices, requiring me to push the cell door open a crack in hopes of catching the exchange between him and Shapley. Even then, there was too much noise for me to decipher more than an occasional muffled word. To my horror, however, it was clear that the order had been given for everyone to return to their cells. As soon as that happened, I would be missed and no explanation I gave would be enough to keep me from solitary confinement.

It was imperative that I remained at liberty to speak to Holmes when he returned that evening.

With no other choice, I nudged the door open just wide enough to allow me egress and pushed my way between the nearest two prisoners. Instantly, a dozen pairs of eyes swivelled towards me and a collective hiss of recognition washed over me. I stared straight ahead, knowing Shapley could not give me away without also surrendering Galloway and his men.

So it proved. With a barked order, the collective mass of prisoners, including myself, were split into groups and dispersed to their cells.

I had much to tell Holmes. I only hoped that I could avoid Galloway for long enough to do so.

Chapter Twenty-Three

D oing so proved simpler than expected. The guard escorting us remarked on my injured ankle and though it was not enough of a sprain to need to see the doctor, it was sufficient for me to avoid that day's exercise period. As a result, I stayed in my cell all day, and was still there when the sound of a key in the lock announced the arrival of Holmes, once more kitted out as Mr. Andrews.

"Really, Watson, can I not leave you alone for more than a few hours, but you must injure yourself in some fresh manner?" he grinned.

"I am glad I amuse you, Holmes," I snapped, irritated at his good humour when I had spent the day in nervous anticipation, "but I have a great deal to tell you, and little time in which to do so."

To his credit, he immediately pushed the door closed behind him and took a seat on the vacant bed.

"My apologies, Watson. I have had some success in my endeavours outside these walls, but I should have known that you had not been idle. In spite of my request that you be so."

He frowned as he spoke, but I had already begun to tell him of Galloway and the meeting in the attic, and he had no chance to continue his thought. His expression lightened as I spoke, and on several occasions he asked me to repeat Galloway's words as exactly as I could.

When I had finished, he unfolded his long frame and jumped to his feet, suddenly alive with energy.

"This is excellent work, Watson, and tells us much we did not know, but I fear that you have so compromised your position that your safety is now imminently at risk." He began to pace up and down in his usual manner, only to come to a sudden halt as the constricted dimensions of the cell constrained his long-legged stride. "I have already tried every avenue open to me to have you set free until your trial, but the twin influences of Major McLachlan's objections and the note sent to Potter have rendered that impossible. My second thought – to remain close by, in the guise of a prison warder – has also proven less than ideal, for if I am to prove your innocence and so gain your more permanent release, I must be out and about in the city and not confined to one location."

"I can look after myself, Holmes," I protested, unwilling to be completely mollified by his concern.

"Generally speaking, I should have no doubt of that, my dear fellow," he agreed with a smile. "But this is a special case, one where every man's hand is turned against you and you have no way to defend yourself effectively."

I could not deny the truth of that, of course. The various wounds and abrasions I had suffered since entering the prison were painful testament to my success – or lack of it – to date.

"Even if I grant that to be true, what would you have me do, Holmes? Short of staying in my cell all day, I fail to see how I can avoid confrontation, especially now that Galloway knows that I have been watching him."

Holmes eyed me thoughtfully. "Perhaps that is the answer," he said slowly. He crossed to the door and risked a quick look outside. "We are agreed that I cannot be here as Andrews all the time in order to lend official weight to your protection. Nor can we arrange for you to be released pending your trial. Therefore, we must ensure that when I am not here, you are not available either."

"That would be most helpful," I agreed, "but how do you intend to manage that?"

Holmes stiffened suddenly as we heard footsteps approaching, but they passed by without disturbing us.

"My guard duties tonight do not require me to be in your section, so I shall explain quickly then be on my way. There are two ways in which we can keep you away from the other prisoners. Either I, as myself, can persuade the governor that your life is at risk from the other inmates, or you can commit some infraction of the prison regulations that leads to your being placed in solitary confinement. As the latter generally involves a fair degree of violence, I think it best to try the former approach first."

He straightened his uniform tunic and placed his cap on his head. "I am on the night shift throughout this week, so I shall return in the morning and speak to Governor Keegan on your behalf, stressing threats made against you by criminals we have jointly placed in prison. It would not do, I think, to mention Galloway directly, given the result of your previous accusation." He straightened the cap precisely. "I shall bring Lestrade with me. He will add an official flavour to the request."

"Lestrade?" I queried. "Would Potter not be more likely to be listened to, assuming he can be convinced to speak for me?"

Holmes grimaced. "Inspector Potter has proven… uncooperative, I am afraid. He has already refused to aid you in any way."

Just then I heard a doorway being opened somewhere nearby and in a flash, Holmes was gone. Only as he locked the door and his footsteps receded from me did I realise I had failed to ask him about the success he had mentioned regarding my own case.

The next morning dawned cold but bright.

Holmes arrived, as he had said he would, at around nine, transformed from the beetle-browed guard of the night before. He and Lestrade were already seated in Keegan's office when Shapley brought me to join the meeting. To my surprise, Inspector Potter was also present, standing to one side of the governor.

"It would seem that there is some concern for your safety," the governor began without preamble, indeed almost before the office door was closed behind me. "Mr. Holmes here – in company with Inspector Lestrade of Scotland Yard, for reasons which I admit elude me – claims that there have been threats against your life. Is this true?"

"It is," I replied.

"And these threats have been prompted by certain assistances you have supplied Scotland Yard during Mr. Holmes's work as a… what was it again, consulting detective?"

I glanced down at Holmes, who stared implacably ahead, a freshly lit cigarette dangling from his fingers. "Yes, I believe that to be the case."

"Hmm." Keegan coughed and Potter handed him a sheaf of

papers from the briefcase I now saw he had been holding behind his back. He began to read one, his finger tracing the lines as he read. In the ensuing silence, Lestrade took the opportunity to confirm our previous successes.

"Dr. Watson's assistance has been invaluable on many occasions in the past, Governor Keegan. He and Mr. Holmes have provided invaluable aid to the Yard in several high-profile cases, including some whose impact was felt in the highest positions in the land."

I was grateful to the little inspector, for I knew it must have pained him to describe Holmes's role in such glowing terms. It mattered little, however, for Keegan had evidently found what he was looking for, and replied in the most dismissive tone.

"The highest positions in the land, is it? Mr. Holmes hinted as much before the prisoner arrived but I assume now, as then, you are unable to provide any detail of such cases? For reasons of national security, was the phrase you used, if I recall correctly?"

Grudgingly, Lestrade nodded. He opened his mouth to speak, but Keegan was not finished.

"And the other cases in which these two gentlemen have been of help to the police? Those involving a less exalted clientele? Are those the sort of things Dr. Watson writes about in the popular periodicals? The... ahem, *Sign of Four*, for instance," he asked, stumbling deliberately over the title.

"It is," Holmes interjected before Lestrade could reply. "I have upbraided Watson more than once for his tendency to sensationalise our already fascinating work, but I cannot deny the accuracy of the bare facts he presents in each case he reports, once shorn of what he tells me is necessary literary licence. I do not flatter either Watson or myself when I say that we have a high success rate in our investigations, and have been responsible for the capture and imprisonment of numerous vicious criminals. Which is why he is in need of special protection while he remains temporarily incarcerated in this establishment."

"As you said," Keegan responded smoothly. "Yet, when I contacted Inspector Potter this morning – in his role as the detective actually investigating Dr. Watson's crimes – he informed me that Dr. Watson plays only a very minor role in such affairs. And as I read through these summaries the inspector has placed before me, it is clear that Watson is simply a useful if cavalier man with a revolver, who otherwise appears to spend much of his time on purely administrative errands, or applauding his colleague's own apparently limitless intelligence. In fact, I cannot see a single case in which he might be said to have played an essential part in the capture of anyone." Both his tone and his smile were mocking. "Would it not be fair to say that in every case, events would have unravelled exactly as they did were Dr. Watson to have been absent throughout?"

Holmes made no reply for a long second. He leaned forward and ground his cigarette out in the ashtray, then brushed the tips of his fingers together.

"First, Governor, I would remind you that it is more proper to say 'Watson's alleged crimes'. He has been convicted of nothing to date – at least not by any court. But to answer your question, no, that would not be fair at all. I shall go further. It would require an almost wilful misreading of every case in which we have been involved to draw such a conclusion. It is true that Watson often downplays his own essential contribution to our investigations for reasons of literary effect, but even someone taking his tales at face value could not fail to see the many and varied ways in which he provides insight and suggests new approaches in times of difficulty.

Any policeman worthy of the name would advise you of the truth of that assertion."

As he concluded, Holmes allowed his eyes to wander across to Potter and rest there, his final sentence directed at the inspector and not the governor. Potter did not miss the implied insult.

"How would you know what makes a decent policeman, Holmes?" he spat, stripping all courtesy from his voice. "You don't have what it takes to be even a poor one, and deep down you know it. Police work is difficult and it's frustrating – and it's without reward more often than not. There's no picking and choosing of clients, and neither can you ignore the dull cases and only involve yourself in the interesting ones. It's long nights spent in the rain and the wind, watching and waiting, and longer days tramping round the city, poking your nose in where it's not welcome and hoping nobody decides their life would be easier if the interfering copper were dead in the gutter. Mostly, though, a policeman deals with stupidity all day long, and you could never bear that, could you, Holmes? I've never investigated a snake trained to climb up ropes – yes, I read some of Dr. Watson's doggerel before I passed it to the governor – but I've seen any number of big buggers beat their wives to death because their tea wasn't ready, or there was no money for beer, or just because they could. What would you do with men like that, Holmes? How would you investigate them? And how would you get on if you had half a dozen like that a week? No criminal masterminds. No cunning plans. Just brutes being brutes, and a policeman coming along later to pick up the pieces and try and make something of them."

Holmes said nothing throughout this tirade. He stared at Potter through a haze of cigarette smoke, then suddenly rose to his feet and stalked across the room, until the two men stood almost toe to toe.

"I have never hidden my... disappointment with Scotland Yard, Inspector Potter. Lestrade will tell you, and Watson will no doubt back him up, that I am often less than complimentary about the efforts of his colleagues and himself. To my mind, they are ponderous and flat-footed, slow in both wit and action, and inclined to accept the easiest solution rather than the correct one. But..." he continued as Lestrade flushed with colour and opened his mouth to speak, "it is those very qualities which make them so well suited to the work you have just described. You ask how I would investigate the thug who beats his wife to death? The answer is obvious. I would not. There would be nothing to investigate, only injuries to be healed and punishment to be meted out. I am not temperamentally suited to either role, Inspector, but the likes of Gregson, Bradstreet and Hopkins are ideally fitted to the task. Plodders to a man, but diligent, and dogged too. As, I suspect, are you, Potter. Perhaps if you had not over-reached yourself, allowing your ambition to outstrip your ability, you might not be in the position in which you now find yourself."

Potter's voice was shrill with rage and his face flushed red. "The position I find myself in? What do you mean by that? It is not I who over-reaches himself, Holmes, but you. In your hurry to defend your friend the killer, you defame a police force whose members are your superiors in every way, and a man like Lestrade who has risked his very career to assist you in that foolishness. I wonder what he has to say to your contempt?"

If Holmes was concerned by this appeal to Potter's fellow officer, he did not show it. "Lestrade knows the value I place upon him," he replied. "Indeed, hand on heart I can say that I have described him in the last few days as the ideal detective. And if he does not know that I owe him a debt of gratitude for his help in recent weeks, then he is as poor a detective as you are yourself. To be clear, I very much doubt that to be the case."

"Thank you, Mr. Holmes," Lestrade said quietly, "but I can speak for myself. Whatever relationship exists between Mr. Holmes and myself is no business of yours, Potter," he continued, squinting at his colleague through narrow eyes. "But you mentioned the risks I've taken in helping Dr. Watson, and I'll tell you why I've taken them, shall I? Not because of Mr. Holmes or the help he *occasionally* gives Scotland Yard, nor even because he's saved my life before now. I've helped because he's a good man, who I know never killed that old woman. For one thing, only a fool would think the evidence points to him. But, nearly as important, he's not got it in him. He's a good-hearted man, is Dr. Watson, for all that he's been personally responsible for the apprehension of criminals far more dangerous than your friend the governor's ever likely to see inside Holloway."

As soon as the words fell from Lestrade's mouth, I knew that he had made an error, and from the look on his face, that he knew it too.

So it proved.

"You make Governor Keegan's point for him, Inspector," Potter responded quickly, before Lestrade could retract his statement. "The criminals Holmes and Watson capture do seem to die quite often, one way or another. And as for those who do not end their days dancing on the scaffold, are they not far more likely to be found in Dartmoor or Newgate than Holloway? Are there currently, in fact, any prisoners at all within these walls whom Holmes and Watson placed there?"

"There are none with whom we have dealt directly," Holmes reluctantly answered in Lestrade's stead. "But that is hardly the point. Watson is known to be an ally of the police force. He is, as you have admitted, responsible for sending sundry criminals to the gallows. The attacks by Isaac Collins and others are surely evidence enough that a prisoner may not necessarily be directly linked to our cases for Watson to be a target of retribution!"

It was clear that Keegan believed Potter had trumped us. He was not to be swayed. His smile became a grin, and he settled back in his chair with a small sigh of satisfaction.

"You could say that of almost every man in here, Mr. Holmes," he shrugged. "If I were to give special consideration to everyone who might be targeted for some offence committed outside these walls, the punishment cells would soon be overflowing. No, I am sorry, Inspector," he continued, turning to Lestrade, "but my hands are tied. And frankly I would be remiss if I did not take a moment to question exactly why a Scotland Yard detective who is not attached to this case sees fit to bring a civilian into my office to plead for such special treatment? I am a busy man, as I am sure you must be, and it strikes me as a waste of both your valuable time and mine to spend half an hour listening to the random entreaties of what – now I have met him in person – seems to me to be nothing but an amateur with an over-inflated sense of his own competence."

Holmes's back stiffened at that, and he rose quickly to his feet.

"Clearly the time being wasted is our own, Lestrade," he said coldly. "The governor's obvious preconceptions make it unlikely that Watson will be granted equitable treatment, which makes it all the more pressing that we spend our time more profitably." He stared down his nose at Keegan, who remained in his seat, an insolent smile still visible on his face. "But before I go, it would be remiss of *me* not to demonstrate exactly the calibre of man I take him to be, and exactly how little Watson should fear his opposition."

So saying, he bent forward across the governor's desk. Keegan leaned back in sudden fright and I heard Shapley take a step forward from his place by the door. Lestrade too moved, shifting to one side, so that he stood in between Shapley and Holmes. "Best to let him have his say, I've always found," he said quietly, as Holmes went on in a sharp, clinical voice.

"You are a vain man, Mr. Keegan, but you have never attracted a wife. You spend almost all your salary on satisfying your expensive tastes, which causes you to worry that you will have no means of support when you are too old to work. You employ no servants, possibly for financial reasons. You are not liked by your men, obviously. And of course, you play billiards frequently but remain a poor player."

The governor stared at Holmes, the colour slowly suffusing his face. "How dare you speak to me in such a manner–" he began, but Holmes cut across his bluster with a cold fury, such as I had rarely seen in my friend before.

"I dare, *Governor*, because I am not one of your lick-spittle lackeys, nor one of the poor unfortunates who suffer under your lamentable 'care'."

"To my infinite regret, I assure you," the governor spat out. "If you were to present yourself in this office, spouting such a pack of falsehoods in an official capacity–"

"You and I both know that there is no falsehood in anything I have said, but for the benefit of my colleagues, I shall explain, if you wish."

Allowing Keegan no chance to demur, Holmes pressed on with what was swiftly turning into a character assassination.

"Your vanity is undeniable and all too clear to the thoughtful observer. You have shaved recently, in the last few days, but missed a single hair on your chin. It is rather too long to be the result of one day's growth and since you could hardly present yourself in this office unshaven, you must have had a beard until recently. The skin around your chin and under your nose is of a slightly paler colour than the rest of your face – which, given that you must spend most of your time within these walls, indicates both that you were bearded for a considerable length of time, and that your beard was of the fashionable Van Dyke variety favoured by members of the artistic community. That the errant hair is grey in colour – unlike your unnaturally black hair – suggests to me that vanity caused you to remove your beard. Add to that your suit and shirt, whose quality must strain the purse of any public servant, and the faint aroma coming from them of extremely costly cigars, and I struggle to think of any other description than vain."

"What of the lack of a wife?" Lestrade encouraged Holmes, evidently enjoying the spectacle.

"Surely even you noticed the second button down on Mr. Keegan's expensive French shirt, Lestrade? It has come astray and been sewn back on, but the thread is not quite the right shade. It does not match the buttons above and below it. No wife would make such an elementary error. Nor would any servant worthy of the name, hence he has none such, though his salary would undoubtedly allow him one should he wish it."

"And the billiards?" I worried that I would be punished later for my interjection, but watching Holmes in full spate was the first real pleasure I had felt in days.

"A mere trifle, Watson, I assure you. But if it will amuse you... the indentation on his left middle finger and the less noticeable callus on the forefinger of the same hand could only be caused by a billiard cue held frequently. The small trophy on the shelf above his head declares that he came third in an intra-prison competition seventeen years ago; the absence of any other trophies indicates he has not improved in the meantime. As I said, a mere trifle."

The familiar rhythm and tone of one of Holmes's explanations soothed me, I cannot deny, and I found myself looking even on the governor with a little more kindness, helped in large measure by the extreme displeasure evident on his face. It was swollen with indignation, and reddened to the point, I both feared and hoped, of apoplexy. He said nothing while Holmes spoke, but as a brief silence fell on the room he seemed to come to his senses and, with an enraged cry, barked an order at Shapley.

"Take the prisoner back to his cell!" he ordered, "and escort Inspector Lestrade and his companion out of the prison. Now!" he concluded, his voice raised almost to a bellow.

The officer gave me a shove in the back, propelling me towards the door, before with only marginally more politeness asking Holmes and Lestrade to follow him. As I was marched away from my friends, I had just time to hear Lestrade ask Holmes how he knew that his men disliked Governor Keegan, and Holmes's reply that, having met the man, need he really ask?

There had been an undeniable pleasure in watching Keegan humbled, but any satisfaction I felt was only fleeting. Within minutes I was once more in my cell, with the mechanical routine of the day ahead of me and, in the not too distant future, a trial which, for all Lestrade's supportive words, I might well lose.

I held fast to those encouraging words throughout the long day, intending to ask Holmes about the progress he had mentioned as soon as he arrived for his shift as Andrews. In the event, however, he appeared at my cell door in the early afternoon, with an order in his hand to take me to the infirmary. It seemed the morning meeting with Keegan had at least prompted the governor to have my injuries examined by a doctor.

"Fortunately for us, there are staffing difficulties in the prison at the moment. One of the warders on today's roster failed to appear this morning, and so a runner was sent round to my lodgings requesting my presence for a portion of the day shift." He allowed himself a quick smile. "The absence may be connected to an anonymous telegram to the local constabulary giving warning that a certain guard had republican sympathies and planned a bombing atrocity in the near future. Don't worry!" Holmes quickly stifled my objection. "I have also asked Lestrade to ensure that the fellow is treated well and only held in custody until I give the word for his release. But this way I can be present as often as I wish for the next few days."

"Which I appreciate, Holmes, but when do you intend to sleep?"

"You know me better than that, Watson! I have trained myself to manage with very little sleep when required. A few days without will not impair my faculties. But quiet now!"

The warning was unnecessary. I too had seen the guard approaching. Like Holmes he was escorting a prisoner.

"Afternoon, Andrews," he called cheerfully. "What you doing in?"

"Pulling a double, ain't I?" replied Holmes with a sour grimace. The two men stood and chatted for a period, and I glanced across at my fellow prisoner, who nodded in greeting.

To my surprise, it was Isaac Collins, but he gave no indication that he knew me. He eyed me curiously for a second then turned his attention to his right boot, which he rubbed against the back of his calf. I thought to say something to him, to ask why he had tried to kill me and for whom, but as I opened my mouth he frowned in warning and shook his head sharply in a tiny, quick movement, then resumed the buffing of his filthy boot.

The moment passed and Holmes bade his colleague goodbye. We moved off towards the infirmary.

Only once we were far enough from the other guard not to be overheard did I speak.

"That prisoner was Isaac Collins, Holmes!" I exclaimed.

"I am aware of that fact, Watson. I have kept an eye on him since your first encounter with him. He is no more than a small-time handler of stolen goods, though with a reputation for violence. He is on his way back to the punishment cells, having been found with a home-made knife in his cell. But here we are at the infirmary! I shall hand you over into the custody of the doctor there, then I must be off to attend to other matters." He pulled out a battered pocket watch. "I shall return in thirty minutes to take you back to your cell."

He stepped past me to open the door, but I placed my hand on his arm to stop him. "Wait a moment, Holmes," I whispered urgently. "The busy turn of events had driven it out of my mind, but I meant to ask – what progress have you made in your investigation into Miss McLachlan's murder? You said last night that you had had some success."

"Forgive me, Watson," my friend immediately apologised. "I have allowed myself to become too much caught up in the role I am playing, and forgotten that you are not at my side at all times, as is more usually the case in our investigations." He glanced down the corridor, then pulled me to one side, so that we would have a moment's warning should someone open the infirmary door from the inside.

"I have discovered what happened to the girl who led you into the murder room. As yet, I have been unable to identify her, but I have hopes of doing so very soon, and knowing how she contrived to evade recognition until now has opened up a most profitable avenue of investigation. It is not too much to say that that fact, combined with her identity, will lead me to the solution to the case, and your freedom. In the meantime, be wary of Galloway and if–"

Just then, the door to the infirmary swung open and in an instant, Holmes was Andrews once more.

"Thank you, sir," he muttered obsequiously to the doctor who stood in the doorway. "I were just about to bring this prisoner in to see you. He's complaining of a busted ankle, and the governor'd like you to take a look at him, if you've time."

The doctor looked me up and down and nodded wearily. "As if I didn't have enough to do," he muttered, then, "Leave him with me. It shouldn't take more than ten minutes to strap him up. You needn't wait. One of your colleagues is already inside, about to return another man to his cell. I'll have him stay a little longer and kill two birds with one stone."

He kicked the door wide open, and gestured inside. "In you go then," he said, without looking in my direction. "Have a seat and I'll take a look at your ankle in a minute."

I did as I was bidden, and shuffled to a seat. Within, however, I exulted at Holmes's words. Perhaps my nightmare would soon be over!

Chapter Twenty-Four

❧

It has been my experience that, no matter how unpleasant, eventually every situation becomes commonplace. So it proved over the next week in Holloway.

For one thing, our meeting with the governor had turned out not to be entirely disastrous after all. As a result of the formal warning issued by Holmes to Keegan that a fresh attack might well take place, May – the guard who, alongside Shapley, had taken me to the treadmill – had been assigned to keep watch over me. Needless to say, this action was motivated entirely by self-interest and not at all by concern for my well-being, but it did mean I could relax a little. Unfortunately, it had the disadvantage of preventing Holmes from exchanging more than the briefest of formal greetings with me. A week passed in this manner, then "Andrews" disappeared completely and I, unable to draw attention to our relationship by asking after him, had simply to trust that he was working on my behalf outside the prison.

In any case, I spent most of the next few days moving back

and forth from my cell to a private room where Osmont Marcum detailed his intentions for my legal defence.

"It is my opinion, Dr. Watson, that the very prospect of this trial is a terrible indictment of the judicial system in this country!" he muttered disapprovingly. "It would not occur in Scotland, I assure you. Why, there a gentleman such as yourself... but I ramble, and time is pressing."

He flicked through the pages of his notebook without reading a word, then caught and held my eye. "As you know, the evidence against you is circumstantial and rests in large part upon an anonymous note and your presence in a room locked from within, with a mutilated body adjacent to you. The note is of little weight, in my opinion; juries mistrust any communication to which a man is afraid to put his name. But the matter of the key... that is not ideal, not ideal at all. I suppose you have had no thought as to how the room came to be locked and the key on the inside? No? Well, never mind, we must proceed with the facts as we have them.

"I shall call you to speak in your own defence, if you are willing? A professional man, with a degree of popular fame, and wounded in defence of his queen, no less. Yes, the jury will like that, they will like that a great deal. Naturally, I shall be at pains to contrast your good, upright self with your craven, faceless accuser! Yes indeed, there is much cause for hope even before I raise the name of Alistair McLachlan, the ravisher of serving girls!"

I shifted uncomfortably at the mention of McLachlan but Marcum moved on before I could again re-state my belief in his innocence.

"There it is then! My intention is to discredit the anonymous IOU letter and to present John Watson as he undeniably is – a solid and honest member of the community, with ties to the police force and links to the gentry and even the aristocracy. It is a pity, a great pity indeed, that I cannot do more than hint at your service to the Crown itself, but there you are.

"I shall allude to Mr. Holmes, although I shall not call him to the stand, and Inspector Lestrade has agreed to speak to your good character. I shall avoid, as much as I may, all mention of the murder room itself, except to stress the lack of time you had to commit the killing and the identity of the knife used in the bloody deed. That will then naturally lead on to a discussion of Alistair McLachlan's inheritance and his lack of an alibi, at which point I shall task the prosecution with providing a motive other than that proposed in the, by then worthless, IOU."

He sniffed loudly and closed his notebook. "Does that meet with your approval, Doctor?"

I nodded. Put like that, it seemed impossible that any jury could believe me to be the killer, but I knew that the prosecution would place a far blacker slant on each item of evidence, and could call on a Scotland Yard detective of their own who was certain of my guilt.

In the absence of further discussion with Holmes, I was forced to seek other avenues of news. Fortunately, unconvicted prisoners were allowed to purchase the better quality newspapers and thus it was in *The Times* that I discovered we had saved the life of Adams, the individual nominated for death by Galloway some days before. The report was a small one, but I cut it out and have it still.

WOULD-BE KILLERS CAPTURED ran the headline, and underneath appeared an account of the arrest of two masked gunmen who had broken into the home of George Adams, one of London's foremost collectors of fine art. An anonymous telegram alerting Inspector Lestrade of Scotland Yard of the potential attack had led to the arrests, which were believed to be the work of notorious gang leader Matthew Galloway, the report concluded. I allowed myself a small smile at the irony.

I remembered Lestrade's description of the man who had informed on Galloway – a rival, he had said – and wondered at the heights to which the capital's criminal leaders aspired.

According to the date of the clipping, that was the twenty-eighth of the month, exactly one week before the date set for the commencement of my trial. I had still received no word from Holmes. I could only hope that he neared a breakthrough, but if he did, he was cutting things fine. I continued to seek out what information I could regarding Galloway, and attempted, late at night in my cell, to construct a chain of events and movements which would put him, or one of his men, in the cell alongside poor Hardie. The thought of the little shake of the head he had given me on the stairs, gloating in the knowledge of what he had done, burned inside me. He believed himself untouchable, and perhaps he was right. Certainly, he had the free run of the prison, and who knew how many warders were in his employ. I slept fitfully, increasingly consumed by the idea of his never-ending immunity from punishment.

I have heard condemned men describe the days preceding their execution as passing by in a trice, while the night before dragged on for an eternity. So it seemed to me in the final week before my trial.

The first few days came and went in a blur and I am unable to pick out a single memory that I can definitively place in that short period. I know that each day passed in similar manner to the ones before, in an unchanging series of meals eaten alone in my cell, hours spent in worship or exercise, but all I can say with certainty is that whenever I was not locked inside I obsessed over Matty Galloway. In chapel, I made sure to sit somewhere behind him, so that I might better watch him. In the yard, I stood by the wall, shifting my back along the brickwork so that he was always in view. Even on the way from my cell to the visitors' room to meet with Marcum, my eyes were in constant motion, seeking out Hardie's killer to the exception of everything else.

Only after Marcum shook my hand on a cold Friday afternoon and said that he would see me in court on Monday did events finally slow from the blur of the previous week to a more comprehensible speed. I had seen Holmes neither as himself nor as Andrews, though in my obsession I had barely noticed his absence, but now, as my senses returned to something approaching their normal state, the lack of any word filled me, perversely, with optimism. No news was good news, they said, and I knew my friend would only desert me at this time if he were following a promising path from which he could not deviate. In his absence, all I could do was prepare for court.

It was while I lay in bed considering what I could do to help myself that my guardian angel, Mr. May, opened my cell door one night and slipped inside. It was past midnight, and there was no reason why he should be there. I sat up and pushed my blanket away, but before I could speak, he held a finger to his lips.

"Quietly, Dr. Watson. I have something which I think might be of interest to you."

He gently closed the door behind him and took a seat on the spare bed.

"I've bin watching you, Doctor, as you know, on the orders of the governor, and I don't reckon there's much evil in you. Not enough to do the terrible things they say you did, anyway. And I got to thinking that mebbes I could do you a good turn, on account of I don't like to see a good man done down like you've bin."

His little speech done, he fell silent and stared across the empty space at me. And a speech it definitely had been, rushed out in a single breath, as though rehearsed but imperfectly remembered, and the speaker keen to get the lines out before he forgot any more.

There was a full moon that night and by its light I could see sweat glistening on May's top lip. His fingers drummed on his thigh and his foot tapped against the floor in an uneven rhythm. He was plainly nervous, which was to be expected if he was breaking the rules to do me a kindness – but perhaps too nervous if all he intended was to pass me information in my cell and then be gone. Whatever he intended, he did not believe he could easily explain it if he were caught during its execution.

"A good turn?" I said carefully. The more I could entice him to explain, the better armed I would be in the coming days. For there was no doubt that I intended to go along with whatever he proposed. Only a fool would not expect a trap, but better willingly to enter the trap than remain in darkness and risk being taken completely unawares later.

"I can show you proof that Matt Galloway is a killer."

Trap or not, May spoke now as though he believed what he was saying. His fingers and foot had stilled, and his voice was natural and unforced. If this was the bait, it was at least convincing. I slipped my feet into my shoes and stood. May also rose, suddenly tense.

"If that is true, Mr. May, then you shall have my undying thanks. But I take it that you do not have the proof on your person?"

He shook his head. "No, not on me. But if you come with me, I can take you to where it is. It's hidden in the governor's office."

I was almost offended that I should be considered sufficiently dim-witted that I would fall for so transparent a ploy, but I had already decided to go along with May. "Very well," I said. "Will you lead the way, or should I go in front?"

He hesitated, then pulled open the door. "It'd be better if you go in front, Doctor," he muttered.

I stepped out into the corridor and noticed the door at the end was ajar. I turned towards May – and a blinding pain arced across my head as a heavy cosh struck the side of my face. I stumbled forward, one arm outstretched for the wall, but before I reached it, everything turned black.

Chapter Twenty-Five

When my head cleared, my first thought was to wonder that I was still alive. My second was to consider how long I was likely to remain in that happy state.

I knew at once where I was. The abandoned attic room in which I had seen Galloway order the killing of George Adams was unchanged, save that the late hour had necessitated three lamps to be lit and instead of a box in the centre of the room, there was now a chair, to which I was securely tied. I could taste the iron tang of blood in my mouth, and one eye throbbed painfully and was swollen shut, so that I could only squint through the other at the assembled gang who surrounded me. My head, too, ached and every breath was painful – the earlier damage to my ribs had obviously been exacerbated by new injuries.

A voice spoke from my left, the side on which my vision was impaired, so that I was forced to twist my neck round to confront the speaker. As expected, it was Matty Galloway.

"I hope you will accept my apologies, Dr. Watson," he said,

moving round until he stood directly in front of me. "The lads can get a bit... over-enthusiastic." He smiled, but there was no warmth in it. "Still, you're a man of the world, and I'm sure you realise that any discomfort you currently find yourself in is only temporary in nature."

From behind me I heard the laughter of Galloway's men and their hope that my death would be a painful one, but I felt no fear, only anger with myself that I had failed Albert Hardie, and that his murderer would also be my own. I strained at the ties that bound me to the chair, and instantly recognised the futility of the action. The rope was too tight around my wrists and ankles to allow even the most minute of movements. Instead, I concentrated on keeping my head held high and holding Galloway's gaze. Whatever transpired, I was determined that I would show no fear. That I would deny my killers.

Galloway seemed to understand. "Plucky, I called you once, Doctor, and I'll say it again. It's a pity that you've proven so bent on my destruction, for I'd be happy to have you in our little enterprise. A man like you'd be a useful addition to our company... but there it is. You've no more control over your role in our relationship than I do. One of us was bound to be the victor and the other the victim. And I've too many men rely on me to risk an outcome other than the one we're engaged in now. You can see that, I hope?"

I assumed the question to be a rhetorical one, but Galloway paused, as though waiting for a reply.

"Just business is it, Galloway?" I said finally, unable – and unwilling – to keep silent. "Was it just business when you slit the throat of a mere boy, too? Do you tell yourself that? Is that how you live with the memory of your own butchery?"

I was becoming enraged again, I knew, and I struggled to prevent myself screaming in fury at the bloodless creature before me. Better to give Galloway no satisfaction whatever, to add nothing to his victory, but the sly smile that played across his lips almost caused me to abandon that resolution.

"Perhaps it is true what everyone says, eh? That Sherlock Holmes keeps you around as a plaything; that it amuses him to see you dance attendance on him and understand nothing. You surely don't continue to labour under the idiotic delusion that I had Hardie killed? Why would I?"

"Because I made a terrible mistake!" The words were forced from my throat. I could not hold them in. "Because I failed to stop him spying on you!"

Pain lanced from my ribs to my shoulder as I pressed against my restraints, but the anger that had boiled inside me since I had been confined in Holloway would not be quelled, no matter how much I might wish it to be. "I should have prevented him, but I did not. And so you slaughtered him, as though he were nothing!"

Now Galloway's smile became a full-bellied laugh. "Spied on me? You said it yourself, Watson. He was no more than a child. I have killed more than one man and perhaps I am the butcher you claim, but I don't kill children for *watching* me. At worst, I would have had one of my people warn him off." He shook his head. "You disappoint me, Doctor. I've laboured under the misapprehension that there was more to you than bravery and a willingness to be hurt in the cause of Mr. Holmes's games, but it seems I was mistaken. Spied on *me*, did he?"

He laughed again, and there could be no doubting that his amusement was genuine. But if Galloway had not killed my friend, then who had?

I had not long to wait to find out. Galloway composed himself, and crouched down before me, so that his face was level with my own. Close to, I fancied I could actually see the moment at which amusement left his eyes, to be replaced by a cold hardness. Galloway was all business once more.

"I'll tell you who killed your young friend, shall I? Because I know everything that goes on in here. I knew the boy was dead before the guards did. One of my boys saw the act take place, you see. Did Potter not tell you that? I told him to give you fair warning of what lay in your cell. No surprise there, I suppose; he's no better than a dog, that one. But still… I know who killed the boy. Do you want me to show you?" He stood and stretched, caring little how I replied. "There's no reason why I shouldn't do you this one last favour. Your life is assuredly forfeit for saving George Adams, but I am not so cruel as you believe, and won't send you to your grave unsatisfied. Not in that respect at least."

He beckoned to one of his unseen compatriots. "Bring the good doctor his gift, and then we can be done with this business."

The man, whoever he was, did no more than grunt, then shuffled past me into the corridor beyond. I heard a door open, I assume the same storage space in which I had watched the earlier meeting of Galloway and his gang, then a muffled thump, as though something heavy had fallen to the floor. In the dying light of the evening, the man entered the room with his back to me, dragging something that I was unable quite to make out. With a final sigh, he allowed his burden to slip to the floor, then stepped back into the shadows.

A burlap sack lay crumpled at Galloway's feet. As soon as I saw it, the shape of it, I knew that it must contain a corpse.

"Here's your murderer, Dr. Watson. I'll own up to this killing happily enough."

He indicated that the bag should be opened, and one of his men knelt down and pulled at the rope that bound it, then manoeuvred the top of the sack down, exposing the boil-encrusted face of Isaac Collins.

"You look surprised, Doctor. Were you expecting someone else?"

"I don't understand," I said weakly. "Why should this man kill poor Hardie, when he could as easily have killed me instead?"

Galloway's laughter cut through me like a knife. "You think a great deal of yourself, Doctor, don't you? You're not quite so important as you believe, not in a place like this. There are any number of reasons why a man might get himself killed inside a prison's walls, and what you consider your fame is not high on that list. Why, I doubt one man in a hundred has even heard your name, never mind be able to identify you in a crowded prison yard.

"But steal from any man in here and you take your life in your hands. The lad paid the price he should have known he would when he stole booze from Ikey Collins."

Stole booze? Suddenly, I remembered the rough alcohol Hardie and I had shared on my first night. Of course, he had stolen it. He had told me he had just arrived. Where else could it have come from but theft?

"But the G carved on his cheek?" The question sounded redundant, even as I asked it, but Galloway nodded anyway.

"Not a *G*, Doctor, a *C*. You think I got where I am by signing my corpses?" He chuckled at the thought. "But Collins wanted every inmate to know who killed the boy. I doubt he even knew who you were at first. Probably made it his business to find out after I… intervened, but by then he knew better than to touch you, even if he wanted to. Which I also doubt. I'll say this for Ikey Collins, he didn't go looking for trouble. Ran an efficient ship, kept himself out of trouble, didn't give any warder a reason to bother him. A cut of the takings to Shapley and one or two others, and a blind eye was turned in his direction. But he couldn't let some wet-eared boy steal from him, now could he?" Galloway's smile was now as cold as the air in the room. "'Cos if it got about that a miserable nothing like him could take even a portion of what was Ikey's, and escape without punishment, well – what was to stop someone like me deciding to take it all?"

There was nothing I could say. I stared blankly at Galloway, my mind empty, aware only that I had begun to shiver. I knew at that moment that I would die in this squalid room. Nothing could save me. That was why Galloway had shown me the body, had admitted to the murder. He wanted me to know that my life would soon be over.

"So now you know," he said, still smiling. "Consider the information a last thank you for the favour some say you did me with McLachlan's aunt. Not that I really believed you did it. Not for long. But I've long wished to do Mr. Sherlock Holmes a bad turn. I could hardly ignore an opportunity dropped in my lap like you showing up in the yard at Holloway. And accused of a killing which everyone would otherwise have thought my doing? It was too good a chance. So I made sure that the world was certain you were my man. Shook your hand for all to see, extended my wing over you, claimed you as my own. And then sent that IOU, just to be sure. We did laugh at that, I can tell you. I don't know who put your head in the noose, and that's the truth, but I've done my level best to make sure it stays there.

"But that's all done now, and I've pressing business to attend to. I'm afraid I can't waste any more time on you, Dr. Watson. My boys need to be putting the word out that I'm the man to see for booze now. Time waits for no man, they say. I'm sure you understand."

Casually, he kicked the corpse at his feet. "Take this away and dump it in a corner somewhere it'll be found," he ordered the man nearest to him. "And you," he continued, pointing to another, "put an end to Watson here, and leave his body in the same place. There'll be a bit of noise when they're discovered, but everyone knows I did all I could to protect the poor doctor. Besides, what am I paying Keegan for, if not to cover up the likes of this? Mind and leave the blade you use beside the bodies. Stick it in Ikey's hand, maybe. That should help."

He turned briskly, and the second man he had spoken to stepped in front of me, a length of sharpened metal in his hand. I willed my eyes to remain open as he approached, determined at least to face death head on, when the most unexpected voice broke the silence.

"Take one more step towards him and I shall be forced to shoot."

I twitched my head towards the speaker, and was astonished to see the man who had dragged in the body step from the shadows, a revolver held steadily before him. Had I not recognised Holmes's voice, I would not have known him at all. Dressed as he was in the same filthy uniform as the rest of us, his face dirty and partially covered by long stubble, only his eyes, when the last few rays of sunlight caught them, were those of my friend.

"Cut him loose," he went on, his voice as calm as if he were discussing the weather. "Do it now, or Mr. Galloway dies at the count of three."

He moved the revolver slightly, so that it pointed directly at Galloway, then softly said, "One."

Galloway was no coward, I'll say that for him. For a moment, I thought he would rush Holmes. He leant forward, taking all his weight on the balls of his feet, but Holmes murmured, "Two," and, obviously realising that the distance between them was too great, he rocked back and snarled, "Do what he says. Cut the doctor loose."

My would-be killer stepped around me, and I felt the bonds at my wrists and then my ankles loosen and fall away. I pushed myself to my feet and swayed to one side as the blood resumed its interrupted course, sending a sharp pain through my legs.

"How–?" I muttered, but Holmes shushed me quietly.

"In a moment, Watson," he said, taking my elbow with one hand, while the revolver in the other retained its steady aim at Galloway's heart.

Slowly, we backed out of the room. Once we were outside, Holmes slid a bolt across and locked the door behind us, trapping the men inside. The circulation had fully returned to my legs by then, and I was eager to be away, but Holmes held fast to my elbow and bade me wait.

I had not long to do so. No more than a couple of minutes passed before I heard footsteps climbing the staircase towards us and then, emerging from the gloom, the eager face of Inspector Lestrade, with two uniformed constables behind him.

"Inside is he, Mr. Holmes?" Lestrade asked, glancing across at me as he did so.

"He, sundry members of his gang, and the body of one of his victims, Inspector. At least one of them is armed with a home-made knife, so I suggest you take this." He handed Lestrade the revolver. "There will no doubt be other charges, but for the moment, the murder of one Isaac Collins will suffice."

"And Dr. Watson?"

"To the infirmary would be best, I think. With a police guard, to be on the safe side. But first, I must have a word with him in private."

My head was still heavy and my hands still shaking, but I had strength and will enough to take a seat on the top step of the stairs and wait for Holmes to join me.

"I feared I would be too late," he began as soon as he was seated. "I was delayed returning from a necessary errand, and though I came straight to your cell dressed as Andrews, you were, of course, already gone. Fortunately, there are only so many places you could have been taken at one o'clock in the morning and I gambled correctly that it would not be the pump house.

"I rushed here, and discovered a large sack where we now sit – the same sack you saw containing the late Mr. Collins, of course. I was just wondering how best to effect entry when Galloway sent his confederate out to fetch Collins. After that, it was the work of a moment to render him unconscious and take his place. The rest you know."

I still had many questions, but I knew they could wait for now. Holmes gestured to a nearby constable for assistance and, with an exhausted sigh, I allowed him to help me up, then preceded him down the stairs.

Chapter Twenty-Six

In the infirmary, the doctor I had seen earlier took me efficiently in hand. To my relief, none of my injuries were serious, only a second cracked rib and a deep cut to my scalp requiring no more treatment than antiseptic ointment.

As my ribs were being re-strapped, word arrived from Lestrade that I was required in the governor's office. The doctor protested that I needed rest – a distinct change in attitude from my previous time under his "care", I noted – but I assured him that I already felt much recovered and he, with a great show of reluctance, eventually agreed to release me. With the constable who had escorted me at my side, ready to steady me if I should stumble, I made what haste I could to Keegan's office.

Here too, much had changed from my earlier visit. Of Keegan himself, there was no sign, though as the hour was still early, that was no great surprise. Lestrade sat in the governor's chair, with Holmes perched on the edge of another, still in the begrimed prison uniform he had worn during my rescue. Galloway, too, was present, handcuffed to the wrist of a burly police sergeant, standing before the governor's desk. As I entered the room, Holmes looked up and in the artificial light I saw a look of relief flash across his eyes.

"Take a seat, Watson," he said. "Galloway has been telling us a most fascinating tale. I am certain that he would have no objection to recounting it again for your benefit."

I sat, and examined the man who, not an hour earlier, had ordered my death. He appeared composed and alert, and perfectly willing to look me in the eye as he spoke.

"It's straightforward enough, Doctor. I'm not keen to swing for Collins's death, but I won't give up any of my lads to prevent it. Loyalty is everything in a business like mine, but it's only through trust that you breed loyalty. And how could any one of my lads trust me again if I did that? No, I'd rather be topped myself than send one of them to the rope.

"But that don't apply to everyone. Some of them I employ, they don't understand loyalty. They just put their hands out and I fill them with money or information, or whatever they need. They'd turn on me and mine in a second if they thought it'd save their skins, so I reckon I owe them nothing in return. That's reasonable, wouldn't you say?"

I said nothing, and Galloway gave a tiny shrug. Holmes waved a hand, encouraging him to continue.

"Like Governor Keegan, for instance?" Holmes said. "Even allowing for all the palms you greased among the guards, I realised as soon as I worked my first shift that the degree of freedom you had required collusion from the very top." He turned to me, his face downcast. "I attempted to warn you not to trust him, but we were interrupted, and then I was unavoidably called away."

Galloway looked at each of us in turn, ensuring he had our

attention, before he replied. "Keegan? Of course. I've been greasing his palm for years. Regular payments too, to make sure that any of my lads who end up passing through his gates gets treated right. And a bit more now and again, when special arrangements need to be made. A prison can be a dangerous place – well, I don't need to tell you that, do I, Doctor? – and if someone happens to fall down a stairwell now and again, or manages to hang himself in his cell, well, who's to say what happened? Not Governor Keegan, that's for sure, and not his guards. Not the ones who count, anyway. Same goes if I want to see someone sweating on the treadmill for a bit. Teaches folk respect, doesn't it?"

"Let's be quite clear here, Galloway," Lestrade interrupted. "You are saying that you've paid Governor Keegan to turn a blind eye to torture and murder inside his own prison? And you'd be willing to put that in a statement, and repeat it in court?"

"I said I would, didn't I? I told you, I owe him nothing. Nor Potter."

Inspector Potter's name was obviously a new addition to the conversation, for I heard Lestrade suck the air in through his teeth, and Holmes moved forward, until he was all but crouched in front of his chair.

"Thank you, Galloway. I wondered when you would mention Inspector Potter." Holmes spoke before Lestrade could respond, his eyes glistening brightly and his mouth set in a thin-lipped line. "I would be obliged if you would allow me to lay out what we already know in respect of the inspector, and you can make additions and corrections as necessary?"

Galloway shrugged, as though the matter were of supreme indifference to him. Lestrade glowered, but remained silent, as Holmes re-settled himself in his chair and began to speak.

"You have been working with Inspector Potter for some time; since his original fall from grace, in fact. You approached him, I think. No matter the flaws in his character, a man such as Potter would not turn to one like yourself of his own volition. Not readily, at least. But you caught him at his lowest ebb; betrayed, as he saw it, by those who should have supported him.

"So you contacted him, offering to provide information which would help him recover the standing he had lost. Something small, at first. Details of a crime to be committed by one of your rivals, an unpleasant matter, but a trivial one in the grand scheme of things. Evidence of your good faith, as it were. Perhaps you presented yourself as that most illogical of beasts, the honest criminal. One of the old school, a man who respected the unspoken rules of the game. I can imagine Potter reacting well to an approach of that nature.

"And thus you cultivated the inspector. You supplied him with a steady stream of information, and watched his fortunes rise once more. Always, however, alongside your own. For you too benefited; how could you not, for every blow he struck against this gang or that was a blow against one of your competitors. Your business expanded as each rival fell, the vacuum created in their wake filled by you or one of your men, until you were in a position to spring the trap you had built around him."

Holmes's recital came to a halt, and he looked across at Galloway, one eyebrow raised, seeking confirmation. Galloway nodded once. "That's about right," he said. "He thought he had me in the palm of his hand, told me to my face that he could break me any time he wanted. But he was wrong there."

Holmes returned the gesture. "Because though Potter is no fool, he is, at heart, a simple man. Even the professional reversal he had suffered had not taught him caution. Just as he had once set himself up against the establishment, convinced that because he was in the right, he could not be gainsaid, now he allowed himself to believe that his own honesty provided him with a shield that would protect him against you. But it did not; it could not. Watson will tell you that I do not generally care to conjecture, but it is safe to say that some of the arrests he made, using the information you provided, implicated him in a degree of illegality which, if made public, he would struggle to refute."

Again, he stopped, and waited for Galloway to speak.

"Something like that. I made sure that I had witnesses to certain of our dealings. Men of good character who would swear, if need be, that Potter was a bought man, who took my coin knowing that he was working for me."

"But he took no money from you, did he?"

"Not a penny. But who'd believe that? Even if they did, would his own vanity seem a more acceptable price, once the newspapers twisted the story? It's no secret, there's more than one newspaperman who'll print anything if it brings a copper low."

"So we discovered. But whatever the cause, Potter found himself trapped, unable to retreat from his acquaintance from you, left with no choice but to move forward, the little services he had once done you growing ever larger. What I cannot be sure of is when you first realised that you could use Potter to manipulate Major McLachlan."

Finally, Lestrade found his voice, interjecting an outraged exclamation before Galloway could speak. "You've gone too far now, Mr. Holmes, really you have! Keegan, even Potter, if the trap was cunning enough, I grant you – but Sir Campbell McLachlan? A decorated war hero and a member of Her Majesty's government? No," he said, shaking his head vigorously, "that I'll not believe, and nor will anyone else."

"As ever, you misunderstand, Lestrade," Holmes replied calmly. "Sir Campbell acted throughout for the most noble of reasons. He trusted Potter implicitly, and believed him when he whispered that action needed to be taken against the criminals who plague London's streets. If he is guilty of anything, it is simply that he was *too* trusting. But why should he not have been? Potter had proven true in the past, after all."

"In the past?" I had remained silent until now, but I knew my role well enough.

"You recall the nature of Potter's original fall from grace? His over-zealous pursuit of certain younger members of prominent families? It required only a few minutes' browsing through my scrapbooks to uncover the reason Sir Campbell places so much trust in Potter. I confess I gave the case little mind, either at the time or since, for it seemed unconnected to your current travails. But when we spoke to McLachlan, he implied that his positive view of the man was based on more than mere opinion, and I began to wonder what had brought them together in the first place. After all, Potter, for all his fame in the police force, was only an inspector, and would be unlikely in the common way of things to have many dealings with a decorated knight of the realm. But when McLachlan described the wayward character of his younger brother, and his efforts to curtail his activities, the association was clear.

"Potter suffered for his part in an investigation which potentially implicated several of the greatest families in the land in a scandal of a moral nature. The matter was not widely reported, hence my lamentable failure to make the link earlier, but one or two of the more radical journals printed what detail there was, and fortunately I included those reports in my own library. Alistair

McLachlan was one of the names mentioned in the very earliest reports on the scandal – a raid on a house of ill repute on the outskirts of the city – and note was made that the police had been working on the basis of information supplied by a person or persons unknown. That person, I have now discovered, was none other than Sir Campbell McLachlan.

"McLachlan knew that a blind eye was routinely turned to the more regrettable actions of young men of a certain standing, but wished to scare his brother into reformation before the family name was irrevocably sullied. Crucially, however, as a member of the government, he could be confident that such an affair would be hushed up. So he contacted Potter, a man with a reputation in the force for a strong sense of duty and morality, and provided him with the information he needed to lead a raid on the disreputable premises. This Potter did, and though the matter ended up damaging his career, the younger McLachlan's name featured in no official report. Sir Campbell was obviously impressed enough by Potter's discretion to keep in touch and, later, to take his advice on how best to deal with the gang problem. Advice that came directly from Galloway."

"That's about right, Mr. Holmes," Galloway announced in the silence that followed Holmes's explanation. "Potter already had McLachlan's ear when I got in touch with him. In fact, it was that what put the idea in my head. I'd heard that there was a policeman, a right eager sort, who'd joined with some old duffer, and intended to put an end to businesses like mine. I admit, I thought to have him done away with, first off, but it doesn't do to waste something useful, I always say, and I reckoned the two of them could prove very useful indeed."

Galloway had obviously decided that his best chance of avoiding the rope was to divulge as much information as he could without implicating any of his own men. He appeared at ease, standing before us, almost amused by Holmes's recital, in fact. We could have been a group of friends discussing a play we had seen, or a trip to the country. But I remembered the bodies he had left in his wake, and the thought brought bitter bile to the back of my throat.

"And Miss McLachlan?" My voice cracked as I spoke, anger making me indistinct, but to my surprise it was Holmes who replied.

"Galloway did not have Miss McLachlan murdered, Watson. I thought you would have realised that by now. Why would he? McLachlan was already doing exactly what he desired. Why would he risk that by killing his aunt? Besides, even if you do not trust his words just now, he had already told you – albeit unknowingly – when he had no reason whatever to lie. What was it that you overheard him say while you spied on him from your little storeroom? *No public demonstrations. Avoid making too much noise.* Obviously, Galloway had no part in the death of Miss McLachlan."

He turned to Galloway. "But do you know who did kill the unfortunate lady?"

Galloway shrugged, a thin smile playing across his lips, and in that instant I profoundly hoped that whatever help he was to the police, it would not be enough to keep him from the scaffold.

"No idea," he said. "It was a bit awkward, if I'm being honest. Potter came to see me. Said that if I'd killed the old bird, he'd go straight to the authorities, tell them everything, and take whatever punishment he was due. I had the devil of a job convincing him it wasn't any of mine did the deed. Look to the other gangs, I said. They're the ones who want to nobble McLachlan."

"You did send the note regarding Watson's alleged debt, though?"

"Yes," Galloway said slowly. "In fact, I got Potter to do that.

That did make me laugh; sending Potter to deliver a note that we both knew would end up back in his hands. It was too good an opportunity to miss, what with the doctor already the only one suspected. All it took was that, and a bit of play-acting in the yard, and every man, inside and out, believed he was a murderer. Telling Potter to drag his heels and obstruct you helped, of course. A silver lining to a sticky situation, you might say."

"But why, Galloway? What did it really gain you? You did not kill Miss McLachlan. Why blame me?" There was no doubt he was telling the truth – with Collins's murder irrefutably laid at his door, he had nothing to gain by denying another murder. I would soon have to consider the question of who *had* killed McLachlan's aunt and gone to such lengths to implicate me, but for the moment I would settle for the answer to that one question.

"I already told you," Galloway said, shaking his head, as though disappointed in me. "Don't you remember, the first time we had one of our little chats? I told you then. Our paths have crossed before now, only you didn't know it. Looked at in one light, in fact, you're the reason I'm here right now."

At this unexpected statement, Holmes jerked upright, and his eyes snapped open.

"We are the reason?" I asked before he could speak. "But there is no case of ours in which you were involved."

"I realise you have had a trying time, Watson, but do pay attention," Holmes barked, his interest evidently reawakened. "He said we were unaware of the connection. Go on, Galloway. How did our paths cross? Presumably as a result of an investigation in which you were only tangentially involved?"

"Well done, Mr. Holmes, well done. Exactly that. And more than once, in fact. The first time was when we were doing a bit of work for the Mendicant Society, ten years since at least. You broke up that little club, and the police happened to catch up three of my men who were unfortunately delivering to the premises at the time. Then there was Charlie Milverton. We'd put out a handy pile to buy a juicy tale from a certain under-butler and sold it on to Milverton, but he got croaked before we could collect our payment, and no way of making it back."

Holmes's fingers drummed on the desk. "Fascinating," he murmured, then, "but though undoubtedly vexing to you, neither occasion led to your current confinement?"

"That was more... indirect, you might say. You remember Andrew Tankard, who you sent to the gallows in the spring? Well, he was another who owed us money – a great deal of money, in fact – but defaulted on account of his inconvenient demise. Writing off his debt as we had to left us in urgent need of funds. So I went cap in hand to that backstabbing swine Adams and asked to be cut into one of his schemes. And he betrayed me the first chance he had." He shook his head ruefully. "I can't really blame him – I might have done the same thing myself – but I only had to approach him at all on account of you. Anyway, I reckoned I owed you for that, even more so once I realised the good doctor here hadn't offed McLachlan's auntie after all."

I could remain silent no longer. "You condemned me in revenge for something I did not even know had occurred?" I exclaimed, outraged.

Galloway shrugged. "You and Mr. Holmes, you treat what you do as a game. It's something to amuse you, to pass the time. The game's afoot, isn't that what he says? But you're wrong. It's no game, and people get hurt when you act like it is.

"I told you, crime is a business, no different to any other. Most people work for me because there's nothing else they can do, but you act as though they've got a choice. You think the scum of the rookeries and the dregs of the slums could do whatever they wanted, be whatever they wanted, if they just worked harder. I'm telling you, they can't. Surely you learned that in here? The honest ones try, and they end up dying in the same rotten houses they were born in, with no more money in their pockets or food in their bellies than they had then.

"Join up with me, though, and you might still die in a gutter, but you'll have a life worth living in the meantime. My men rely on me to feed their families and keep a roof over their heads. They'd be in the workhouse or in the streets if it weren't for me and my business.

"Answer me this, Doctor: why does it matter to you if a bank gets robbed or a lord has to pay through the nose to get back the letters he wrote to some pretty factory girl? Who's injured? The bank's insured and his lordship can afford it. But the money taken makes its way down from me to my boys, and from them to their families, and because of it people are fed and have somewhere to live that isn't quite as full of filth and disease.

"I said to you before, you only see two types of criminals, and only concern yourself with one. Gents like yourself and Mr. Holmes, playing the same game as you, only doing it from the other side. But I told you, there are other types too. Only we're not the sort you'd put in one of your books, and maybe you're right, maybe we're just sprats swimming among sharks. Still, though, you interfere in our business, even if you don't know it, not giving a thought to the consequences. Because there ain't any consequences for you."

As he spoke, the veneer of amused detachment slipped for the first time, and I glimpsed the truth of the man underneath. There was genuine indignation in his voice and a ring in his words of the low station from which he had come.

"But watching you hang? That'd teach Sherlock Holmes that his little games have higher stakes than he thought."

After that, Galloway would say nothing more, except to provide the name of an eminent lawyer and request that he be contacted as soon as possible. After a fruitless few minutes of questioning, during which Holmes looked thoughtful but said nothing, Lestrade threw his hands up in annoyance and ordered the sergeant to take him away, leaving just we three alone in the governor's office.

"He'll swing, of course. Keegan has already offered to turn queen's evidence, and knows enough to condemn him," the inspector said, offering me a cigarette. I leaned across to take it, and Holmes gave a start and reached into the pocket of his soiled prison jacket.

"My apologies, Watson. I had almost forgotten that I had brought you this."

In his hand, he held my pipe and a pouch of tobacco.

"Lestrade is confident that you are a free man, too, for now at least," he added as I lit the bowl and inhaled deeply.

Lestrade smiled in confirmation. "You are indeed, Doctor. Potter is being taken into custody as we speak. All his outstanding cases will be viewed as suspect. Indeed, though I would not like my saying it to go beyond this room, I would not be surprised if they are all abandoned and Potter himself allowed quietly to retire. It's not that long since Palmer and Meiklejohn brought the Yard near to ruin; I doubt the authorities will want another scandal."

When I had previously considered that moment, I had imagined that my primary feeling would be of relief, tempered perhaps by indignation that I had ever been suspected, but in the event I most keenly experienced a sense of disappointment that my name would never now be entirely clear of suspicion. Granted, due to the efforts of Mycroft Holmes, my shame was not widely known, but I would much have preferred that any doubts be unequivocally laid to rest.

Still, the prospect of walking out of the gates of Holloway a free man was a wonderful one. I smoked my pipe, and thought of Hardie, who would never do so, and gave thanks for the friendship of Sherlock Holmes.

Chapter Twenty-Seven

The rest of the morning passed in a frenzy of paperwork and interviews, as I first told Lestrade everything that had occurred, then repeated myself in a formal statement to a sergeant from Scotland Yard. After that, Holmes harried the red-faced official who had been sent to run the prison in Keegan's soon-to-be-permanent absence until all the relevant forms had been completed for my immediate release.

As I stood in the reception area Holmes walked up and handed me my final release paper. His face was grim, however, as he passed on shocking news.

"Inspector Potter somehow managed to convince his escort to allow him to return home to collect a change of clothes rather than go directly to Scotland Yard. Left alone for a mere minute, he took a revolver he had secreted in his bedroom and shot himself. He died instantly." He shook his head sadly. "Whatever his sins, he is beyond our judgement now."

Though Potter had played a significant role in extending my

recent misery, when I thought of him, the thing I remembered most clearly was the look on his face the last time I had seen him, when he had said he bore me no personal ill will and was only following orders. His expression had been that of a man weighed down by sorrow and regret. Now that those orders had come to naught I found that, more than any other emotion, I pitied him. Holmes was correct. It was no longer our place to judge him.

"The others?" I asked quietly, handing the gate guard my release form.

"Shapley, May and seven other guards have been taken into custody," Holmes replied. "All Galloway's men are currently being processed by Lestrade's officers for a variety of offences. Meanwhile, Keegan and Galloway each wish to give evidence against the other. It is not yet clear who will be granted that particular boon, but while Keegan is corrupt to the core, Galloway is a killer. He will hang, I'm sure."

We passed through the gate and out into the road where, as before, a hansom stood waiting for us. This time, however, Lestrade was not present; he had a great deal to do at Scotland Yard and had left in the early hours of the morning. He had promised to meet with us at Baker Street that evening.

I lowered myself into a seat and felt the exhaustion I had been fighting press down on me like a physical weight. I could not sleep, however, before asking Holmes if he had any idea who had killed Sarah McLachlan. He stared at me for what seemed an eternity, then slowly shook his head.

"I am truly sorry, my dear fellow, but though I have spent the last two weeks on what I thought was the correct trail, it proved barren in the end, and I am no closer to a solution than I was when last I saw you."

I could see it pained him to make such an admission, and I hurried to remind him that I would have died in that attic had he not so timeously appeared to save my life. He nodded, but I knew Holmes well enough to know that he would not be so easily consoled. I had no energy to do so, however, and so allowed my eyes to close as the carriage rocked its way back to Baker Street and home.

I barely made it to my room before I collapsed onto the bed and slept the deepest and most contented sleep of my life.

When I awoke, it was evening. Outside, the night was foggy and grey, but a fire burned brightly in the hearth. Holmes greeted me with a vague wave of the hand, as though I had only been away for the afternoon rather than for weeks. I had a great deal to ask him, but first I was in grave need of a long bath and a good meal.

Once I had completed my toilet and dressed in more civilised garb than I had lately been used to, Mrs. Hudson appeared with a pot of tea and a fine supper of chops, which I fell upon with relish. It was only as I completed my meal that Holmes came over, and dropped the day's newspaper, open to an inner page, in front of me. The section he wished me to read was largely taken up with a report on Harrods' new stepless escalator, but underneath, in a small box, he had underlined a report that Inspector Jonathan Potter of Scotland Yard had been tragically killed in a domestic accident. There was no mention of Galloway or Holloway Prison.

"It was inevitable that Potter's betrayals would be buried along with him," Holmes observed, as he slid into a chair opposite me and lit a cigarette. "Nobody who counts would be well served by full disclosure, and several would be badly affected. Mycroft is of the opinion that Keegan will be convicted of a minor charge, something of a technical nature he suspects, and will serve no time in prison. Only Galloway will feel the full weight of the law."

He blew smoke thoughtfully towards the ceiling. "I am no political animal, as you know, Watson, but I find myself somewhat dissatisfied with that. I reject his claim that I give no thought to the consequences of my activities, of course, but still... I am inclined to give some consideration to his claim that a certain type of person has no choice but crime, and that it is this sort who inevitably pays the price, one way or the other."

I too had given some thought to Galloway while I waited for my release. That he was a violent man was beyond dispute. That he was a callous killer I had seen for myself. But he was fiercely loyal to his own – as loyal to his men, in fact, as Major McLachlan was to his. How many of us would have chosen the noose over the betrayal of our friends? I hoped that I would if it came to it, but still I preferred not to be put to the test. And he had killed the man who murdered Hardie – the very task I had promised I would do myself. In extremis, were we so different?

I decided not to dwell on the question. Besides, I had others to put to Holmes.

"It would certainly appear that every mystery raised by Holloway Prison has now been neatly put to bed, but I do wish, on a personal level, that we had been able to shed more light on the murder which placed me there in the first place."

I hoped that I did not sound as though I were accusing Holmes of failure, for I was sure that he had done more than any other living man could have, but even so, I could not keep a note of disappointment from my voice. Holmes at once picked up on my tone.

"I can only apologise, Watson. It pains me greatly that on the one occasion when you most had need of my deductive and analytical powers, I failed you. Worse, in my hunger to discover the answer, I was forced to abandon you for the past week, when I should have been at your side. You were almost killed because I chose to follow a barren trail. I would never have forgiven myself if my negligence had led to your death."

"But it did not," I pointed out. "You arrived at the most opportune moment! Though I am curious to know exactly where you had been?"

Holmes ground out his cigarette and shook his head. "Nowhere useful, Watson. A blind alley in which I wasted several days to no great purpose." He pinched the bridge of his nose, and sighed. "Rest assured that I will not cease my investigations, but for the moment, there is nothing positive I can tell you."

I could have pressed him, but he was obviously fatigued (I wondered suddenly if he had slept at all) and had no wish to discuss what he perceived as a failure. I nodded my understanding, and turned the subject to less painful matters. I must be content with my freedom, I thought – twenty-four hours earlier I would have been satisfied with my life, after all.

A week later, I received official confirmation via Lestrade that no further action would be taken against me in relation to the death of Sarah McLachlan. Major McLachlan was reportedly outraged (I could hardly blame him, in the circumstances) and threatened to bring a private prosecution against me, until Mycroft again intervened. Whatever he said, the major let the matter drop entirely and with nobody else interested in revisiting what had become an extremely embarrassing affair for the government, the death of an elderly lady of uncertain wits quickly faded from the memory of those few who had ever known about it. It was not exoneration, but I told myself it would have to do.

Galloway was hanged for the murder of Isaac Collins just before Christmas, though the trial was little reported. Keegan was sentenced to one year in prison, suspended for two years, and retired to Ireland of all places. In between times, I arranged for Albert Hardie's body to be interred in a small London graveyard, which I intend to visit each year on the anniversary of his death.

With that, I believed I was done with the whole nightmarish experience. Holmes and I returned to our previous life and were soon caught up in a wide range of cases. I cannot say that the absence of a definitive resolution did not bother me, but I believed I had moved on, and left the McLachlans behind me.

And then one evening more than a year later, as I sat at the table reading over my notes on the affair of the Napoleon busts, and Holmes dozed by the fire, I heard the sound of raised voices from downstairs and the thunder of booted feet running up to our rooms. The door was flung open, exposing a red-faced and panting Lestrade.

"He's back in the country, Mr. Holmes," he gasped. "Alistair McLachlan's come home!"

In an instant, Holmes was transformed. He leapt to his feet and had his coat in hand before I could react. His agitation was something to behold, for all that Lestrade stood in the doorway grinning like the Cheshire cat.

"Come, Watson!" he commanded, but I had now taken a moment to process what Lestrade had said, and I was determined to go no further until I knew exactly where we were going, and why.

"Come where, Holmes?" I snapped. "What interest have any of us in Alistair McLachlan now? Or are we to set off into the night every time a fragment from the unlamented past washes up in England?"

"By no means," returned Holmes, gathering up my coat and hat and throwing them to me. "But there is more than one fragment of our past in England tonight."

"How–?" I began, but Holmes was in a fever to be away and had already chivvied Lestrade to the top of the stairs.

"Time is of the essence, Watson. We must not let McLachlan slip away or all is lost!" When he saw I still hesitated, reluctant to open old wounds to no obvious purpose, he went on, "Did I not tell you that I would not cease my investigations until I had solved the case? McLachlan holds the key to the resolution of the murder of his aunt, and your own absolute exoneration! Do not forget your revolver!"

He did not wait for further response from me, but followed Lestrade down the stairs at a run. I pulled on my coat and retrieved my revolver from my room, then raced after him, a wild hope flaring in my breast that I had spent the past year attempting to subdue.

Chapter Twenty-Eight

The police carriage in which Lestrade had arrived stood waiting in the road, the horses' breath steaming in the cold night air. As soon as we were inside, Lestrade poked his head out of the window and ordered the driver to move off.

"You know where to go," he shouted. "And be quick as you can about it!"

He fell back into his seat as the driver took him at his word, and whipped the horses forward with a jerk. Soon we were thundering through London, then out of the city and into the country. Decent town roads gave way to country lanes and finally rain-sodden tracks, but neither Holmes nor Lestrade would explain where we were going. The most that Holmes would say was that tonight could be the moment at which a conclusion was reached, or it could be the end of any possibility of success. Either way, he asked me to wait until we reached our destination and to trust him that all would be revealed there.

Fortunately, it was not a long journey and, having waited twelve months already – and having given up any hope of resolution – I was able to curb my impatience for the hour it took.

Finally, at five minutes before eleven, we turned onto a dirt track, at the end of which I could see a low farmhouse, and stopped directly behind another police carriage.

"Almost there, Doctor," said Lestrade with the same grin that he had worn at Baker Street and which had reappeared on his face every time he looked at me. He opened the door and jumped down, before crossing to the other carriage and engaging the driver in conversation.

Holmes also alighted and I followed, so that we stood together in the freezing darkness. Not a sound could be heard but the panting of the horses and the low murmur of Lestrade's conversation. The only light visible for miles around came from the windows of the farmhouse.

Lestrade concluded his business with the other driver and returned to us, still smiling.

"Our quarry is inside, Mr. Holmes," he whispered. "Jenkins followed McLachlan here and saw them both at the window not two minutes since." He gestured to the driver of our carriage. "You and Jenkins go round the back, in case they make a run for it. I don't expect any rough stuff, but the doctor and I are both armed, if there is. Mr. Holmes," he said, turning to address my friend, "perhaps it'd be best if I led the way."

Holmes nodded. Lestrade pulled a pistol from his jacket pocket and held it in front of him as he walked slowly down the path to the farmhouse door, Holmes and I in his wake. The two police drivers quickly split off from our party and disappeared into the darkness.

Viewed close up, the farmhouse itself was undistinguished. Single storeyed, it was around thirty feet long, with a shingle roof and a heavy wooden door, bracketed on either side by long, shuttered windows. A small vegetable garden ran along one side with what looked like peas growing in tall rows just visible at the rear. Light shone through the cracks in the shutters on one side of the door.

Lestrade walked up to the door and rapped on it hard with the butt of his revolver. The sound was louder than I expected, but not so loud as to drown out the sounds of surprise from within. I gripped my own weapon more tightly as one of the shutters was pulled slightly open for a second and then as swiftly closed again.

A moment passed, before the door to the farmhouse slowly opened and a figure emerged, lit from behind by lamps hung in what looked like a kitchen.

Alistair McLachlan looked tired. His jacket was crumpled and his eyes dark with shadows. His mouth hung open and he panted slightly as he spoke, as though from exercise, or fright.

"Good evening, Inspector Lestrade. This is an unexpected visit. And Mr. Holmes and Dr. Watson, too! Quite the party, indeed." He gave a tiny bow in my direction. "I heard, of course, that you had been released, if not actually acquitted. My congratulations, sir. I did say that I knew you to be innocent, did I not?"

He made no move to invite us in, although a light drizzle had begun to fall. I was puzzled, I admit, that Lestrade did not simply arrest McLachlan where he stood, if he and Holmes were so certain of his guilt, but I had travelled this far based on my trust in my two companions. I was willing to travel a little further.

"What brings you back to England, Mr. McLachlan?" Lestrade asked.

"A family visit, Inspector. I shall be here and gone within a day, I hope." McLachlan smiled nervously and ran his palm across his thin hair.

"And yet you choose to come straight from the docks to this remote farmhouse? You did not think to stay with your brother in town?"

"He... he does not know I am here. I wished to surprise him. We have been estranged since the death of my aunt, you know," McLachlan's voice grew stronger as he continued with more conviction, "but I have reason to believe a reconciliation may be possible."

Holmes ostentatiously turned up his collar beside me and settled his hat more firmly upon his head. "Might we continue this conversation inside, Mr. McLachlan?" he asked. "I cannot speak for my friends, but I am becoming quite soaked in this rain."

He took a step towards the door, but McLachlan pulled it close to him. "It is not convenient, I am afraid," he protested. "I am extremely tired after the voyage from France. I am sure you understand. Perhaps in the morning...?"

Something fell in the shadowed room behind him and we all heard a door open, followed by a muffled exclamation and the sound of the door closing again.

"It would only be for a moment, and only we three, sir," Lestrade said pointedly. "My men will remain outside, of course."

He put a hand on the door and began to push it open, while McLachlan attempted to keep it closed with his foot, all the while complaining indignantly. I was about to add my own weight to Lestrade's when the door was dragged open from inside and a girl stepped into the light.

The girl – a young woman really, now that I saw her more clearly – was the same one who had left me with the corpse of Sarah McLachlan. There was more colour in her cheeks and her hair was darker than I remembered, but there was no mistaking her, even illumined only from behind by lamplight. Nor was there any mistaking the shotgun she held in her hands.

McLachlan took a step back, his face set in a grimace. "Mary…" he said, but the girl gave no sign she had heard him.

"Stay where you are, if you please," she ordered, allowing the shotgun to weave menacingly in front of her. "There's nowhere to go, Alistair. They would not be here if they did not know the truth, but I'll not go anywhere before I've had my say."

The thought crossed my mind that we could potentially disarm her by rushing at her all at once, but before I could make such a suggestion to my companions, Holmes stepped in front of me and addressed the girl in quiet, measured tones.

"You are Mary Parr, I presume?" he began, and though the name seemed familiar, I could not place it exactly. More than one fragment of our past, Holmes had said, but whatever the exact nature of our earlier acquaintance, it remained a mystery to me for now.

The girl nodded sharply. "I am. And if you know my name, you no doubt also recall my sister?"

Something imprecise stirred in my memory. I reached for it, but it slipped away even as I thought I had it.

Holmes obviously knew who she meant, however. He had expected this woman to be here with McLachlan.

"I do indeed. An attractive girl, as I recall, though somewhat unfortunate in her choice of sweethearts."

Unexpectedly, Mary Parr scowled in my direction as Holmes described her sister. "You may think so, Mr. Holmes," she countered, switching her gaze to him, "but that says more about you than it does about my sister."

"Indeed." Holmes seemed apologetic. He gave no indication that he was even aware of the gun or the fact that Mary Parr held it a scant foot away from his midriff.

"Yes, indeed." She shifted her feet on the wet ground and took a half step backwards, as though in recognition that Holmes had strayed too close. "But let's leave that to one side for now. You undoubtedly have questions for me, and I am happy to answer them, where I can. I do not," she concluded without obvious emotion, "expect to escape the consequences of my actions."

It was an odd scene altogether. Holmes held his hands behind him, his head cocked slightly to one side, while Mary Parr stood straight-backed three feet or so before him, the two of them as composed as if they had been discussing the weather or tactics for bridge. Lestrade shuffled from one foot to the other at my shoulder, and McLachlan coughed in the silence, but other than that there was no sound in the farmyard. Had it not been for the weapon pointed at us, we might have been visitors stopping for directions to the nearest inn.

Holmes broke the silence almost apologetically. "You do not deny the murder of Sarah McLachlan, then?"

"Would there be any point in denying it? The act is hardly important, only the reasons. But yes, I killed the old lady. She's been addled in her wits for years, you know. She's called me her sister before now, when I helped dress her, so it was easy enough to convince her to come with me, even though I'd been away for months. I waited until everyone was out or asleep and let myself in by the kitchen door, then made my way to her room. I knew she'd have been made ready for bed, and right enough, there she was, sitting by her mirror, talking to herself as she often did at night. I told her that we were going on a holiday, a few days away in the town. She was so happy to see me, I thought she might bring someone running, the amount of noise she made.

"I put her good robe on her, and we left the same way I came in, with nobody any the wiser. I'd picked up the knife from the drawer on my way in, alongside a couple of other familiar bits and pieces, and she followed after me like a faithful hound. She'd wandered before, you see. She liked to be outside in the night time. We slipped out the kitchen door and into a cab I'd arranged to collect us, then straight to Grandma's, simple as that."

"Once there you murdered her. Though not straight away, I think. You hesitated."

"No, not straight away. I'd brought along some meringue since it was her favourite, and she was eating it in the bed while I hung the picture and whatnot. And she smiled across at me, and called me a good sister, and I didn't think I could go through with it. She was a decent sort, really, only unlucky to be so convenient to me right then. But it had to be done. So I sat on the bed and brushed her hair until she was sleeping and then – when I couldn't see into her eyes any longer – I stabbed her in the chest."

"Using a rag to stem the initial flow of blood?"

"Yes. I kept my coat on, too, as I couldn't risk getting any on my dress, for fear that Dr. Watson would spot it. But there was more blood than I expected."

Holmes shrugged. "There always is," he said simply.

She glanced at Holmes with sadness in her eyes. "She didn't struggle, but the blood got on my coat, even with the rag. She just lay there with her eyes closed, and her breathing got quieter and then she was gone. I felt her sag under me."

"The other wounds were post mortem?" Holmes asked. "You administered them after she was already dead?" he clarified, catching the girl's look of confusion.

"I think so. She twitched a bit at a couple of them, but I couldn't stop, even if I wanted to. I needed a horror, you see. I wanted nobody to doubt that the killer was a monster."

"Of course," said Holmes. "But first there was the murder weapon to discard. You could not leave it in the room. You had intended to take it away with you, but your coat was too bloody to wear."

She nodded.

"So you stripped a pillow case and used it to slingshot the knife into the scaffolding next door?"

"I couldn't think what else to do. I had to meet Dr. Watson, and had no time to bury it, nor the nerve to stand mid-street and throw it away. I would have come back for it later, but I hadn't reckoned on there being a policeman there all the time. As it was, I barely got him back to the room and locked inside before a constable turned up in the street."

"You slipped the key to your grandmother as you left, of course? And she returned it to the inside of the lock as Constable Howie and the others stood in the room with Watson."

The girl said nothing, but tightened her grip on the shotgun. Holmes did not appear overly concerned. "You will not implicate her? That is commendable, I suppose."

"Not that it matters. She's long gone now. Alistair's money paid for that. You'll never find her."

"Ah yes, Alistair's money. Thank you for bringing that up, Miss Parr. I had feared I would have to tease from you the second bird you killed with your single stone, and I would be interested to know which motivation came first. Did you kill your former employer so that Mr. McLachlan would come into his inheritance and so be free to marry you, or did you do so in order to punish Watson for what you perceived as his offences against your family?"

In the past, observing Holmes in full flight had often been a pleasure, but on this occasion, for the first time, I recognised that it could be a painful experience too. The bare facts of the murder had been exposed, and my own innocence established, or so I thought. But now it seemed that I had in some way been responsible, if only as a motive.

I remembered Lucy Parr.

A few years previously we had taken on a case in which a wealthy banker had believed his son to have stolen a famous gem, the Beryl Coronet. The family, I now recalled, had employed a maid by the name of Lucy Parr, given to ill-advised romantic assignations. She was not an especially memorable person, though I had given her a small part in the version of the story published in *The Strand*. But I could not see why the girl's sister should have any enmity towards me on account of the case. Lucy had not been involved in any criminality and besides, Holmes was the detective, not I.

While I had been thinking, McLachlan had pushed himself forward, and now stood alongside Mary Parr.

"Do not answer that, Mary," he said in his soft voice. "My fiancée suffers from nerves and is prone to flights of fancy. She has nothing more to say until she has spoken to a lawyer."

Mary Parr was not, however, a woman who was easily silenced, even by a man for whom she had killed.

"Don't be ridiculous, Alistair dearest," she said with a smile. "Involving that animal was a late addition to my plan, Mr. Holmes, but an inspired one, I think. Originally, all I wanted was for Alistair to be free of his brother and able to marry me, as we both desired. I see you looking at me doubtfully, Inspector. What would one of the gentry want with a mere maid, except a momentary dalliance, you're thinking. But we were in love, and love knows nothing of class."

As though to prove her assertion, McLachlan placed a hand on her shoulder, and she briefly pressed her cheek against it.

"Even after I was dismissed from service and Alistair warned to have nothing more to do with me, we continued to meet in secret. I might have been happy with that, but Alistair wanted more than a few snatched hours here and there."

"I had had enough of the rake's life," McLachlan interrupted. "I had met the woman I wished to spend my life with, and I intended to do so, no matter what the cost to me socially and financially."

"You see, Inspector? How could I not love a man like that? But for all his willingness to give up all he had, my Alistair was not built for the poverty that would ensue if he simply ignored the wishes of his family.

"It did not take me long to think of his aunt, who barely knew her own name, but who held the key to his freedom. If she were to die, everything would be as it should. I planned how best to do it, so that Alistair could not possibly be suspected, choosing a spot far from the house and a night when he was known to be at home. It was a risk using my grandmother's, but she had long spoken of leaving London and going back home, and I knew that Alistair would well be able to afford to send her, if all went to plan.

"And then, as I turned out of Linhope Street one evening, wondering what night would be best to carry out the deed, who should I see but Dr. John Watson, the heartless brute who had so grievously wronged my sister. The rest, I have already told you."

I had heard as much of this insinuation as I was willing to accept and so, before Holmes could say another word, I stepped forward, ignoring the gun entirely in my anger, and confronted Miss Parr.

"That is twice now you have described me in inhuman terms and I am at a loss to understand why. What have I done to you or your sister, that you feel such loathing for me, and wish me so much harm?"

Holmes answered before she could. "Because she blames you, and not I, for her sister's death, of course. That is correct, is it not, Miss Parr?"

The look the girl turned on me was filled with a hatred so intense that I almost flinched. She began to speak, though not to answer either of our questions directly.

"My sister never worked again after she was dismissed by Mr. Holder. No reference, you see. Precious little chance of a decent marriage either. So she moved to the country, and hid away, waiting for time to pass. Waiting for people to forget what was only a few lines in a tale most of them hadn't even read. That's what she thought, anyway.

"But people didn't forget. They didn't get the chance to, not with Mr. Sherlock Holmes in all the papers, and Dr. Watson turning his adventures into entertainments. So one night she took herself into the woods round the back of the house she was staying in and cut her own throat. It was snowing so hard that even when she was missed it took them two days to find her under the drifts. I didn't even hear about it for a fortnight, not until my next free Sunday. No point. I wouldn't be given leave for a suicide. Nor a wanton woman, neither. Major McLachlan's got *views* on that sort of thing."

She spat out "views" as though it were the foulest profanity imaginable. But she was not finished.

"That is the third reason why you chose Miss McLachlan as your victim," Holmes interrupted. "To damage Sir Campbell."

She tilted her head to one side, considering the suggestion. "A little, perhaps," she admitted. "Maybe there's something in that. But mainly she was the one who could give Alistair his life back.

Everything else followed from that."

She stared at each of us in turn, daring us to speak.

"Does that answer your question, Doctor?" she asked. She gripped the shotgun stock so tightly that her knuckles stood out white against the redness of her skin as though bleached. "Maybe not," she continued, "but I've got one of my own to ask you."

Her mouth twitched as though she intended to smile then decided not to, but there was no warmth in her face, and she gave no other sign of relaxing her guard. When she spoke, her voice cracked and wavered, in an excess of pain.

"Would you have recalled my sister at all, if you hadn't been reminded by your friend and I?"

I hesitated to reply, for I was unsure in my own mind whether I would have recollected Lucy Parr unaided. I hoped so, but had to admit to myself that what I mainly recollected, even now, was my own writing about the case, not the girl herself.

"Did you think my sister wanton, Dr. Watson?" Mary Parr broke into my thoughts. "Is that why you painted her as entirely fallen when she had simply been unwise? Is that why you destroyed her life for the crime of being foolish and gullible and believing herself to be in love?"

The accusation was as venomous as it was unexpected and I flinched inwardly as she spoke. But I could not deny there was a degree of truth in her assertion, once I had placed her sister in my mind. I had indeed exaggerated the girl's nature, adding a little spice, as my editor put it. Readers loved Holmes's deductions, he'd said with an ingratiating smile, but it was my own little artistic additions that set the stories apart – and besides, a scorned woman of low morals never went amiss. I should have said no, but he had just bought me a splendid lunch and in the glow of several glasses of excellent port his flattery seemed no more than credit given where it was due.

I knew, of course, that I could not offer that as excuse, nor did I want to. Two women were dead and at least one more would join them in due course. I had no excuses to offer.

"Miss Parr," I began but I found I had no explanation beyond the bald truth, and wretched though I felt I had no stomach for that. The irony of the writer being bereft of words did not elude me.

Not that it mattered. I had delayed my reply for too long.

With a snarl, Mary Parr took a single step forward and jammed the barrels of the shotgun into the flesh below my chin. Obviously, I could not see her finger tighten on the trigger, but I fancied I heard the smallest *click* as it was pulled back.

McLachlan staggered backwards in shock and from the corner of my eye I saw Lestrade raise his revolver, but I knew it was too late to do anything. Of the two police drivers who had gone around the back there was no sign. Only Holmes knew what to do.

"I am sorry, Miss Parr," he said loudly, "but you are about to kill the wrong man."

For less than a heartbeat, my life hung in the balance, and then I felt the shotgun barrels move imperceptibly away from my throat.

"Whatever his other faults, Miss Parr," Holmes continued in a steady voice, "I have never known Watson deliberately do harm to any woman, nor do I believe he has done so now." His voice was soft, almost sorrowful. The girl tried to speak but he held his two hands up, palms out. "Please, let me finish. It has been suggested to me recently that I give insufficient consideration to the impact my investigations have on those involved in them only at a remove."

He took a step forward, and carefully moved the shotgun until it pointed it at his own chest. "If Watson embellished the role of your sister in one of his scribbles, then the fault lies not with him, but with me. It was I who involved him in my work and I who encouraged him to write down the circumstances of my cases. He has on occasion paid greater attention to the more sensational aspects of a case than I would have liked, but on some level I was content with the elevated role he created for me. And for the 'genius' Watson created truly to stand out, he needs must populate the background with lesser figures, with whom his readers can more fully identify. That they are, at least in part, fictional, he and I both know, but obviously that is not true of everyone." He gave a tired sigh, and pinched the bridge of his nose as though in pain. "I can only offer my most heartfelt apologies, of scant consolation though they may be, for allowing Watson to paint so false a picture of your sister, as a result of which she was so grievously harmed."

For a long moment, everything was silent. The thin rain continued to fall and in the backlight from the farmhouse, Mary Parr's figure seemed to waver in the mist like spray. One of her feet slipped backwards in the mud and the shotgun dipped slightly, but Holmes made no move to take it from her. Instead, he held out his hands in an oddly penitent manner, palms upwards, and she laid the heavy weapon into them. His long fingers closed round it, then he lowered it to the ground.

"If you will go with Inspector Lestrade," he said quietly, "he will have further questions to put to you."

Lestrade raised his head sharply, as though surprised to be mentioned, but quickly remembered his duty and pulled her round in order to place handcuffs on her. Alistair McLachlan hurried to take her hand before the inspector could do so, however. "I never wanted any of this, you know," he said unhappily. "But once she'd done it, what could I do but try to protect her?"

He put his jacket around Mary Parr's shoulders and I watched them trudge away into the darkness, Lestrade vigilant but unobtrusive at their side.

Holmes and I stood in the increasingly heavy rain, saying nothing, for some time, each alone with his thoughts. I should have felt a huge relief that it was all over, but in truth I felt only numbness and a great sadness for the Parr sisters – and shame for my part in their ruin.

Eventually, I felt the cold rain seep past my collar and run down my back. I turned to Holmes, barely visible in the dying light.

"Time to go home, Watson," he said. "Mrs. Hudson will be waiting up, and I am in need of a pipe and a good night's sleep. Tomorrow evening, we should invite Lestrade to Baker Street, and I shall provide the full explanation I know you desire."

Chapter Twenty-Nine

The next day, Lestrade visited Baker Street once again.

On this occasion, however, he arrived more sedately and accepted a whisky and a seat by the fire. At first, he seemed uncomfortable to be in Baker Street as a guest. He sat stiffly and silently in his chair, glass balanced on his knee and his bowler still gripped in one hand. It was Holmes, unexpectedly, who cajoled him to relax a little and gradually, and perhaps under the influence of a second whisky, he settled back and became more animated in his speech.

We talked for a short while of recent news, then Holmes stretched out his long legs, lit his pipe, and offered the explanation he had promised.

"Do you remember Potter saying that the urchins of the streets come and go and nobody can say where or when? That is not entirely true, as he would have known. It is true that *we* do not value them, but they do value themselves. Not a single street Arab disappears in this city, but his friends know it. I set Wiggins and his associates about the task of tracking down any of their kind who had vanished on the day after the murder of Miss McLachlan. They found no one for whom they could not account, but Wiggins did discover something connected to another matter I had placed before him.

"It seems that three days after the murder, a carriage drove into Linhope Street and picked up Mrs. Soames, the landlady who was so concerned for her elderly tenant's safety. You will be interested to know that a young woman was observed already to be in the carriage. You will, I think, be even more interested to learn that on the doors of the carriage were emblazoned the twin horns of the roebuck."

"Alistair McLachlan!"

"The very same," Holmes confirmed. "Initially I had instructed Wiggins to take part in the search for the girl and had discounted the younger brother entirely. However, after hearing of your meeting with him, I asked Wiggins instead to watch out for any unusual activity at the McLachlan house. He rightly assumed that the family carriage leaving in the dead of night counted as such an activity."

"All well and good, Holmes, and obviously in hindsight you were correct, but nothing that McLachlan said in our meeting struck me as suggestive of guilt. Quite the opposite, in fact. What did you see at second hand that I, who was actually present, did not?"

"I believe I remarked at the time that I had no faith in your ability to judge personality without supporting evidence. Any man may commit any crime, in my experience. As to Mr. McLachlan particularly, I was immediately struck by two things. First, the certainty with which he proclaimed your innocence. No man could possibly be so certain about a matter so important on so brief an acquaintance. The only explanation was that he either knew the identity of the real killer, or knew for a fact that it could not be you."

"And the second thing?"

"McLachlan called the girl Mary. Not Parr, as one might expect from a notorious degenerate describing the poor girl he has ruined for his sport. No, he knew and used her Christian name instead. There is an intimacy there which spoke of strong feeling."

"I see," I said. "But news of this carriage journey came to you only some time later, long after the event?"

"It was. I had no way of ascertaining where the carriage had gone and, after our abrupt removal from Major McLachlan's house, no way in which to find out. Of course, I went to the back door in the guise of a destitute man looking for work, hoping to obtain the information from a servant, but the door was slammed in my face. Clearly, the major, or Murray more likely, had warned the staff to be on their guard.

"I did, however, have one avenue open to me."

"McLachlan's address in Paris!" I exclaimed, recalling the card I had given Holmes.

"Quite correct, Watson. It was for that reason that I had to leave you so abruptly. I had no way of knowing how long McLachlan would stay in the same hotel, so I rushed to catch the first boat to France. As it happened, he had moved on by the time I arrived in Paris, and it took me several days to track him down to a small pension in the Rue Blomet."

"What did he say? I assume that Mary Parr was not present?"

"She was not, and McLachlan denied even knowing her name. He simply repeated that he was happy to write on your behalf to the courts, pleading for clemency and stating his own belief that you were innocent, but he could not help with my search for a missing maid."

"Could you not have brought Lestrade along? He might have been able to convince the French police to arrest McLachlan."

"On what charge? Besides, even if somehow he had been convicted of a crime, it would have brought us no nearer the real killer, and your exoneration. Better instead to wait, and hope that his murderous mistress would attempt to join him in Paris. It is to that hope which Lestrade and I have clung for this past year."

"There has been a notice with her description posted at every port for twelve months now," Lestrade added. "Mr. Holmes was sure that Mr. McLachlan had her hidden away somewhere, waiting for you to be hanged and any interest in the case to disappear."

"I was not sure, Lestrade," Holmes chided the inspector. "I merely hoped. It was for that reason that we could not tell you, Watson. Imagine the tension you would have felt, every day hoping for news and yet none arriving."

I understood his reasoning, and was thankful to both of them for the pains they had taken to clear my name. But one question still nagged at the back of my mind.

"Why did you assume that the maid had killed Miss McLachlan? Why not Alistair McLachlan himself?"

"Do you have so little faith in me, Watson? It was obvious from very early on that the killer was a woman. Sarah McLachlan may have wandered somewhat in her wits, but she remained a lady, and would hardly have thought it proper to appear dressed for bed in front of a strange man. From there, the strong likelihood was that the girl who bade you treat her ailing grandmother and the murderer must be one and the same." He stopped, and tilted his head in consideration. "I would have arrived at this conclusion earlier, had I not erroneously assumed that Potter acted in good faith. His insistence that you – or someone of similar stature – was to blame, caused me to wonder whether two people were involved, the girl to settle the victim and a man to carry out the deed. But if that was the case, why did Miss McLachlan not struggle? Of course, once I had the opportunity to examine the room in which she was killed, I was satisfied that only one person had been present, and confident that that person was female."

"Due in some way to the recovery of the knife, and the manner in which it was hidden? Or was there something which you did not pass on to Lestrade and me?"

"On the contrary, I relayed everything that I saw. Only the conclusions I presented were incomplete. I said that a man had crouched down to look out of the window – you recall the fingerprints on the glass? – but as we knew a girl had been in the room, the obvious conclusion was that it was she who had left her imprint. The discovery of the murder weapon where it should not have been simply confirmed my theory."

"Where it should not have been?" All Holmes had said made perfect sense, but I was in no mood for riddles. Holmes, I think, recognised this, for he hurried to reply.

"On the scaffolding. You recall that I did not initially find the knife, but had to descend and re-ascend the structure via a different ladder? I had calculated the distance that both a man and a girl would be able to cast a bag containing a dagger of the type required to inflict the wounds we saw. The far ladder represented the distance conceivably reached by the toss of a man of average strength, the nearer that of a girl as described by you. As soon as I had confirmed that there was no knife at the far point, I knew that I had been correct all along, and that Potter had been mistaken."

"Ingenious," I said with approval, then frowned as a thought occurred to me. "But why then were you so interested in the loafers who helped Constable Howie break down the door?"

"As I said, I was initially led astray by Inspector Potter. I have only myself to blame. I assumed that he was simply mistaken in his belief that you were guilty and, leading from that flawed assumption, that another man must be involved. At that stage it did not cross my mind that he could be misleading us deliberately."

"You wondered if the smallest man might have been the killer?"

"Exactly. It was improbable, I admit, but if he were of sufficiently diminutive size, it was conceivable that he, and not the girl, had left the fingerprints, thrown the bag, and murdered Miss McLachlan. In the end, he did indeed prove to be an imposter, but not the sort I had hoped."

"I admit that I wondered whether you thought the little man an assassin, hired by one of your enemies," Lestrade piped up, with a smile.

"You have evidently taken to reading fiction, Inspector," Holmes chuckled. "Had I known, I would have advised against it. A limited intellect can only hold so much information before it begins to confuse the real and the imaginary."

"Holmes!" I chided my friend. "Lestrade has been invaluable in recent weeks. He deserves better than to be insulted."

I fancy I saw a flicker of contrition cross Holmes's face. "My apologies, Lestrade," he said contritely, "I spoke in jest. But I hardly think it likely that any enemy of mine would employ a hired killer in order to carry out so convoluted a strike against me. Far simpler to walk up behind me in any London street and shoot me in the back – or lure me to a convenient waterfall and cause me to fall!"

He laughed, but I repressed a shudder at the thought, and turned the conversation to a less morbid topic. Sometimes Holmes's sense of humour left much to be desired.

About the Author

Stuart Douglas is the author of numerous short stories and novellas, as well as the Sherlock Holmes novels, *The Albino's Treasure* and *The Counterfeit Detective*. He is one of the founders of Obverse Books, and was Features Editor of the British Fantasy Society journal. He lives in Edinburgh.

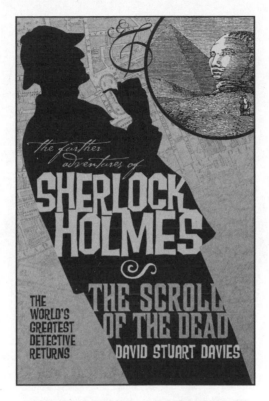

THE FURTHER ADVENTURES OF SHERLOCK HOLMES

THE SCROLL OF THE DEAD

David Stuart Davies

In this fast-paced adventure, Sherlock Holmes attends a seance to unmask an impostor posing as a medium. His foe, Sebastian Melmoth is a man hell-bent on discovering a mysterious Egyptian papyrus that may hold the key to immortality. It is up to Holmes and Watson to use their deductive skills to stop him or face disaster.

ISBN: 9781848564930

AVAILABLE NOW!

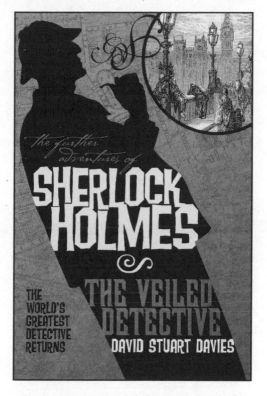

THE FURTHER ADVENTURES
OF SHERLOCK HOLMES
THE VEILED DETECTIVE

David Stuart Davies

It is 1880, and a young Sherlock Holmes arrives in London to pursue a career as a private detective. He soon attracts the attention of criminal mastermind Professor James Moriarty, who is driven by his desire to control this fledgling genius. Enter Dr John H. Watson, soon to make history as Holmes' famous companion.

ISBN: 9781848564909

AVAILABLE NOW!

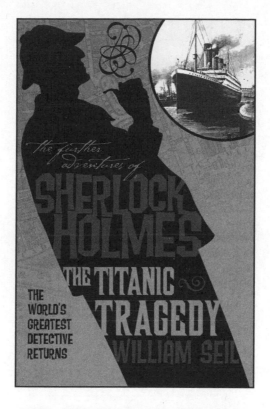

THE FURTHER ADVENTURES
OF SHERLOCK HOLMES

THE TITANIC TRAGEDY

William Seil

Holmes and Watson board the Titanic in 1912, where Holmes is to carry
out a secret government mission. Soon after departure, highly important
submarine plans for the U.S. navy are stolen. Holmes and Watson work
through a list of suspects which includes Colonel James Moriarty, brother to
the late Professor Moriarty—will they find the culprit before tragedy strikes?

ISBN: 9780857687104

AVAILABLE NOW!

THE FURTHER ADVENTURES
OF SHERLOCK HOLMES
THE STAR OF INDIA

Carole Buggé

Holmes and Watson find themselves caught up in a complex chessboard
of a problem, involving a clandestine love affair and the disappearance
of a priceless sapphire. Professor James Moriarty is back to tease and
torment, leading the duo on a chase through the dark and dangerous
back streets of London and beyond.

ISBN: 9780857681218

AVAILABLE NOW!

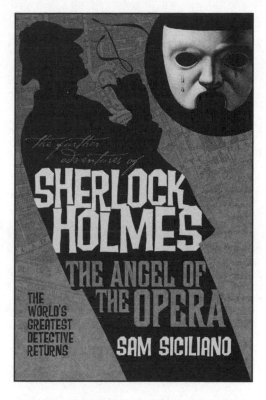

THE FURTHER ADVENTURES
OF SHERLOCK HOLMES

THE ANGEL OF THE OPERA

Sam Siciliano

Paris 1890. Sherlock Holmes is summoned across the English Channel
to the famous Opera House. Once there, he is challenged to discover
the true motivations and secrets of the notorious phantom, who rules its
depths with passion and defiance.

ISBN: 9781848568617

AVAILABLE NOW!

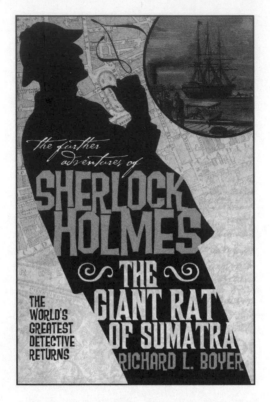

THE FURTHER ADVENTURES
OF SHERLOCK HOLMES

THE GIANT RAT OF SUMATRA

Richard L. Boyer

For many years, Dr. Watson kept the tale of The Giant Rat of
Sumatra a secret. However, before he died, he arranged that
the strange story of the giant rat should be held in the vaults of
a London bank until all the protagonists were dead…

ISBN: 9781848568600

AVAILABLE NOW!